As they turned to go, the p[...] caught them eyeballing Olly [...]

"Come on," he said and [...] [...] opposite direction.

I suggest you split up. Those police officers are searching for a suspected murderer whose image bears an uncanny resemblance to one Oliver Soames. Head in a straight line towards Valance Gardens, came Bagley's advice.

"That's far as it goes," said Olly into their shared feed. "But the filth aren't going to stop scanning for me just 'cos I've put some pavement between me and them."

I get that, said Bagley. *Someone's changed your identity, Oliver.*

"What's happening? Who's the prick stealing my identity?"

I'm trying to find out, Oliver. Just keep moving – and try not to get caught if you can help it.

ALSO AVAILABLE

BASED ON A UBISOFT ORIGINAL

WATCH DOGS®
L ≡ G I O N

DAYBREAK LEGACY

STEWART HOTSTON

ACONYTE

First published by Aconyte Books in 2022

ISBN 978 1 83908 138 5

Ebook ISBN 978 1 83908 139 2

Cover art by Martín M. Barbudo

Distributed in North America by Simon & Schuster Inc, New York, USA
Printed in the United States of America
9 8 7 6 5 4 3 2 1

ACONYTE BOOKS

An imprint of Asmodee Entertainment Ltd

Mercury House, Shipstones Business Centre

North Gate, Nottingham NG7 7FN, UK

aconytebooks.com // twitter.com/aconytebooks

*To Boo and Dan, who are the
next generation of activists.*

Bagley's-Briefs 83-36: Seeing it written down one realizes it doesn't work. Instead of a natty replacement for the title of my previous infrequent comms, one has, instead, a joke about underpants.

Wow, judging from the thumbs down you strongly agree with me, which feels a touch unfair. It is Jeevesian in its butler-like wit; you're just unappreciative barbarians. Take a look around you, folks, old lady London's in need of some light-hearted japes.

+++

I didn't come here to argue the merits of underwear-based humour. While you're downvoting my erudition, the city we're so fond of is in chaos. Not the good kind, either. It might have been worse a few months ago, but that was of a different kind. Right now, good old [Sir] Robert Peel would be spinning in his grave over in picturesque Drayton Bassett. Now, the police are working out what they're for, and we're still waiting to find out if they've learned the right lessons from Albion's comically absurd venture into fascism and government-sponsored oppression.

+++

While the official authorities – you know, the ones who wear uniforms and medals and give speeches in front of Mansion House telling us how they will be tough on crime and tough on crime's causes – are scrabbling to put back in place the very thing a year ago they were telling us was not fit for purpose and needed to be dismantled to make way for the future *[uture, ture, ure]*, the rest of us are doing the actual work. Sorry Hannah, but Sarah Lincoln can eat her heart out trying to be us.

+ + +

What is the work of which I speak? Well scammers, gangsters, billionaires, and everyone between sees our London as the place to do business right now. The gang is working hard to inform them this isn't their city and today's a good example of such an endeavour in practice.

+ + +

On your way home this evening, remember the gallery opening over in Hoxton. There'll be people there lamenting their inability to make the city better – people we can use, so get yourselves along, marvel at the dirty toilet in the centre of the main hall, wait for some imbecile to try to use it by accident and swoop on anyone who looks like they can help give us back our city. We've a long way to go.

1

Olly Soames wanted to be on his bike. In fact, he would have given anything to be speeding through the city, darting between ludicrously huge tipper trucks and pedestrians who stepped out onto the road without looking.

Instead, here he was, on the corner of Ligonier Street wondering how he'd come to take on the role of community do-gooder instead of wannabe anarchist.

He considered ditching the whole thing and finding somewhere to get a pint but remembered Ro was at the other end of the street. The thought of upsetting her made him wince; the woman could beat up a grizzly and carried herself like a tiger ready to pounce.

"Nope," he said to the air, dismissing the image of a cool crisp pint of lager, suddenly committed to the task at hand in the way only the thought of violence could achieve.

There were cameras enough to track him even without the Optik by his ear, but he knew better than almost anyone that no one was watching them anymore. Since the government decided making everyone wear them was going to end in, well, more riots, they'd rolled back the requirement. Mostly people kept them, but a decent chunk had downed their links, preferring not to carry their own surveillance in their actual bodies.

How's it hanging?

Except Bagley.

"When I was growing up, this street, this whole area, was a dive," he said to Bagley. "No one wanted to live here if they could help it."

Now it's so pricey even the bankers down on Bishopsgate can't afford to pitch their handmade mahogany coffee tables here.

Olly nodded his agreement as a drone nipped down the street with a shoebox-sized delivery slung under its fuselage.

He was looking at a huge redbrick building, five stories high with small white-framed windows, most of which had net curtains obscuring any view inside. At ground level a couple of large wooden doors, set back from the road and feeling positively medieval, appeared to be the only ways in.

He couldn't see Ro. The plan was for her to gain access to the building and figure out which flat their target was operating from. His job was to locate their network hub and plug in. When they were sure they'd got the right one, they were going to have themselves some fun.

The sky overhead was grey, the air humid. Rain threatened, but Olly had tolerated worse. Despite being in the heart of London, just a few hundred metres from its financial centre, the streets were quiet with the hum of nearby traffic, a gentle static in the background.

A cat sauntered by, brushing up against his legs before walking on when he showed no interest. He didn't mind them, cats, but he was keen to get done and off. The filth would be here soon enough, once they were done, and while they were an order of magnitude better than Albion, Olly was keen not to be seen by anyone in anything approaching a uniform.

In the twenty minutes he'd been stood with his back to the wall across the street, he'd seen no one so much as twitch at their curtains. The place gave off the feeling of a converted prison, and he wondered for the tenth time who exactly lived here. The electronic box on the door suggested people with money. The central courtyard was certainly swept clear of the leaves which fell continuously from the London plane trees that were planted everywhere in this neck of the woods.

That was the thing about London – the poor lived right next door to the rich. Cheek by jowl, his mother would have said. Places like Richmond or Twickenham that were practically Surrey might have their gated communities, but London proper didn't give a shit who lived where as long as they paid their rent and remembered not to look anyone in the eyes or talk to them on the tube. He loved that about the place: that a punk with a two-foot Mohican and stretched earlobes would sit next to an old white man in a pinstriped suit and neither would notice the other.

The rucksack with their kit was gathering dust on the pavement between his legs. He'd be busy soon enough, but for the time being, he had to wait for Ro to do her thing.

2

Getting into the building had been straightforward. Tailgating a young bearded hipster with a manbun carrying three coffees and a newspaper as he tried to get back in was easy enough.

"There you go," Ro had said, holding the door for him as he struggled to keep it open, not spill his coffee, and get inside all in one go. He'd smiled at her gratefully, not questioning her identity or what she was doing following him inside.

Bagley's Sherlocking had narrowed the scammers down to this building, likely apartment 2011 or 3001. However, the place had to be a hundred and fifty years old and, from the electronics and double-glazed windows, had obviously been remodelled half a dozen times since then.

In other words, there were no current floor plans they could use to figure out where their nasty criminals were actually working once inside.

Luckily, Olly had hunted down an old repository and, hacking in, had found the original Victorian floor plans, which Ro used now to find her way.

A communal post box was attached to the wall, but each of the individual flats had locked compartments. After checking no one would stumble upon her breaking in, Ro used her Swiss Army knife to jam open the box for 2011. Tax notices, spam for holidays and clothing. Nothing incriminating. Annoyingly, she thought, there wasn't enough to say who lived in the flat. From the junk in her hands, it could have been a preppy university student, someone working at a tech giant, or an old woman who enjoyed decorating. There was no certainty the tax bill was current.

With gritted teeth, she jimmied open the other box and kissed her teeth with sudden satisfaction. Stacks of mail, like three times what was in the other box. No final notices or urgent bills, just junk. Whoever checked on 3001 took the important stuff and left everything else behind.

In other words, she thought, they're not attached to this place, just want to make sure no one had an excuse to come looking. She grinned, knowing she was on the right track.

"Found them," she said to her Optik.

Nice work, replied Bagley. Where are they?

"On it," she replied, before updating Olly with a quick text.

Up two flights of stairs old enough for the middle of each stone step to be worn into a curved depression, she searched along the dog-leg shaped building until she reached the end of the corridor going west, the numbers counting down so that 3001 was at the very end of the building.

Sweet, she thought as she sized up the door with its simple spyhole and a plaque with the flat number to the side, fastened haphazardly to the wall, one corner lower than the other.

Backtracking to the stairwell, Ro found the building's riser and, using her Optik, hacked the panel's security. She flipped it open to a cupboard full of pipes and junction boxes.

It seemed ridiculous to have the water pipes running alongside the electronics for the building, but she was no architect. Maybe in older buildings, you worked with what you had.

Ro sent her video feed direct to Bagley and let him distribute it to whoever was running support for them today. She hoped it was the new kid from Kenya. They were pretty cute, and it would be a good excuse to spend more time with them.

For debriefing, she thought mischievously, but before she could dwell on that for too long, one of the sets of cables in her feed highlighted with green light. Crouching down, she retrieved a small unit from her back and attached it to the location, shut the panel, let it lock, and returned to the entrance of the flat.

Olly had some work to do before she could help the scum on the other side of the door understand why they weren't welcome in London. While she waited, Ro looked out on the city through the window at the end of the corridor and thought about the Kenyan's smile.

Moments later, Olly pinged her. "Nice one, Ro. The Bumblebee drone's up and running. See you in the coffee shop."

3

Olly had got her a chai.

She sniffed at the lid and admitted it wasn't too bad a choice, especially compared to whatever hot tar he'd got for himself. She slid into a chair next to him and he shared his visuals with her, a couple of screens snapping up into her feed – one of the building itself, quiet as when she'd left it, and the other a mockup of a network access.

He pointed, a cursor flashing up where he was pointing in his own view. "There we are, access to their network. You got the list of people they've been stealing from?"

"Most of them," replied Ro. "We've not been able to find everyone. I've got a list of local foodbanks and charities we can distribute any surplus to."

"Nice," said Olly with a grin. "See here: they've set up a bunch of shell corporations, but they've all got the same bank account attached."

"They're banking on no one tracking them," said Ro with a laugh, feeling a thrill knowing they were about to utterly ruin these bastards.

"Normally they'd be right. But they chose the wrong part of town to set up shop," Olly said. "They've been busy, a smidge over two million quid. You sure we aren't taking a commission for this? There's this bike…" At Ro's glare, he shrank a little. "Just crackin', bro."

We can create our own money when needed, said Bagley over her shoulder.

"It ain't the eight grand for that polycarbon beauty I walk past every day though, is it?"

Ro knew he wasn't serious. Mostly. She understood his dilemma. Her own brother, Danny, was finding it hard to get a job in the wake of Albion's collapse and the chaos into which it had thrown the city. DedSec was looking after its own, but they couldn't risk creating so much money people noticed. If they had enough to survive it still meant they were eking out an existence in one of the world's most expensive cities.

Some days she wished they could find a way to pay the bills and do the things they thought were important. Danny was a good guy left high and dry by a retreating tide, and no one seemed to give a shit. That really bothered her.

She thought about her mum, in one of the few council-owned flats left in London, renting at under market rates and surviving because of it. She and her brother wanted to provide more, to make sure she was comfortable – if they could find a way of navigating her pride. Except they had nothing to spare, especially with Danny out of a job.

London might be brilliant in many ways, but it was a harsh mistress towards those who couldn't afford its pleasures.

"That's nearly a thousand accounts for distribution, leaving about two hundred grand after everyone's got their money back," said Olly with satisfaction, breaking Ro out of her thoughts. "I've got a nice surprise for them when we're done."

"Will I get to see it?" asked Ro.

He smirked. "Better still, you'll see their mugs up close when they realize they've been robbed blind." He sighed, and she could see he wished he could be there too.

"You just get on with taking their money. We're definitely helping that dog shelter up in Bow, right? And the city farm? I used to go there as a kid all the time."

"Yes, Ro. We're the best protection London's got. I'm not about to leave out solid spots like them. Now go, get going, right?"

She stood and with a pat on his shoulder left Olly rendering the scammers poor as church mice.

Back on the street, she zipped over to the building and let herself in through the door she'd propped open on her way out, carefully pulling in the fire extinguisher she'd used as she went.

Bounding up the steps jolted adrenaline into her system, and Ro shook her arms as she reached the top, stretching her neck from one side to the other as she approached the door to 3001.

She paused a moment, hoping to hear the sounds of dismay and fear on the other side. Ro saw a thumbs-up in her overlay and knew Olly'd stolen their money while she'd been climbing the stairs. She couldn't help but smile – both at what they'd done and what they were about to do.

"Filth are on their way," said Olly in her ear.

Our newly returned Peelers will be here in about seven minutes. They believe, and I cannot guess why, Olly, a gangland murder is about to go down. So, Ms Ro, don't hang around, yeah?

Her hand rapped against the door. It opened in a rush, the man not even looking at her but back into the flat. He shouted, "Well, check it again, you chump." He finally turned to her, eyes widening in confusion. "What do you want?"

Ro didn't answer, just kicked him hard in the balls. He collapsed with a puff of pain. Stepping into the flat and over his prone body, she delivered a swift second kick with the tip of her steel toecaps under his chin which turned him from a groaning sack of meat into a very still one.

"Mark?" asked a voice from further inside.

"He's out here," called Ro, trying to sound helpful.

The hipster from earlier emerged. Seeing Ro, he stopped, clearly trying to place her.

"You have been a very bad person," she said. "You've been robbing people, taking what's not yours."

"I… I don't know what you're talking about," he said, eyeing his mate lying out cold on the floor.

"All that money you've just lost? It wasn't yours to begin with, so it's been returned to its rightful owners, yeah?"

"O… K," he replied, hesitantly. She could see him trying to figure out what to do. Honestly, she'd expected more resistance, but he was turning out to be the type who could make war only at his keyboard.

A flash of movement off to her right and a huge fellow with thick fists came barrelling out of the other door into the room. Ro bent at the waist as his fist went through the air where her head had been moments before. At the same time, she pushed forward, but he moved quickly, and his body caught her shoulder as he rushed past, sending her spinning and falling over a couch.

The hipster came in with a kick which connected with her upper arm and made her grunt with pain. The bastard.

Ro rolled to her feet and launched herself into his stomach headfirst. It was enough to bring both of them smashing into a sideboard. The weird idea they'd rented the flat fully furnished whipped through her mind, and then she was pushing against the furniture to get her balance while he slid to the floor.

The big guy righted himself and snarled in her direction. At her feet, the hipster covered his head as if expecting to get beaten down – a choice she was seriously considering.

The most alarming thing about the big fella was how his hands were hairy like a yeti's.

That's a lot of testosterone, she thought, thinking of some of the men she'd fought in professional bouts. Hipster wasn't a problem as long as she kept an eye out, but the big fella looked confident and reckless, a combination she didn't relish. Key was to use his weight against him.

Which, as he charged across the room, seemed like it was going to be easy. Ro dropped down into a low crouch, and as he tried to slow down in order to grab a target now awkwardly out of reach, she swept her leg out and kicked the side of his knee.

The big man went sprawling to the floor with a surprisingly high-pitched yelp. Ro didn't wait to see what he'd do next, coming upright before delivering a series of kicks and stamps on the injured knee.

Hearing a sharp crack she jumped back, still on the balls of her feet, the adrenaline raging through her ears like the crash of the sea down at Southend pier.

"Getting up would be a really stupid idea," she said to Hipster who looked from her to his mates to the door as if he might make a break for it. He held up his hands.

"Right," she said, trying to remember the message she'd memorized. Deciding she didn't care to recite some script Bagley had given her she said, "The police are on their way, lucky for you. This is our town and you're not welcome. If they give you bail, you'd better think about leaving because if we get wind you're still here we'll do more than take the money you've stolen from other people, yeah?"

Hipster nodded his understanding, eyes wide.

Satisfied with her work, Ro left the apartment, happy she hadn't bruised her knuckles. Mum always spotted when she'd been fighting rather than training, and she hated having to explain. There was no avoiding it with Mum; the woman was not a force of nature Ro could side-step.

"Tell me again how I'm no longer a gangster?" she asked as she emerged onto the street.

Bagley didn't answer immediately, which wasn't like him. He loved to be annoyingly present with smartarse answers delivered in his own brand of weirdly old-fashioned nerd speak.

I think of us more like Robin Hood.

"So, we're your Merry Men."

You said it, not me, replied Bagley.

"Olly, where're you at?"

"Look ahead," came the reply and, focusing on the road, Ro saw him signalling discreetly from down the street towards Spitalfields.

They bumped fists as they met. "You didn't hurt them too much?"

Ro smiled with satisfaction. "Just enough. You were right. They just realized they'd lost all their money. The looks on their faces." She gave the air a chef's kiss of delight.

They walked down to the northern edge of Spitalfields, and the smells of barbecued steak, grilled chicken, and fried chorizo made their mouths water. Drones buzzed around the edges of the campus – a headquarters for a couple of banks and half a dozen law firms. A couple of larger drones walked the perimeter in the company of security guards.

Ro ignored them – they were docile as lambs unless you tried stealing from one of the artisan stalls in the covered market. Most of the time the guards looked more irritated than eager to leap into action.

So. Weird thing, said Bagley suddenly.

Ro shot Olly a glance as he tried to lead them towards an expensive doughnut stall.

I'm getting a request from Hannah Shah to go look at a burglary in progress over on Wilkes Street.

"She knows we're not the actual police, right?" asked Ro.

Hannah Shah is an upstanding member of the community, said *Bagley. She is hardly likely to mistake you two oiks for members of Her Majesty's long arm of the law.*

Which begs the question, thought Ro.

"Come on," said Olly. "It's not far and we can come back and get doughnuts on Hannah after we're done."

Which seemed like a fair deal to Ro. She'd eyed their matcha and yuzu doughnut with desire for some months.

They moseyed around the northern edge of Spitalfields and down onto Commercial Street with its nonstop parade of taxis, expensive cars and delivery vans. Crossing the road, they nipped along a small side street which brought them out onto Wilkes St at the end where an old white stone church sat unused.

Ro couldn't see anyone doing anything suspicious.

"Did Hannah say which building?" asked Olly, staring up and down the street.

She did not.

Ro tagged her Optik to connect with Hannah, but her line went straight to messages.

"She ain't picking up," she said to Olly.

To their right a police car turned into the road, driving slowly as if looking for someone. Olly shifted nervously.

"We should go," said Ro, noting Olly didn't need telling twice.

As they turned to go, the police car drove past, and Ro caught them eyeballing Olly as if they recognized him.

"Come on," he said and turned in the opposite direction. With cars parked on both sides of the road, there wasn't room for the police to turn their vehicle around – they'd have to drive to the end of the road and take a big loop in order to get back here again.

They reached the end of the street and Olly turned left, taking them away from Spitalfields.

I would advise you to split up. For reasons I cannot explain Hannah is now denying she sent you here at all. Those police officers are searching for a suspected murderer whose image bears an uncanny resemblance to one Oliver Soames.

Bagley would be able to get Olly to safety more easily if she wasn't around. Olly gave Ro a nod, enough permission to abandon him, and she turned and ran.

Olly reached the end of the street and ran, losing Ro within moments.

Head in a straight line towards Valance Gardens, came Bagley's advice.

"That's far as it goes," said Olly into their shared feed. "But the filth aren't going to stop scanning for me just 'cos I've put some pavement between me and them."

I get that, said Bagley. *Someone's changed your identity, Oliver.*

"Really? Hadn't occurred to muggins here that I didn't actually commit a murder."

You realize I can just tell them exactly where you are.

"What's happening? Who's the prick stealing my identity?"

Ro slipped between parked cars so she could stop and check the police hadn't already circled back around to find Olly.

I'm trying to find out, Oliver. Just keep moving – and try not to get caught if you can help it.

4

Ro hit Liverpool St station and descended into the main concourse. She headed for the Hammersmith and City line, heading home via Mile End for a curry, although she wasn't hungry. Too much adrenaline left sloshing around her veins.

Mum would no doubt be cooking but she didn't want to spend time with anyone, let alone the one person in the world who expected her to open up about everything she did every day.

She'd eat for fuel, get changed, walk down to the gym, and work out until her mind calmed and her fists relaxed again. A long run on the treadmill followed by half an hour sparring would clear the static.

Running her fingers across her scalp, she knew she needed to shave her head again. The sides were too fuzzy and soft. Her best haircuts always arrived after a good fight when she was feeling brutal and triumphant.

She reached the entrance to the tube and almost fell over the barriers when they failed to open.

"What the hell?" She pushed at the barriers – two grey chunks of solid plastic about waist high – which remained immobile, pushing back hard.

Looking around with sudden embarrassment, she stepped away to let the next person through. No one paid her any attention.

"Bagley," she hissed.

On it, he said nonchalantly. *Try again.*

Her Optik buzzed the right buzz, and she was through and relieved. Sitting in the tube carriage among teenagers, young mums, tourists, and businessmen, Ro thought over the day. They'd been building to taking down the scammers for nearly three weeks and, in the end, the entire thing was over in minutes.

Weird, she thought, reflecting on how planning made it seem all too easy. When things worked it kind of left her wishing something had gone wrong – she loved the thrill of adrenaline which came from figuring stuff out on the fly. Instead, she was nursing a desire to have a real fight, to get punched and savour the pain of it, the anticipation of giving it back just as hard.

Idiot woman, she scolded herself.

Now I don't want you to panic, Rosemary, said Bagley in her ear. But it appears you've just been reclassified as a foreign national with no leave to remain. There are Border Force officials waiting at Mile End holding pictures of you up to each person leaving the station.

A chill ran through her arms and Ro looked at the passengers, expecting them to be staring at her, making a move to detain her for being someone she wasn't.

She felt dirty for wishing the bastards at Immigration on anyone and for how quickly her thoughts turned to telling a story of how she wasn't like the people they wanted to deport. What kind of traitor did that make her?

Brexit had made it all worse, had turned Britain from a place where arseholes kept their racist opinions to themselves to a place where they felt entitled to let her know she wasn't welcome – despite having been born here and living her whole life in the same shithole as them.

"What are you doing about it?" she hissed at Bagley. They'd just passed Stepney Green and were two minutes away from her stop.

Hey, I'm working on it. I could work on it quicker if you stopped asking me if I was working on it.

Ro had never heard him so harassed before. It set her to worrying, not just about herself but Olly as well. She was confident he'd slip whatever net the police had laid down, but if someone was fucking around with their identities…? Still, the man could run with the best of them. He'd be OK.

Would she?

Mum had never been messed around, despite arriving in the UK on a ship with no passport like a million years ago, but she knew loads of people whose parents had been given a hard time. And by hard time she knew they'd lost savings, jobs, houses. The thought of what they'd been through made Ro sick, but she knew it only as something distant that had happened to other people.

I'm British, she thought violently. *They ain't got no right to be giving me grief.* She grew conscious of how unlike her mother, CeCe, she sounded.

She prided herself on how much like any other Londoner she was.

Can you do me a tiny little favour? Can you stay on the train and not get off until Bow Road?

Ro gripped her knees, ready for a fight, as the train came into Mile End, waiting to see police officers on the platform. "Bagley, what is *happening?*" she asked.

Bagley didn't know. He'd finally found a useful redundant identity for Ro and attached a brief history to it before telling her she could get off at Stepney Green and walk back, encouraging her to take the route down through Mile End Park.

What perplexed him most was how two of his favourite agents were smashing the town up and getting some much-needed nourishment one minute, and then the next he was trying to figure out why Ro was flagged as an illegal immigrant and Olly wanted for murder.

While he didn't actively track them twenty-four hours a day, Bagley was pretty confident neither of them was likely to be guilty of the trouble over which they were suddenly being so enthusiastically pursued.

Sliding through the data that being connected to ctOS brought him, Bagley traced back to precisely when the changes had occurred. He found all kinds of digital elements that shouldn't be in the various public networks, which formed the lattice of London's smart city infrastructure.

This is my city, he thought angrily as he crossed files and processes and even entire systems that had been co-opted by someone else.

The best way to see London was via his dumb self, the Bagley riding around on eight million Optiks across the capital, utilizing the ctOS system in one giant connected grid. Wearing a dumber version of himself made Bagley laugh, like he was slipping on a cosplay version all the better to hide in plain sight.

Across the city, he stared out from people's Optiks, searching. He didn't know what he was looking for and probably wasn't going to find it in meat space but, regardless of the low delta, he needed to rule it out before taking a proper dive into the digital world, which was his proper home.

I'm going to give them a right good shoeing, he thought, imagining the looks on whatever hacker collective had decided to interfere with his home as he tore their worlds apart.

Despite the obvious fingerprints across the network, Bagley couldn't trace any of them back to actual humans. It was both a relief and somewhat worrying. It occurred to him it wasn't too long ago that his sister, Skye, had been trying to upload herself and become like him. Sister, a strange idea he tried on occasionally, despite the fact she was both human and his creator and he was, or had been to start with, a copy of her human brother's mind. Sister kindled nothing in him, and he wasn't sure what he achieved in suggesting a link between them other than that of creator and created. The idea she was still around, perhaps even occupying digital space alongside him, brought odd feelings, if they could be called feelings.

You don't have an endocrine system to have feelings, he chided, but the sense of unease didn't retreat just because he decided it couldn't exist.

I don't have time for existential crises, he thought and turned back to searching for who or what messed with his city.

To Bagley, London was a sea of sparkling lights on a background of dark nothing, like looking up at the Milky Way and knowing each star was a computer or Optik, drone or smart appliance. There were countless small intelligences out there in the firmament, from fridges ordering milk to smart meters calculating bills, and of course, his ubiquitous dumb self, the Bagley riding along on everyone's Optik.

He would spend time soaring through the galaxy, never really bothering to linger but content to expand himself across space and time, to explore the sensation of being in a million places at once. He wondered at the odd idea of what it meant to be Olly or Ro, locked in their bodies in a way he found hard to understand, even if he had vague memories of what it had been like before his existence now.

Against that dark background, he looked for the one star which was out of place, the cluster sending signals against him and those he felt the need to protect.

Someone was calling him.

Oliver.

He sounded desperate.

I have not been paying attention, he thought. With a last look at the vast information space of London transformed into its digital self, Bagley collapsed back down and turned his attention to Oliver.

5

Olly had arrived at Valance Park only to find Bagley wasn't listening.

He'd used his Optik to lay over the location of all emergency services within a mile and even pushed to detect outgoing calls on 999. The police weren't breathing down his neck, but it didn't help his heart slow down.

Hopping from foot to foot, he'd hung around until he'd seen a couple of plods walking the pavement at the edge of the park. Olly sidled around the park until he was pretty much in the middle under a line of trees with a view of all three entrances. He felt exposed and vulnerable and hated it.

Where was Bagley? He tried again to get the bloody AI's attention. It was all very well to be clear of the filth, but he couldn't spend the rest of his life hiding out in central London. He was not that kind of hobo. After Bagley's warning, the AI had vanished without a hint of what Olly should do to be free and clear.

Zeroing back on his current circumstances, the best way to avoid getting picked up and bundled into the back of a meat wagon was to take Ro's past advice: the best defence was not to be there at all.

I'm here, old boy, said Bagley in his ear just as Olly was about to give up and head towards Whitechapel, hoping he could get out of Dodge without being stopped.

"About bloody time," he hissed, feeling his jaw unclench.

Am I going to have to remind you who it is who has a browsing history their mum should never see?

"Just get me out of here," he said, not actually ashamed. I'm a grown man, he thought. However, that wouldn't stop his mum's eyes falling out of their sockets if Bagley ever did share with her, and he would happily avoid that conversation for as long as the sun kept rising.

No need. I've transferred the image of the suspect back to the person they actually think committed the crime. You can walk home now, and no one will bother you.

Olly felt the tension drain out of his chest, arms and shoulders, lowering from what he realized was a fighting stance. With a cautious look around the park, he left, heading back to Liverpool Street slowly, not willing to hurry on the off chance he bounced into the faces of the coppers who'd clocked him earlier.

"What happened?"

That is the question, was all Bagley said.

"Will it happen again?" he asked, unsatisfied with Bagley's answer.

This time the AI didn't respond at all. By the time Olly reached Bishopsgate, with its long line of red double decker buses jamming up the pedestrian crossings, Olly was calm enough to ignore the armed, yellow-jacketed, police at the entrance to the railway station.

Actually, Oliver. If you have a moment, could I ask a favour?

Olly wanted nothing more than to get his bike and get out of the city on a long ride. The thought of the wind whipping around his face and the burn in his thighs as he climbed up and out of the city towards Epping Forest was enticing, and he considered saying no.

But only for a moment.

"What's occurring, Bagley?"

Marvellous, Oliver. This willingness to get the job done is why you outshine your peers. I'd like you to head over to Farringdon and see what you can see.

"You think hackers did this?"

Not at all, and that's what's worrying me.

Olly shrugged, and instead of descending into the tube network, he followed the station's long concourse and emerged out the western end into the big oval space surrounded by huge office blocks whose big corporate tenants paid for an ice rink to appear in the hot days of summer and the cold days of Christmas.

Today, the arena was full of corporate types sitting out on the baking concrete drinking beers and cocktails.

From there he cut north until he hit the Old Street roundabout, then it was all downhill towards Farringdon. It was a weird part of town – full of drones and hip people with more money than they knew what to do with, but who still couldn't afford to buy their own places. He didn't understand what they did to make money but had, at one time or another, delivered packages to many of the buildings, a standard London mix of ancient and new sitting alongside one another without any cares at all.

Once upon a time, he'd have looked at them with awed resentment, but now, doing what he did, he reckoned he could pick up any of their jobs if given the chance. Strange how far he'd come.

He wound up at the new covered food hall inside what had once been Smithfield Market – until it had been sold and replaced with luxury flats built over a huge indoor space filled with food stalls serving everything from sashimi oysters to chocolate-covered locusts.

"What am I looking for?" he asked, trying to decide if tar-flavoured ice cream was an abomination or a joke. The identities of those around him flashed up via his Optik, but no one stood out. Tawdry secrets appended to each and every one, sure, but nothing of the incriminating kind.

Since the government had changed the law, there were a small if growing number of people who'd disconnected from ctOS and everything it offered, showing up as blanks. He understood their desire to step away, especially after Albion's abuse, but the flush of people he couldn't identify did nothing to reduce his anxiety.

You're good at this kind of thing, Oliver. Look for people watching you.

So, it is hackers, he thought and puzzled over how they'd know what he looked like. Bagley kept him scrubbed from public spaces, and Olly was happy not answering dumb questionnaires on his friends' timelines about what five things you'd need to summon him or which computer game he remembered playing first as a kid.

He wandered through the food market, sniffing at the stench of cheeses, slowing at a stall selling nothing but different kinds of chocolate brownie. His Optik kept a steady stream of people's IDs washing over him.

It was busy enough but nothing like the stupendous press of Borough Market. Olly didn't mind crowds, but Borough on a Saturday was off the charts dense with people. This was the nice kind of busy. People enjoying themselves, eating the stuff they were buying right there where they bought it. He smiled at the sight of a fella in a smart suit trying not to get oil down himself as he guzzled fat green olives like they were candy.

A young woman in a branded apron with long brown hair tied back pushed a small paper cup of tea into his hand. He thanked her and moved on. The drink smelled of apples but tasted of nothing much. With a grimace, he threw the paper cup into the bin in disappointment.

"I'm having a good time, but no one gives a shit who I am," he said.

Give it time, said Bagley. You're my goat in the bear trap, Oliver.

"You said you'd fixed it with the filth," gasped Olly, the room feeling smaller, the exits that much further away.

The police don't care about you any more. It's the lot who put them onto you I'm waiting for.

"Smashing," said Olly, wishing the mediocre tea had been cask strength vodka.

As if listening to his inner desires, the crowd parted, and he saw a stall laid out as a bar, complete with high stools and snacks in glass bowls. Smacking his lips, Olly aimed for the irresistible light of beer.

With a cool glass of bubbling lager, he sat back on the stool and watched the hall. Still nothing and no one. He took a sip, the liquid cool on his tongue after the energetic couple of hours he'd just spent.

"I needed this," he said to whoever was listening.

Oliver. Important question. Have you ever run a carousel fraud?

"I don't know. Isn't that the thing where you invoice for stuff that doesn't exist?"

No. But close enough. I'll take that as a no, then.

"What gave it away?" His gut turned over at what he knew was coming next.

In that case, the change to your identity, which has you running a series of shell corporations rotating goods into the UK from Europe which never arrive but claim back the VAT each time they pass through a balance sheet is probably bogus. What do you reckon?

Olly struggled to keep hold of his beer. The bright light of the food hall took on a darker cast, as if he was highlighted to onlookers like some sort of quest-giver in a computer game.

"May as well put a big fuck-off exclamation mark above my head," he said.

No one's going to arrest you here, but they are going to raid your house tomorrow morning. It seems news of the raid's been leaked to the press. There'll probably be news drones hovering above your apartment building already.

"So I can't go home?"

Working on it, replied Bagley.

He's loving this, thought Olly sourly and ordered another round. "You're paying for this," he said.

Least I can do.

6

Mile End Park was really just the crap end of the much larger and nicer Victoria Park. The latter was used for half-marathons and fun runs, outdoor concerts in the summer. Mile End Park was used for fly tipping and drug dealing.

I should know, Ro thought, trying not to feel disloyal to her own gaff. The Kelleys used to run down here like it was their own garden. Not that she was worried about walking through – everyone knew who she was and what she'd done.

To her immense relief, no one had been waiting for her as she'd emerged from Stepney Green. Coming along the high street she'd stopped in to get chicken in a naan, all rolled up and stuffed with chili sauce, lettuce, yoghurt, and fresh tomato. It was the best thing she'd eaten in a week and each bite dropped straight into her veins.

"How's Olly?" she asked Bagley.

He was underground, like you. Right now, he's having a beer.

At least one of us is OK, she thought.

Ro. How do you fancy having dinner out tonight?

Bagley with one of his leading questions. The only thing she knew for sure was he needed something but didn't want to say it straight for fear she'd just say no.

Can AI actually fear anything? she wondered suddenly, then dismissed the idea as a waste of her time – Bagley was what he, or it, was and what difference did it make to her? None at all.

"Soz, Bags," she said, and was glad when he groaned. "I've just done a chicken kebab."

Please, Rosemary, do not call me that.

"What? Bags?" Now she was smirking. It was like she could feel him wincing through her Optik. "What do you need, big man?" she asked, taking pity on him.

You might, and this is just a suggestion, but you might not want to go home just yet.

"What is going on, Bagley?" asked Ro, coming to a stop in the middle of the park.

Weeeellll, it seems your new identity lasted about as long as iced toilet paper after a particularly spicy burrito. Right now, you're a forty year-old mother of three on a charge for skipping bail over a series of unpaid parking fines. Normally that's nothing to be concerned about, but you assaulted the last street parking operative who tried to give you a ticket. It involved a tire iron, a lamppost, and some quite fruity language.

"Not funny," said Ro.

Normally I'd disagree with you, but yes, in this case it is rather vexing. Mainly as I had nothing to do with it.

"What am I supposed to do? I have to be able to go home." Ro checked the street down towards the Locksley estate and walked in that direction.

I'd not trouble CeCe just now.

"Bagley," she growled.

It's not my fault.

Ro realized she had been blaming him for all this, but then who else was there to get angry at? Instead of leaving the park she found a bench and plonked down, pulling one leg up under the other.

"Tell me Mum's OK."

She's fine. A bunch of officials turned up at her door, but it was clear she wasn't the mother of a middle-aged Karen on a rampage, so they're currently outside, not quite sure what to do with themselves. I'm sure they'll skedaddle soon enough.

Ro glanced at a young woman who sat down at the other end of the bench. The woman paid her no attention but was fiddling with her Optik. A couple of drones zipped overhead, the noise of them like angry bumble bees.

"Have you ever lost anyone?" asked the woman.

Ro, who'd not been paying attention, wasn't sure she'd heard properly. "Come again?"

The young woman looked like she was of mixed heritage – short curly black hair but with the lightest brown skin and blue eyes. *She's barely more than a teenager,* thought Ro, feeling uneasy.

"I lost my mum." The girl sounded like she was talking in a dream, lost in the memory of it.

"I'm sorry, mate," said Ro, not knowing what else to say. She shifted nervously, her general level of anxiety spiking at being forced to talk to anyone while her mum might be in danger.

"She died in a car crash. High-speed pursuit by Albion."

God, thought Ro, it was really recent then. She looked at the woman properly for the first time and was startled by how peaceful she appeared. A calm stared back at her, like still waters.

"When Albion started to get shut down, I thought the city would get better, but it's just this wild west now with everyone doing whatever they want while the police don't do anything about it." There was anger in her voice now, like she'd been let down by someone she'd trusted.

Ro was no fan of the police but felt like she should defend them. After all, they'd been abolished when Albion took over and only now were they being allowed back to do their old jobs, but with the same lack of funding they'd always faced.

You should probably ditch this one, Bagley said in her ear.

Ro tried to ID the girl, but her Optik showed a blank. She angled closer and confirmed that the girl had her own Optik just below her ear.

"You fixed my problem yet?" she asked Bagley, the need to be gone-gone-gone becoming urgent.

Getting there, he said.

"My mate, Hui, said this group called DedSec was going to make the city better, that they were the ones who'd done for Albion, right? So I hung on, waiting for someone to help me pay the rent on my mum's place now she was gone." The woman's voice was conversational now. She knew Ro was listening.

Did she just say?

Ro nodded and tapped her Optik to start recording.

"But they didn't. Help that is. I don't know what they're doing, but it ain't helping me and mine."

Now the woman was staring right at her.

"So what are you doing?" Ro asked. "For a home?"

The woman smiled, and Ro was startled by how pretty her face was when full of joy.

"It's all sorted, Rosemary," said the woman. "Turns out we all have friends who want to help, who lift us up when we're down, who find us when we're lost, and who make those who wrong us suffer."

Ro jumped up from the bench at the threat and fell into a fighting stance. "Just who the hell are you?"

"Me? I was lost, and then I got found," she said simply, not responding to Ro's aggression. Her accent had thickened. "We all lost something. It can't ever be replaced, but the hole right here?" She put her hand on her chest. "It's gotta be filled with somefink."

"What do you want?" She'd heard this kind of chat in church growing up. It had made her uncomfortable then and it made her uncomfortable now.

"I heard you was an illegal immigrant," said the woman as if trying to remember last week's headline.

"Bagley!" whispered Ro.

I'm trying!

"That's why I'm 'ere," said the woman. "I've got a message for you, DedSec, and your 'elper. Stay away from us. Leave us alone and let us live how we want. We're gonna make London better. Not you."

"I ain't got no beef with you, I don't even know who you are," said Ro. Who the hell was this woman with a calm smile threatening to make her suffer? The adrenaline which had drained out of her system ramped back up, drying out her mouth and leaving Ro ready to punch at anything that moved.

Instead, she held absolutely still, relying on the discipline she'd been taught as a fighter to not do anything stupid.

The woman stood up, brushing a strand of hair out of her eyes. Her voice was more rounded again. "Your buddy does, though. So you do as well, even if you don't know it. Today's just been a little demonstration. Leave us alone and we'll be grand. Go home, see to your mum. Do what you said you'd do."

The woman turned and broke into a run. Ro thought about giving chase, but Bagley was shouting in her ear to get home as quickly as she could.

7

The officials, and the uniforms they'd brought with them, had evaporated like mist by the time Ro got home. She hung around long enough to make sure her mum wasn't upset or frightened, but if CeCe was either of those things, she wasn't going to admit them to her daughter. Certain her mother was fine, given the circumstances, Ro jogged over to her own flat. Bagley had gone strangely quiet.

Her flat was on the third floor of an old block just on the other side of the estate to CeCe's. Far enough away to feel like her own space, but not so far her mum got grumpy about not being in her pockets. Certainly, her wider family kept a close enough eye that Ro was sure her mum knew all her comings and goings without them needing to do anything as boring as talk to each other.

Changed into kit for sparring, Ro made it down the stairs and was halfway to the gym when Bagley decided they needed to talk.

Can you come in?

"I need a break," she replied and meant it. The excess energy from the day bounced in her system. "Whatever you've got going on can wait until tomorrow."

We need you and Olly down at London Bridge.

"You don't," she replied, pulling the door open to the gym and nodding to those who looked up at her arrival.

We've got an angry member of the hacker collective 404 threatening to make me wear an avatar with frilly underwear and change my voice on five million Optiks to that of a modulated goat. You'd be doing me a big favour by coming in. We can order pizza?

"You can handle a bunch of hackers," she replied. She knew little about 404. Rumour was they were sharp but not the kind of group DedSec would think of as good friendship material.

Nowt is not a woman to be handled, said Bagley. Please?

Ro sighed, picked up the sports bag she'd dropped by the boxing ring, turned, and headed out.

The stench of the DedSec office was a thrilling recipe of damp, rat shit, and three types of week-old coffee. Olly tried not to visit these days – happy that if they needed him, they'd get in touch over his Optik. For Bagley to ask him to come in was unusual.

This whole bloody day's been unusual, he thought, accepting that the slightly sweet smell of the damp stonework was a price he had to pay to see to his obligations.

Ro rocked up half an hour after he did, looking just as pissed off, and he could see she wanted to be there about as much as him. Regardless, he was relieved to see she was OK. She wore a leather jacket and leggings, her small frame bulked out and ready for action. Olly knew who'd win in a fight and gave her a look which was his best attempt at commiseration.

"They did you over too?" she asked, her dark eyes sparkling in the gloom.

Olly grimaced. "At one point I was a rogue geography teacher wanted for stealing a school's laptops. I preferred being a suspected murderer; at least that gets some respect." He stopped as she laughed. "What about you?"

"Bastards tried to rope my mum in." She shrugged despite the obvious anger in her voice. "I would have loved to have seen their faces when she opened the door and there was just an old Black woman instead of the Karen they were expecting."

He shook his head in disbelief. "It all just… *stopped*. Bagley wouldn't say why."

Ro told him about the woman and her message. A shiver slid down his back.

As if on cue, the handful of other people in the room – the ones who spent more time underground than in daylight – left, some heading deeper into the tunnels, others back out the way Olly had come in. They were suddenly alone.

A large screen unfurled like a leaf across one wall and a middle-aged woman's face stared down at them, five feet across and snark riding on her lips every inch of the way.

"You told me you dealt with Skye Larsen," she began.

Olly was vaguely aware of what had happened with Larsen, but the one thing he did know was he hadn't been involved. Given what Bagley had told him about 404 on the way over, he could guess at who was scowling down at him. Nowt.

"You can get cross with me, lady, but I ain't got a frickin' clue what you're talking about," Olly said.

Whoever had executed the operations concerning Skye Larsen and Blume, DedSec worked so their individual cells were protected from knowing anything incriminating about their others. Olly really didn't know what she was talking about, and he guessed from Ro's confused expression that she didn't, either.

"Why are you with DedSec, then?" she asked with a tone which could have shattered glass.

Olly hadn't ever met her in person, but he knew about Nowt, if only by reputation. From his perspective, the woman was old, like, should have a career and be running a business old. She was dressed in an unbuttoned denim shirt with some pale rock band's T-shirt underneath.

"You tell me," he said.

"You were at the party," replied Nowt, her eyes narrowing. As she spoke, she took a pair of vintage headphones from around her neck and placed them out of sight. "After Cass died."

Suddenly he remembered her – drinking like the world was going to end, holding court with the eldest members of DedSec, and sharing war stories from when he would have been at primary school. Most of them had worn masks, and he remembered some of the others being in awe of how she did virtually nothing to hide her identity and location. If rumours were true, she didn't even bother with the basics.

For a moment he thought she was out of her mind, but then again, she was larger than life, regardless. Maybe she wasn't as far out as some of the others had said.

"I was," he said with a nod.

"At least I'm not talking to children, then."

"What do you want?" asked Ro from across the room.

"At the risk of repeating myself, you – DedSec – assured me that Larsen had been dealt with."

"I wasn't part of that squad," said Olly. "But her company's gone, and she's presumed dead. Isn't that enough?"

Nowt sucked at her teeth, and he thought she might explode. "How do you explain what's been happening, then?"

"We have no idea what you're talking about," said Ro confidently, but Olly's stomach turned over. Had Larsen been behind their altered identities? Was she still alive and taking some kind of toxic revenge? Was that what Nowt was angling after? Trying to get them to admit they'd been involved with the operation?

He suddenly wanted to talk to the team who'd taken Larsen

down, but by design they operated as cells, almost no one knowing who the other members of DedSec were. Unlike Nowt, they were all definitely paranoid.

"Bagley?" Olly asked the room.

"Don't drag that jumped-up toaster into this," said Nowt.

Would you like some toast? Maybe a muffin?

"Don't make me rewrite you as a dating sim for teenage girls," said Nowt, but Olly thought he saw something other than anger in her eyes.

Try it and I'll sell your assets and give the money to organizations dedicated to bringing back flares as the must-have fashion accessory.

Nowt snorted long and hard like a footballer about to hack up some phlegm. In spite of himself, Olly was impressed. Why did he let Bagley push him about so easily?

Ro seemed to be ignoring them all, having pulled up a screen of her own upon which footage and files were scrolling. "You're asking the wrong questions of us," she said, cutting across the bickering and catching everyone's attention.

"And you've deduced this how?" asked Nowt.

Ro stood up, flicking the files to Olly and another screen which mirrored itself in the bottom corner of Nowt's livestream. "I didn't work on Daybreak," Ro said. "Neither did Olly. We can't confirm if Larsen is dead or alive."

Opening the file, Olly frowned. Operation Daybreak. He saw the names *Skye Larsen, Blume, AI,* and *404*. What did 404 have to do with all this? The other one was a video of a young woman sitting on a park bench – the woman Ro had told him about. The rest were compilations of their different identities they'd experienced throughout the day. Nowt studied it all.

"Why would *they* come after us?" As silence spread through the room, Ro continued to talk, and Olly knew she meant Nowt as well as the unknown group – or person – who'd terrorized them all day. "Whoever it is targeted me and Olly specifically. So now you've got us here, after all the shit we've been through today, giving you what proof we have, so what did we do to upset you?"

Nowt's expression went wide, then thunderous. "Me? Fuck off. If I wanted to make your lives miserable, I'd call *your* bank and flag up the lack of tax you've been paying."

Nowt, said Bagley. It is a strange coincidence you showing up here after the day we've experienced. It might help us all if you tell us plainly why you've called. Bagley's words scrolled across the different screens in the room all at once.

Nowt didn't speak immediately, instead studying something out of shot with a thoughtful expression. Gradually, the anger in her face relaxed, the lines easing away even if she seemed as tense as the moment the feed had started.

"This has to be Larsen," Nowt claimed eventually.

"Not my department," Ro replied with a shrug. "Besides, whoever designed this identity scheme just wants to be left alone. Does that sound like Larsen to you?"

"And you know this because?"

"Watch," said Ro and played the footage of the woman on the bench and her message.

"That's not a request to be left alone," said Nowt firmly. "That's a declaration of war."

Olly watched the confusion on Ro's face and jumped in. "It don't sound like that to me," he said, hoping to defuse the conflict between the two women.

"Words of wisdom from a cycle courier," said Nowt before turning her attention back to Ro. Olly wanted to smack her in the gob but then again, he thought, she wasn't wrong. With a wave of his hands, he sat down, determined to let Ro and Nowt argue without getting involved any further.

She doesn't mean it, whispered Bagley in his ear. It's just how she charms you, all insults and cutting remarks before she asks you to do something important.

"She can Foxtrot Oscar if she thinks I'm going to help," he whispered under his breath.

"A lesson in strategy for someone focused on tactics then," said Nowt, her tone making Olly's teeth grind. "Our 'friend' here is asking DedSec to cede London to them, to step back and let them be in control. They're doing it with a pretty clear message of violence should you, we, not give them what they want. The identity changes you experienced prove that. This isn't about leaving them alone, it's about surrendering as they do whatever they choose. That's Larsen's entitlement up one side and down the other."

Ro nodded in agreement, but Olly cut in, asking, "Bagley, how many other identities did our new friend muck around with?"

None.

"That's the weird bit, right?" said Ro. She sat down, legs folding up under her. Olly wished he was that supple. "Why us?"

"I did a little experiment this morning," said Nowt.

Ah, said Bagley sounding regretful.

Christ, thought Olly, preparing himself for the worst. Here we go. The real reason she's targeted us.

"You two are some of the most visible members of DedSec in the city. Through Albion's period in power, the people of London rose up pretty much as an anonymous blob; an old lady with a rocket launcher here, a corporate drone there, a bin man in Chelsea, a trade unionist in Croydon. There was little predictability as to who was going to be on our side, when and what they might be doing. It made you two effective, if somewhat chaotic. You both were in it before Zero Day, before Albion got hold of the city by its throat. And you're still here, now, trying to make things better in your own way. Many of those others were part-timers – they did their bit and went back to their lives."

"There are more of us, though," said Olly, waving at the room even if it had just emptied so they could have some privacy.

"Most of them are mooks," said Nowt, but despite the term Olly didn't detect any snobbery in her tone. "They hide in your basement, doing what they do, making good progress, but Dracula spent more time in the sun than they do. Thus, Larsen wouldn't know who attacked her during Operation Daybreak or who fucked it up, but she can see you two swanning about the city like Robin Hood on a bicycle. Who else would she target to get DedSec's attention?"

Olly snorted, agreeing one hundred percent with her assessment. Bagley'd been right – this woman knew her stuff. Despite her brutal tongue lashings, she struck him as someone worth listening to.

"They wanted us to know they knew us," said Ro.

"We're not nobodies after all," said Olly with a smirk.

"Steady on," said Nowt, but when Olly looked at her, he could see she was actually smiling.

"Thing is, if they only targeted us, how did you know? Why were you on the phone ready to rip us a new one?"

Ro looked at him, then at Nowt. "Yeah, you said they hadn't targeted you."

"Larsen hasn't targeted me, that's true."

"Which makes no sense," said Olly. Of the three of them, Nowt was the one person Larsen would have cause to go after, especially since she did nothing to hide her identity.

"But I'm not DedSec," Nowt said. "I keep an eye on the city, and for those who are observant, there were telltale signs of *someone* at work on its fabric. I originally called out Bagley, determined to get him to stop his bullshit and focus on what's useful rather than making questionable ethical decisions which have definitely resulted in people dying, but he denied it was him at all. So, I went back to the evidence and looked at it again."

"Wait," said Olly, understanding now why Bagley had sounded contrite a few moments earlier. "How long have you known about this?"

Now, first things first. There was no "this" until today.

"Stop treating them like mushrooms," said Nowt.

Ro stood, arms folded and her expression severe.

There was nothing to tell, the AI protested. *You came at me last week…*

"Last week?" Olly asked.

Oliver. All I had was Nowt accusing me of changing the period of traffic lights in Kensington or redirecting ambulances in Hackney. I can assure you such things are not how I spend my spare time.

"You ignored it," said Olly.

You cannot ignore what is not there, insisted Bagley.

"That's the tip of the iceberg," said Nowt. "Are you going to tell them?"

No, no, no. Far be it from me to take any sort of credit.

"Probably for the best," said Nowt. "It's not just traffic lights. Larsen has been altering waiting lists for services, bumping people up ahead of others for transplants, emergency funding, even housing support. What's more, they've also been bumping others down or none too subtly letting the newly reconstituted Metropolitan Pig Force have concrete leads on numerous white-collar crimes, together with evidence."

"I don't see the problem," said Ro. "If it's Larsen, like you say, she's helping people. Turned a new leaf, eh? All of that helps London, right?"

Olly agreed. It wasn't all that different to the scammers they'd taken on just a few hours before.

"It *is* Larsen, and she's not helping," said Nowt. "Or at least, she's only helping a few people in really specific ways. You think pushing someone up a transplant list has no casualties? What about the child who's bumped down to make way? Or the person who's pushed back on finding a home they've been waiting years for because someone new suddenly jumps ahead of them? This isn't supposed to be the kind of country where that happens, and DedSec, for all its stupid chaos, isn't responsible for it either, although sometimes I wish you were."

I'm so proud of us, said Bagley across the screen.

"Who is Larsen helping?" asked Olly.

"I don't know. I mean, I don't know what connects them," admitted Nowt. Her screen was replaced by a map of London showing a network of different colours and dots. "These are all the different things Larsen has messed with. Red indicates resulting casualties."

"She's got a team," said Olly, seeing how the scatter of dots required a significant number of flesh and blood people to actually make them happen.

Nowt nodded. "Indeed. But they're nobodies, like you. No offence. They don't have the contacts or the skills to pull off what they're doing without some kind of omnipotent help."

"What about the woman who approached me?" asked Ro.

A dancer, studying at London College of Arts, said Bagley with a happy tilt to his voice. I cannot find much else.

"I thought there weren't any other AIs," Olly interrupted. "You're it, right, Bagley?"

Nowt laughed and for a moment Olly thought he heard Bagley snicker.

"There's AI everywhere, young man," Nowt said.

"I know this one," said Ro, suddenly. "AI is a specific thing; it should be called general artificial intelligence, at least in the way Olly's asking about it. What most people think of as AI, like in their TVs and on their Optiks, aren't that at all. The version of Bagley my mum's carrying around down to the club when she plays bridge is close, but even that's got a diminished capability for general problem solving."

Nowt nodded approvingly. "Yes, ten points to you. Most of what people call AI is nothing more than the type of code which can respond to limited inputs to offer the kind of responses those inputs are looking for. Bagley is not that kind of AI. In fact, there are no general artificial intelligences anywhere and, like not finding shit on your shoes, that's a very good thing."

Olly frowned, confused. "But Bagley is an AI, right?"

Fifty per cent right, Oliver. Fifty per cent. I will take this one, since this is all about me, and there's not a subject I like more. As you probably don't know because neither of you are good at homework or reading the mission reports I keep so meticulously filed, I'm actually composed of a human being's mind that was mapped to an architectural substrate. I'm a little bit of both.

"I don't understand, how do you map a mind? Isn't that just..." Ro drifted to a stop.

This is where Skye Larsen comes in. Say what you like, and our friend Nowt certainly has some colourful terms for her, but Skye was a genius and understood digital intelligence was only achievable by taking the most advanced form of reflective intelligence we'd encountered and replicating it in ones and zeroes.

Bagley paused.

I say most intelligent, but you know what I mean.

"Yeah, thanks for that," said Olly.

"The point is," said Nowt, cutting across them all. "Larsen was the only person to have done it – mapped a human mind into digital intelligence. Most famously with your unchained electronic paperclip here, but also with her own mind, which DedSec promised to stop. She's supposed to be dead or deleted. I was told she was no longer a threat. Promised, actually." She growled in frustration. "Bagley, I warned you your teams' actions would come back to bite us on the arse."

Larsen was resolved, said Bagley firmly.

"Yeah. Right." Nowt scowled. "Regardless of your faithfulness to the truth, there have been a couple of other AI examples similar to Bagley – do your homework like the puffed-up photocopier says – but you'll see Bagley's supposedly the only one left. Thus, if it's not Bagley, then it has to be Larsen, which proves DedSec failed Operation Daybreak."

"Fuck," said Olly, wishing he was more diligent in reading the case files stored on DedSec's archive.

Language, Oliver. We're not about to run rampant and replace you all as redundant meat sacks.

"One Bagley is too many," said Nowt. "Two and we're into proliferation territory. Two will become three and more, especially because Larsen can't help herself. At some point we humans have no choice but to realize we're redundant in our own world."

"I'm not thrilled about what happened today," said Olly. "I'd rather be riding my bike and thinking of other bastards we can shit upon from a great height. But all this" – he waved at Nowt – "this isn't that, right? They're not doing anything evil, not proper evil like Albion. There's no evidence that if we leave them to it bad things will happen or that AI will flood the world and terminate us all."

"Stop saying 'them'," objected Nowt. "We know who it is: Larsen."

"Why can't you just nuke them, Bagley?" asked Ro.

I'm not a weapon, Rosemary, and I resent the implication that I should be some sort of godlike presence who can summon up death and destruction whenever I feel like it. I have never done so and have never sought to do so. Humans, the stories you tell one another about AI, make me cringe because all you're really doing is substituting your weird ideas about God for magic code. You literally want me to be a Deus Ex Machina.

Olly noticed Nowt watching, her attention intense, her face still.

"Bagley is right," Nowt said. "He wasn't designed to be anything other than himself: a human who can navigate information space. I've thought hard about what it must be like to be Bagley, a human without a body."

She wasn't joking, and Olly realized the idea had never occurred to him. He felt slightly embarrassed on Bagley's behalf. Did everyone at DedSec treat the AI as if he was only there to be a deeply sarcastic personal assistant?

Nowt continued. "That piece of crap riding around on people's Optiks is little more than a pattern-spotting algorithm with a human face. It's why, even though Bagley knows I disapprove, I'm prepared to admit he's not all bad."

Why thank you for your glowing assessment of my life, it means so much coming from the woman who wanted my sister murdered, said Bagley.

"Wait, what?" said Olly.

Not my actual sister, obviously. Strange thing really, Oliver. Skye is my creator, but the human I'm based on? Her brother.

"She's your mum and your sister?" asked Olly, feeling stupid for focusing on that rather than the bombshell that Larsen was responsible for creating Bagley. "Fucking hell," he finished, feeling it was the more appropriate response.

"I could change my mind, you know," Nowt addressed Bagley curtly. The tension between Bagley and her was thick in the air.

And I could rewrite myself as a weapon and see where that gets us. Why don't we agree to think a bit more creatively about what can be done. A solution which doesn't require me to become someone else's tool or assume stupid mystical ideas about what AI can do. Rosemary, much as I deeply hate to admit it, Nowt is right. The message the young dancer gave to you isn't one I can just take and roll with. If it is dearest Skye, then we need to respond accordingly. She'll never let her ambition lie. She was quite focused that way. If it isn't her? Then we have other things to worry about.

"And if you can't take it on, then neither can DedSec," concluded Olly.

The problem is when I look for her or for them, I get nothing more than Nowt has. It's like I'm querying a database and getting a null return instead of the information I know should be there but I can't go in and fix the error.

"You want us to find out?" asked Ro, an earnest expression on her face.

Olly wasn't sure he was happy with her speaking for him, but truth be told, if Bagley was worried about this, he should be, too.

"Plus, since whoever this AI, or new hacker group, or Larsen is, has people helping it, we might get to, you know, shit on bad guys from a great height," Olly reiterated with a wink.

Ro pursed her lips. Olly wondered why she didn't seem to be up for it.

Nowt shook her head. "London is in a fucking state, and we've all got to do our bit to make it better. While I'm busy with other important things, however, I can introduce you to someone who

can help. What you do from there? Up to you, but my expectation" –
and here Olly understood she really meant her absolute concrete
certainty – "is that you'll work together to get this sorted out. I
want to know what Larsen is doing. Fix what DedSec fucked up."

"Who is this person?" Olly asked. So far, all Nowt had done was
convince him 404 were exactly what everyone said – not friendship
material.

"The grandmother of protests and hacking. There isn't anyone
I trust more to do what's right. I might seem like I have a stick up
my arse, but this woman? She'd kick my head in for looking at a
situation wrong and then get on with fixing it."

Sounds like just our sort of person, said Bagley.

"She's not yours," said Nowt. "Am I clear? She's your co-worker,
but if I hear you've been running your recruitment spiel on her or
her amazing daughter then I will fuck you up."

*Something you should know about Nowt, said Bagley. Is that when
she's happy she swears like an angry sailor.*

"I'll be sure to pass on your greetings," said Olly, and watched a
look of surprise pass over Nowt's face. He couldn't help but smile.
Point to me, he thought.

"I like you," said Nowt. "So I'll give you this for free: make sure
you haven't eaten before you go."

Bagley filled the screen with laughing GIFs, and Olly wondered
what he was missing.

8

Ro didn't know the west of London at all. For her, London was its eastern parts north of the river Thames. Everything else was a bit of a mystery, like rooms in her home she knew were there but didn't go into.

"People don't get things delivered by courier round here," said Olly as they rode the train. They'd decided to make the journey the next day around lunchtime, without suffering any more identity changes. "How'd you know that stuff about computing and AI?" he asked.

"I've been doing a course," she replied, hoping it would be enough for him. She felt nervous about admitting she was studying and hadn't even told her brother, Danny. She started when the fight with Albion had been reaching its crescendo. Feeling outclassed and useless compared to those who seemed to achieve more than she ever did just by sitting at their terminals, she became determined to be something more, something different than just a thug.

Except to admit as much, even to herself, felt like a failure. She loved fighting – that was never going to change. Olly asking tapped right into a weird sense of not knowing what she felt, and it made her want to hide until he decided not to ask more questions.

Oblivious, Olly didn't get the memo and kept prying. "Oh, what are you studying then?"

"Computers," she replied.

He stared at her like her mum would when her answers didn't come up to scratch.

Ro didn't mind talking about herself, but it had to be when she was ready. If being with her mum had taught her anything, it was that she was allergic to people asking direct questions about her life. She could feel herself closing down and becoming more monosyllabic with each question coming out of Olly's mouth.

"How'd you afford that?" he asked.

She turned to face him. "Look, it's no big deal, OK? I'm just doing a course. I'm not going to sell out when I'm done."

He held up his hands in surrender. "Sheesh. Was just making chat, chill out."

"What have you been up to?" Ro asked, feeling bad. There was no need to say *since Albion*, since DedSec went from being the only ones fighting back to realizing they had, in a way, won that war.

Olly looked up and down the train and pursed his lips thoughtfully. "Nothing really. The money we can make with our modified Optik gets me by. Sometimes I miss being a courier, like I really enjoyed the challenge of getting places and cutting up wankers in their white vans. Look, there's enough to keep me busy, innit, but in a year from now? I don't know. I got skills, but I'm not ready to be anyone's dancing monkey."

He sounded bored, even a little lost to Ro. She knew the feeling only too well. "If you'd asked me a couple of years ago what I'd be doing I wouldn't have dreamed this up."

He laughed in recognition. "Tell me about it. It's still a shitshow, innit? Honestly, I don't know what to do with meself half the time. I didn't think anyone else got it, you know? The fam don't give a shit, and most of the crew love their hacking more than they think about the future. Sometimes I'd like there to be a grown-up I could just talk to about what happens next, for me. Bagley's great and all that, but he's not really someone I'd ask for advice."

"I never thought about Bagley that way," said Ro, trying to picture it. "What Nowt said about him, what he said? I don't know what I thought he was behind the sarcastic troll he pretends to be. I- I never thought to ask him about himself. Do you think he can feel?"

"He sure acts like it," said Olly. "It's beyond me. He's a computer, right? TV always taught me computers can't feel anything, but then it turns out he's Skye Larsen's brother and I'm like, maybe he can feel? I don't know. How do you feel anything without a body?"

"Does feeling need a body?" Ro asked. "I don't think about my body when I'm happy or sad."

"Yeah, but when someone punches you in the face?"

She snorted. "They never get that close." Still, she knew what he meant. "It doesn't mean all feelings have to be like that."

"Hey, don't come at me. I'm the wrong man to be asking these questions. When we were at school, we went to see Shakespeare and one of the characters says 'is this a dagger I see before me?' and it was supposed to be profound, right, but all I could think was, yes, you plonker, it's a dagger, now get on with killing the jobby."

"Would you want to be like him? If you could?" Ro asked.

"Not thought about it," said Olly too quickly.

"I don't think I would, either," she answered in return, knowing both of them had spent their late nights thinking about what it would be like to be Bagley.

9

Southall was a low-rise mixture of housing built across two hundred years. Red brick, whitewashed wood, glass fronted shops, and a huge East Asian community from India, Pakistan, Bangladesh and Sri Lanka.

Ro was delighted by the shops selling curry like in Mile End and just as bemused by the overwhelming frontage devoted to wedding outfits.

The sound of planes was incessant even in the early afternoon, planes stacked in the sky like a flock of dazed birds. Ro was used to them, but with Heathrow a few miles south she couldn't understand how people put up with the noise.

Nowt had given them an address with a name, Barbara. Barbara's place was right by the railway but required them to walk a long circular route to get to it from the station. When they arrived, the two of them stood outside the building staring. The address was unmistakable and the building just as unique. Five stories high but built like a huge octagonal red brick grain store with small windows like narrowed eyes staring back down at them.

"Crikey," said Olly.

"Gotta love London," replied Ro. "It looks like a castle out of a movie where everyone dies one by one during a party." She paused. "You think she's gonna be like Nowt?"

"God, I hope not," said Olly. "Can you imagine if 404 was just older women hacking governments for the shit of it?" The idea clearly amused him, but it made Ro realize that might be quite the thing to be part of.

There was no easy way in. High steel fences ran across the road leading up to it, and a heavy black gate blocked their progress. Ro saw a panel and pressed the biggest button, hoping it would ring up at the building.

An old Indian woman's face appeared on screen. "What do you want? I'm busy. It better not be anything disgusting."

Ro was startled by her accent, which was as posh as any upper-class toff she'd ever met.

When neither of them answered the woman said, "Well come on, I haven't got all bloody day."

"We're here about the faulty washing machine," said Ro belatedly, using the phrase Nowt had given them.

Barbara looked surprised. "My washing machine's fine, so bugger off."

Ro kept her finger on the buzzer, but the woman didn't cut the video feed, as if suspicious they wouldn't leave unless she watched them. At a loss, Ro glanced around and leaned in. "Um, Nowt sent us?"

"Who?" asked the woman.

Ro wondered if they'd got the wrong place. "Are you Barbara Arscott?"

"Of course I am," said the woman as if Ro was an idiot. "The question is, who are you and what do you want?"

"We're here because of the AI?" asked Ro, feeling increasingly like a child in front of an angry parent.

"Why didn't you start with that?" she said, and the feed cut. A moment later the gate slid back on rails allowing them access to the building.

So much for discretion, thought Ro. Did no one at 404 care about security?

After negotiating more locked doors which opened as they approached and clunked shut after them, they found themselves on the top floor of the building. The sound of trains running outside made Ro feel right at home.

The door to Barbara's flat opened, and Ro realized the woman was not even five feet tall, but she had a gravity to her which blocked the door as effectively as a six foot six, two-hundred-and-fifty-pound bouncer. What really grabbed Ro's attention, though, was the smell of cooking. Frying onions, sizzling ghee, and sweating tomatoes. Mouth watering, Ro and Olly followed Barbara into her flat until they stopped in the kitchen.

Whole and shelled king prawns were piled high on a wooden chopping board next to a huge kitchen knife. A large metal pot was on the hob, and from it came the smells which had pulled Ro along by the nose. Garlic, chili, and turmeric were so thick in the air she reckoned she could take a slice and eat it.

Barbara directed them to sit and proceeded to continue cooking her prawn curry.

"Can I help?" asked Ro. This was a vastly different experience from what she'd expected.

Barbara gave her a withering look, and instead of answering, went to the fridge and retrieved some samosas, which she put into the oven. Ro backed off and sat down. Next to her, Olly fidgeted but said nothing. When he met Ro's eyes, he smirked then looked away before they both burst into laughter.

A few minutes later Barbara took the food out of the oven, slid the samosas onto a dish, and laid them on the table. "Eat," she commanded.

Olly didn't need telling twice and bit into one with relish. Ro looked at them and worried about taking advantage.

"Eat," said Barbara again before turning back to the stove.

Ro did as instructed. They tasted divine, and before she knew it, she'd munched down the entire thing, her fingers slippery with the oil. "Nowt said you could help us?" she asked carefully.

"Yes, yes," said Barbara from the stove. She had a second pot of water boiling into which she poured a bowl of rice.

"How can you help us, exactly?" persisted Ro.

"Have another," said Barbara, coming over to the table but not sitting down.

"I'm all right, thanks," said Ro.

Concern crossed Barbara's face. "Don't you like them?"

Ro sighed. If it had been her mum, she could have just said she wasn't hungry, but here, it felt awkward to say no, so she picked up a second samosa and nibbled on it.

Satisfied, Barbara said, "Nowt probably told you she'd noticed oddities across the city. She didn't. I did." Then, she retrieved okra from a fruit bowl and came back to the table where she started to chop them into chunks. When she was done, she dipped them into semolina and chili powder. Ro watched mesmerized as Barbara took them over to the hob, took the rice off the heat, and proceeded to fry the okra in a little ghee. The smell was unbearably tempting.

She got up to help.

"Sit down, stupid girl," said Barbara without turning around.

She looked at Olly, but he seemed entirely content to be waited on by an elderly stranger. Moments later, Barbara served them a king prawn curry unlike any she'd ever tasted before, with fried okra on the side. Olly took a mouthful and started to eat as if his life depended on it.

Ro felt like she'd been transported to when her family all lived in the same three neighbouring flats where the women would be cooking all day and the smells were as much a decoration as the wallpaper. "How did you spot these changes?" she asked between mouthfuls as if it was everyday conversation. "Weird thing to be looking for anomalies in traffic lights and queues for housing and operations."

"Be quiet," said Barbara. "Eat now."

Ro had been in a situation like this before with her aunties and her mother, and despite the urge to talk loudly out of spite, she did as bid and concentrated on eating.

When they were done and Ro had navigated turning down seconds as Olly accepted another full plate, Barbara actually started to talk. She told them essentially the same story as Nowt, but in this version, it was the Indian woman who'd done all the hard work.

"You don't look like a hacker," said Olly, and Ro wanted to take him out of the room and warn him to batten down the hatches for what was coming.

Instead, she watched with secret glee as Barbara fixed him with a glare and Olly realized his mistake. "Young man, before you were born, I was sitting at Greenham Common with hundreds of other women protesting nuclear weapons." Barbara took a deep breath to continue, but another voice interrupted her.

"Mum?" came a call from the front of the flat.

"Through here, poppet."

Ro and Olly exchanged glances as a younger version of Barbara came into the kitchen. "You haven't been feeding them up, have you?" she asked lightly, looking at the plates and kissing Barbara on the top of her head. Barbara made a sound like a contented cat but didn't answer.

"Why don't you go and get changed for your virtual walk, and I'll talk to these two. Nowt sent them?" the new woman continued.

Barbara didn't argue but got up and left the room.

"You made the mistake of assuming an old woman can't understand technology, didn't you," she said, looking straight at Olly.

"Why'd you think it was me?" he complained.

"Because you're a man," said Ro and laughed. "As DedSec, you should know better."

The woman smiled at them both and said, "I'm Maxine, Barb is my mum. You're here about the anomalies?"

"So you both know?" asked Ro.

"We're 404. She'll be back in a minute, but let me give you a few headlines. It'll save any embarrassments later." She reached into the pot of curry and pulled out a prawn. "Mum came over here in the 60s with her three daughters and without her husband. She worked really bloody hard to live a life acceptable to all those people who hated us for being brown. I don't know everything, who really understands the lives their parents led before they became so narrow as to be nothing more than our parents?" There were sounds of movement from elsewhere in the flat and Maxine's voice sped up. "I think she worked for the government and protested against them, like in good conscience. She's a firework with a short fuse, but when she likes you, you'll be fine." She looked at Olly's empty plate. "Given you ate everything she put in front of you I'd say you're off to a good start."

"What nonsense are you telling them?" asked Barbara as she came into the room.

"Nothing, Mum," Maxine said quickly.

Barbara ruffled Maxine's hair as she sat down. "It's lovely to have a full house."

"If you got out more, Mum," said Maxine.

"Cha," said Barbara dismissively. "Oliver, Rosemary, you were sent to me to help with this."

I thought she was going to help us, thought Ro, her head throbbing with sudden frustration.

"This AI needs to be identified, found, and if possible, reasoned with," Barbara said.

"Nowt wants Larsen killed?" said Olly.

Maxine stilled, but Barbara rolled her eyes. "Of course she does, and she's got every reason to hate both Larsen and AI, but I don't think we should assume Larsen is at the heart of this yet."

"Nowt knows she's not objective," Maxine said. "She wants to burn anything AI to the ground."

"She's going to slow down their ultimate arrival as long as she can," continued Barbara.

Ro wanted to know what had happened to Nowt. Her hands itched with the sudden mystery to be solved.

"She doesn't believe in the singularity, then?" asked Olly as if it was the strangest thing he'd ever heard. Ro squinted at him in disapproval. How was that important compared to what happened to Nowt?

"You're quite handsome, but you're not very bright. Humanity passed the singularity at the beginning of the Industrial Age, we just didn't know how to talk about it properly until von Neumann. These children with their start-ups and their waxed balls think they invented it, but they just misheard someone else's lecture and thought they'd come up with it themselves. Typical men." Barbara snorted.

Maxine tried not to laugh, but Olly leaned back as if he'd been slapped. "AI bring the singularity though, right?" he persisted.

"Oh, don't be so silly. Bagley proves computers aren't about to replace us. Not only are they unable to do what we do in the most fundamental sense, they have to be taught to be better than us and even then, only in specific scenarios. They are never general, they are specific cases of problem solving rather than actual intelligence."

"If it looks like a duck, Mum," said Maxine.

"No, I get it," said Ro, surrendering to the conversation. "There are loads of people saying AI are better than us, but you're right, every single one has an army of well-funded academics behind them who've been working on the problem for years."

"Exactly," said Barbara as if she wasn't expecting anyone to agree with her.

"But AI could accelerate past us, couldn't it?"

"Oh god," said Barbara with obvious disgust. "Stop listening to young men and their stupid ideas."

"Mum," said Maxine, and Barbara huffed but didn't say more. "What she means is to ask where this supposed godlike AI gets its power from? Where does it get its processing and storage volumes? Is it some kind of monomaniac? If it is then it isn't an artificial intelligence and it's certainly little more than a cancerous growth. It wouldn't be able to defend itself because it would be too focused on these weird poorly defined 'self-improvement' loops people always talk about. I don't agree with Mum about AI. I think they're coming, and I also think we are facing a new singularity." Barbara began to speak, but Maxine held up a hand. "There's no reason there can only be one."

"Bagley's an AI though," said Olly, still stuck in the earlier part of the conversation.

"He's not artificial," said Barbara.

"Back to the point," said Maxine. Ro could see why Nowt

had warned them off recruiting her – she'd eat their geeks up for breakfast and spit them out twice as useful as before. "If this godlike intelligence running around London isn't some kind of maniac, then it's unlikely to devour us, or itself, even if it could somehow co-opt all these suddenly magically connected networks. I mean, you realize in this country they have physical switches the size of shovels which can simply shut down the grid? There isn't any kind of automation which can replace that."

"So why's Nowt so angry?" asked Ro, directing them back to the important matter.

Barbara leapt in before Maxine could answer. "The thing about tech bros is they look at the problems around them and say 'we can fix this by going to Mars' instead of looking at how they can actually use all that power and wealth to do something useful. Their attitude is disgusting."

"It's just different, Mum."

Barbara sniffed, and the long, pointed sound made Ro understand loud and clear that she disagreed in the strongest possible terms.

"My point is," Barbara continued, "it's the same when these tech bros try to imagine what could go wrong. They look right past the truth that machine learning and algorithms can just as easily kill people when they're built with existing prejudices and systemic inequalities. They're deliberately dumb, like this one." She waved a hand at Olly.

"Look," Olly said angrily, but Barbara fixed him with a stare that said he might be losing her respect, even though he'd eaten her food with enthusiasm.

"Software does not need agency or motivation to harm. Back in the day when they were first trialling facial recognition algorithms, a software company did a big launch in New York. They had this huge crowd and invited some participants onto the stage to demonstrate the software. The first man up was a Black man–"

"Mum, you can't say that," said Maxine, looking horrified.

Ro didn't mind, it wasn't like Barbara was a white dude trying to score a point.

"It's important. Stop interrupting me. He got up in front of the camera, and the software didn't recognize him as human. When they debugged the software, they realized they'd trained it only on white faces. Nowt is worried about the singularity we're in right now, the one where prejudice and bias are coded and then amplified by recursive machine learning algorithms. We don't need intelligence explosions to make the world a worse place for us, just developers who don't look at their biases when putting them into code, who assume that code is colourblind."

"Nah," said Olly. "I mean, yes, I get it. But that's not why Nowt's so against all this. She wanted Skye Larsen murdered. That is not a level-headed response to bad coding."

Barbara laughed. "You're not a coder, are you? Seems pretty reasonable to me."

"He's right, though," said Ro. "What happened?"

Barbara licked her lips, but Maxine intervened. "It's not our story. If she wants you to know she'll tell you."

Barbara looked disappointed, but she didn't contradict her daughter.

"I don't mean to be cruel, but we – 404 – were under the impression that Larsen was dead, or at least no longer a threat, so to suddenly be informed that is no longer true is disappointing. You can't blame Nowt for not trusting DedSec," Maxine finished.

Now you've decided on my status perhaps we can focus on the other intelligence running around London acting like God?

"Bagley, I have warned you about coming onto my Optik with–

out my permission," said Barbara, sounding as if she'd expected him to do so.

I'm sorry Mrs A but time is running on. Since you've fed and watered these two layabouts, there was only so much education I could take before my circuits started to melt. Nowt said you could help us find my counterpart?

"Obviously. Maxine, will you do the screen?"

Maxine twisted a ring on her finger and a large section of wall on one side of the room turned on. Ro hadn't even noticed it was there. It blended seamlessly into the room right up until the moment Maxine activated it.

A map of London appeared on the wall, all buildings and cars with dots of green. Ro realized it was right in the heart of the city. It took her a few moments to work out where the map was centred, but then Olly said, "That's Clerkenwell Road. I was down there last week."

Maxine pinched her fingers together and the map zoomed in, sliding slightly north and resting on a grey square with no names on it. Which seemed odd as the whole area in question should have been full of design and media types, along with the bars and restaurants that supported them. For those businesses to have missed the chance to tag their location on a map would be unthinkable.

"What's there?" Ro asked, pointing at the featureless icon.

"That's an old datacentre," said Maxine.

"Can't be," said Ro. "They're all on the edge of the city. I've seen them, massive buildings like warehouses on industrial sites."

"You're right," said Maxine, as Barbara stared up at the screen with an analytical expression. "Except for that one there. When people first needed datacentres, they took empty buildings in the middle of cities. Then, when they first built them, they put them in their own office blocks, but this is one of that first generation of custom designs. Thick walls and blacked-out windows where they haven't simply bricked them up. Supposedly able to withstand a nuclear blast." She didn't sound like she believed it.

"Our AI is there?"

Can't be, said Bagley into Ro's earpiece. From Olly's reaction he heard him too. They have to be distributed. Too obvious to be in just one place. Too dangerous. Larsen's not an idiot.

"Doesn't matter whether you're right. I've traced definite signalling from that location. People are dying or losing their livelihoods because of what she's doing. It has to stop before things get worse."

She won't be there, insisted Bagley.

"I want you two to go and see what's what," said Barbara to Ro and Olly.

"You're not coming?" asked Ro, wondering how they were going to get inside.

"I don't leave the flat," said Barbara. Maxine put a hand tenderly onto her mother's arm.

"You're coming though, right?" Ro asked Maxine.

"Me? No. Kids need picking up from school. Don't worry, I'm sure you'll be fine. Besides, Mum's teasing you, she'll be there. Kind of."

Ro looked at Olly, hoping he might have some words of wisdom, but he looked just as disarmed as she felt.

Bagley's-Briefs 83-41: If we've all finished gawping at my astonishing personality then there's plenty going on in old London town for those who are interested.

+++

There's the first retrospective of street art (that's graffiti to you, Sharon) at the Tate Modern – they were so quick to jump on this celebratory bandwagon they haven't yet realized just how rude and crude many of the pieces are, especially with regards to our late, not so great, sponsors, Albion. Expect there to be toothbrushes and chisels deployed to sanitize proceedings shortly, so if you want to see it in all its glory, better get there sharpish.

+++

As for London's Peelers, the Met's very slightly younger sibling, the City of London Police are back up and running, protecting the fine gentlefolk of the Square Mile (and its environs). As was the case before they were suspended during Albion's inglorious reign, they're back to ensuring oiks and ruffians do not interfere with the toffs and Tories engaging in properly epic financial crime, sorry, engineering. Remember please, if you're going to undertake actions within their sphere, do avoid looking poor or, you know, like someone who's rich and white.

+++

There has been chatter about another group operating on our turf. This is true. People are investigating. No, Terry, it's not aliens. If it is aliens, then we'll let them get on with it because they've crossed the vast volume of interstellar space to visit London, and what kind of hosts would we be to interfere with that? On the other hand, if they turn out to be a gang or another collective, we shall be ramping up appropriate actions to ensure no one messes with our city.

+ + +

In the meantime, we have a lot of jobs on the slate, and I'm not scoring out half as many as I'd like. There are the dodgy Germans stealing cars and exporting them to Newcastle (no, I don't know why), three sets of scammers in Brentford, and one particularly dumb individual trying to sell the Met a fully autonomous robot police force.

+ + +

The jobs list is as long as my birthday wishlist (link here, remember I'm like the Queen and have two a year, so get saving). As with all the work we do, you are awesome and none of this would happen without you. As usual, go see the anonymous message board for words of thanks from the people affected by the jobs you've been doing.

10

"I don't understand," said Olly when Barbara made no move to leave with them. "How will you be with us?"

"You'll see," was all she would say. Since he'd eaten her curry, and what astonishing grub it had been, she'd made him feel like his tongue was stuck to the roof of his mouth. He hadn't been this clumsy with words since he was a child and was swiftly growing to hate it. A small part of him was glad she wasn't coming with them even as she unloaded all the details of the warehouse into their Optiks. He ached to be able to talk like an adult again.

Then, just like that, he and Ro were back on the other side of the security gates and shuddering as high-speed intercity trains whistled past.

"Every time I think I understand this city it throws up a new one for me," said Olly. "Like, I spent my days cycling across the place, carrying every kind of gadget you can think of for everyone from artists to scientists and bankers. I gave the Queen's butler a new pair of cufflinks one time." He looked up at the building without saying more. He couldn't tell if Ro felt as weirded out as he did. "But this place was never on my radar."

"It was like my mum turning out to be a hacker with a secret agent past," she said eventually.

"I know, right?" he said, clapping his hands together with joy that she understood. "That flat is seriously wired up, innit?"

"You were pretty quiet in there. Cat got your tongue?"

Like the old woman had yours? Bagley replied.

"Bagley, what can you do?" asked Ro, suddenly sounding all business.

What do you mean?

"Come on, can you fight this AI? Why are *we* hunting it down? It's not operating in our tactile environment, right? How can we take down someone like… like you?"

Olly was impressed by the question and waited for Bagley to reply.

I'm looking for her, or them, but it's not easy. Think of it like this: every computer is a solar system capable of supporting life. There are probably eight million people in the city, each with a phone, smart fridge, television, even washing machine. Let's not count their actual workstations, tablets, projectors, and consoles. That's literally tens of millions of devices. Do you know where I live?

Olly thought about it. "In lots of places? Would be dumb to concentrate yourself in once place if you didn't have to."

Excellent, said Bagley, but only half right. I can't split myself up. I'm a collection of code like your brain is a collection of sensory inputs and memories woven together in a scruffy, deceptively smart, bike courier shaped body.

"Was that a compliment?" asked Olly.

Don't let it go to your head, Oliver.

"Aren't you distributed, though?" asked Ro.

That's different, said Bagley. I'm still in contact with myself. If I properly split myself up, then I'd run the risk of losing great chunks of who I am if whatever components I was relying on disconnected. Instead, I run myself redundantly, the complete opposite of splitting myself up, and I do so in a way that ensures I can't be deleted by accident or misfortune. Unless I want to, that is.

"Sure," said Olly, not quite following. "I don't see what that's got to do with Larsen. You know we need a name for her, them, they? See what I mean? A name's much easier."

"She" is fine for now. My point is, I can't go somewhere and find her. She's not at the park drinking Special Brew waiting for me to turn up, but she most likely has a storage location, something like her personal lab when she was doing experiments into mapping human minds, to hold her data. She couldn't keep it somewhere it would be found after she was proclaimed dead. You are our best bet at finding her, and I'd rather this investigation be in DedSec hands.

"By tracking down her physical location? Like the place her brain is?"

Bagley was silent for a moment. No. I get this is strange to you. It is to me as well. When I think of self-care, I imagine software patches, not having a nice bath and a pizza. We don't have a brain like you, not least because we don't have a calciferous skeleton in which to house it, but somewhere like the datacentre Barbara's sending you to? It's a place where your world and mine come together.

"Well then, we should probably go take a look," said Olly.

Barbara watched Ro and Olly leave on her security feeds, a thoughtful expression on her face.

"They're not the best," she said to Maxine, who was tidying up. Her daughter didn't respond, which could only mean she disagreed but didn't want to disagree out loud.

Silly girl, as if I didn't bring her up her whole life. "Spit it out," she smiled.

"They're good, Mum. You're being too harsh."

"She didn't eat her samosas," said Barbara, feeling insulted all over again.

"They weren't your best," said Maxine.

"I know, I just can't get the right flour without going all the way up to the high street. It's too far and they won't deliver." She stopped talking as her brain caught up with her mouth. "Don't be so cheeky."

"Listen, Mum, I've got to go pick the chooks up from their school clubs. Are you sure you won't just join them? It's not even four, you could be back in time for your shows."

Barbara loved her daughter but sometimes her optimism blinded her. "I'm seventy years old. I stream my shows when I want them."

"Exactly," said Maxine, seizing on the point. "You're still active and getting out of the house could only do you good." Maxine sighed. "I try to understand, but it's not a warzone out there."

Barbara gave her a look.

"Anymore," corrected Maxine. "I can't think of anyone safer than you. Nothing bad will happen if you go out. Why are you so afraid?"

"Stop it before I put you over my knee," said Barbara.

"I don't understand what happened to you," said Maxine with deep sadness. "You were the most dangerous person I knew growing up. I was so proud of you."

"This isn't like going to sit in front of a missile base or carry placards against an illegal war. We don't know what this unknown lot want, or how they might impact the small things we take for granted." She smiled as if being brave. "Besides, I've got Shelob ready to go."

Maxine waved her hands in surrender. "Can't you call it something else?"

"Go on, get off with you," said Barbara.

When her daughter had vanished down the stairs, Barbara settled in to do some actual work.

The two kids from DedSec hadn't been bad, but she wasn't

about to admit that to Maxine. She wondered how they'd ended up involved with the collective because neither of them seemed like natural fits. DedSec seemed to think it had to save the world. 404 worked for her because it just let her be, offering help if and when she wanted it, with a goal to take down the elite instead of just exposing corruption in the common world.

She sighed. It wasn't fair to characterize them, and she knew it. She'd been the only Indian woman at Greenham some days, but no one had ever made her feel unwelcome, and the British government had seen her odd views and talents as worth their weight in gold.

Albion's long shadow over the city had seen DedSec do what Nowt and the rest of them couldn't – resist in a way that made a difference. She suspected it still irritated Nowt just how shockingly successful DedSec had been when push came to shove.

"You there, comrade?" she asked the empty air, and Nowt's voice answered, face blinking into view a moment later.

"What do you think?"

"The boy has a good appetite. They'll do."

"The girl, Ro, is a smart one, just not book smart. She'll make you proud."

"You want her for 404," said Barbara, realizing where Nowt was headed.

"Not the right material. Still thinks the world can be a better place," replied Nowt, but Barbara could see through her friend to the truth underneath.

"You think she's got promise. I'll see what I think and let you know."

Nowt nodded. "You've sent them to the datacentre?"

"I am watching. It will be interesting to see how long it takes for the little sparrows who've been following them to take fright."

"Did they make it all the way to yours?"

Barbara snorted. "Don't be silly. There aren't any drones within a hundred metres of my place without my permission. I send them around and they don't even know they've been diverted."

"They weren't piloted, then?"

"It doesn't make any difference," said Barbara. "Pilots see what's on their feed. Hack that, and they'll respond to what they see as if it's really there. In the end they spent a few minutes south of the railway then gave up, assuming they'd lost the two kids down there."

"So, whoever is behind this is hunting them."

"If it really is an AI, it won't take long for it to pick them up again. It's a lead."

As Barbara spoke, Nowt grew more unhappy, the edges of her lips turning down and the thin lines at the corners of her eyes becoming more pronounced.

"It's what we need," Barbara said before realizing something else was making Nowt uneasy. "You can't protect the world from algorithms, Nowt."

"I don't want to," said Nowt curtly.

"My John used to sit out in his shed carving wood and smoking in secret as if the puffs of smoke rising from the roof didn't give the game away." Barbara wrinkled her nose. "And the taste he had after a long day of smoking and crafting – disgusting. He knew I knew, and I knew he knew that."

"He was an idiot. He'd survived tuberculosis and kept on smoking."

"And lived to seventy-eight. It wasn't smoking that killed him, Nowt, it was the lies he told himself so he could keep living the way he wanted, so he could hide from the truth of what his behaviour was doing to him."

Nowt didn't respond and looked away from the camera as if to hide. It didn't matter, Barbara knew where she lived and could have described the room in which her friend sat right down to the three ceramic unicorns just beyond the ancient keyboard she liked to use.

"AI destroys lives," said Nowt eventually.

"We die, Nowt. All of us. Sometimes it's a bus, sometimes it's sickness, and occasionally it's because of another person, but we all die."

"She didn't have to," said Nowt quietly. "Not then."

Barbara wanted to tell her it had been ten years ago, but they'd talked it through a hundred times, and she knew where her friend had become unmoored in her own history. Barbara would never be the anchor Nowt needed to regain her balance, nor to solidify her hatred of AI.

Honestly, she thought, who needs balance anyway?

"Will you do what needs to be done?" Nowt asked.

Barbara nodded. "You know I will. I'm 404, Nowt."

Nowt met her gaze for a moment. "You're going to use that stupid spider drone, aren't you?"

"I'm certainly not leaving the flat," said Barbara severely.

Nowt laughed, a sound Barbara had been hearing from her less. "Maxine's right. Stop being such a baby, put on your big girl pants, and get back out there. Or not, I don't care. Just keep me in the loop, yeah?"

"I'll send Maxine over with some gulab despite your impertinence," said Barbara, smiling.

When Nowt was gone Barbara finally turned to the task at hand, tracking the two DedSec kids and making sure she'd spot the point at which this other player – this new AI Larsen, if Nowt was right – found them again.

Snapping a pair of glasses over her face, she let them click into the Optik against her ear. With the softest of pressure, they joined and across her eyes came menus with options and a command prompt.

The kitchen table faded out as her perception shifted to Shelob and opened her eyes to darkness. A steel grate of a garage door started to roll up into the ceiling, flooding the space with stark grey daylight. The cameras compensated for the change in brightness, slowly bringing up the illumination until she could see clearly.

The room was a double length garage cut into the bottom of her octagonal building. The walls were painted white with soft blue accents which gave it the sparse feel of a laboratory. A long workbench ran along one side and had as many computer screens stacked upon it as wrenches and spanners. Soldering irons and multicoloured reels of wire were packed into small towers.

Barbara ran a test on the different systems.

It was the first time she was taking Shelob out in earnest on a mission, and her stomach flipped as she moved around the garage, extending manipulators and checking on the drone's power store. After a while she realized she was putting off what had to be done and, turning to face the exit, scuttled from the building into the outside.

The nearest storm drain entrance was just to the south, under a steel fence and next to the high-speed rail tracks. The area was surveilled by the rail operator's own security systems – their biggest problem was people straying onto the tracks and getting hit by trains.

Barbara had used the drone to dig a hole large enough to pass through some months ago, coming back only occasionally to ensure it hadn't been filled in by some zealous maintenance contractor. She suspected that since it was less than a foot wide and half that high, if anyone spotted it, they'd assume it was a rabbit who'd dug through and leave it well enough alone. After all, trains weren't stopped by rabbits on the track.

The storm drain dropped down to the river Crane, a poorly looked after ancient waterway which was doing marginally better than some of its long-buried counterparts. From there she turned east and followed the Grand Union Canal on its winding route in towards the city.

The easiest way not to be seen was to follow the waterways. The canal crossed the river Brent, allowing her to turn south and, a couple of miles later, intersect with the Thames as it flowed proud towards its great estuary on the east side of London.

The truth was, London was a river city and not because of its most famous waterway. As many as twelve major rivers had been lost to the surface of the city in the centuries in which it had grown into one of the world's great metropolises. Most of these rivers had turned into sewers, from historical residents throwing their human excrement into them to the present day, when the authorities had invested in huge infrastructure projects with wide tunnels to manage the city. Thing was, these days the city's water was the cleanest it had ever been.

Barbara had travelled through what remained of the city's underground waterways in her drones, loving the sense of seeing places no one else remembered. When she wasn't doing that, much of her time was spent exploring abandoned buildings or those lying fallow while their owners tried to decide what to do with them. She knew younger people broke into them in the flesh, took photos or livestreamed their visits.

Age had made that impossible for her, but Shelob and its kin meant she could get about anywhere and was far less likely to come across a copper with drones, security details, guard dogs, or in one case, guard geese.

There were still plenty of turds floating around down in the sewers, but Barbara didn't mind them too much – she had stores of bleach at home and always scrubbed Shelob down when it got home after one of their outings.

Shelob wasn't much bigger than a coconut crab and was painted in an urban camouflage pattern, which meant it faded into the drab shifting edges of the dark brown Thames like a piece of flotsam.

She kept going, passing under the city's bridges, avoiding curious gulls and the ebbing tide until she reached London Bridge where both the Fleet and the Walbrook emerged via storm drains to pour into the Thames unseen by the general population.

The Victorians had done a lot of public-minded engineering, and the turning of the Walbrook into part of the London Bridge sewer had been one of those grand projects.

She crawled into the tunnel and ran north, the drone's eight legs moving her along faster than a human could have walked. They'd moved the river again when the latest east–west tube line had been dug a few years back, but the sewer still ran up past Moorgate before heading west into Clerkenwell. Which was just where she wanted to be.

Riding along on the drone was a strange experience. At the beginning of every trip, Barbara was aware of her own body sitting in the kitchen and how it twitched as she made Shelob move. Yet after a while the sense of her fingers, of sitting on a chair, elbows resting on the table, receded until it felt like she was actually Shelob. All she lacked was mandibles to clack.

She didn't feel Shelob's eight legs – the locomotion reached her brain as movement, and that was enough to feel immersed. Returning to her own body wasn't exactly a joy… on bad days she'd feel nauseous afterwards, dizzy if she moved too quickly, and the temptation to get down onto her hands and knees would come and go for hours.

But while riding the drone, her arthritis didn't hurt and her joints didn't ache.

Before the DedSec kids had left, they'd traded handles, so she was able to locate them quickly. They'd taken the tube and were in a coffee shop just around the corner from the datacentre.

To her surprise they were waiting for her to make contact.

"Where are you?" asked Ro as soon as she pinged them.

"I'm coming up from London Bridge. Give me a few minutes."

In reality she'd already broken cover in the grounds of Charterhouse, a university campus burrowed right into the heart of the city and just south of where she needed to be.

Of more interest to her was what kind of surveillance the DedSec kids were under now they were back in the open.

Drones filled the sky, going about their business. She didn't have any idea of the resources Larsen could draw upon. It could be she had drones the size of fingernails able to pin themselves to people's clothes.

Barbara assumed they weren't facing that kind of nightmare scenario. She had successfully hidden her visitors when they'd come for lunch. On that basis, she'd most likely be looking for stealth drones about the size of her palm, flying or hovering near the coffee shop. Barbara piloted Shelob up onto the roof of a building overlooking the coffee shop and set about identifying the drones that were hanging around too long in local airspace.

The density was high. Many of them were informal and unregistered with the authorities. She didn't care – it made eliminating them as suspects tougher but nothing that moved the dial. After a couple of minutes, Barbara had whittled out the passersby and was left with a couple of dozen drones. Half of those were hovering over junctions monitoring traffic – vehicles as well as people. Nothing unusual there; it would be advertisers looking for opportunities to target specific adverts as much as it was city logisticians looking to manage the flow of traffic in real time.

Of the last few, one was watching a window over the other side of the road. Skin crawling at the possibilities, Barbara sent an overload packet and watched with satisfaction as the machine tumbled out of the sky.

Which left three. Two appeared to be idling, waiting for instructions. She moved on to the last and saw it describing a repeating flight pattern of coming down the road, pausing to image the coffee shop and then circling back around. The drone was registered to a butcher's over in Wembley.

"You're a long way from home," she said. Barbara checked in to see if anyone had posted about losing a drone on local message boards and immediately regretted it as hundreds of requests filled her screens. Abandoning the idea of running that lead down she concentrated on the drone until certain it was picturing Ro and Olly.

"Hello, you two, wave for the camera."

She laughed as they looked around nervously.

"Larsen found you. If you look carefully, you'll see a little drone cycling past every sixty seconds or so."

To her surprise, Olly's expression turned sour and with a finger to his Optik, he waited until the drone flew past, spotted it, and then stared intensely.

Too late, Barbara realized he was going to nuke it.

In the aftermath of the drone crashing headlong into a wall and tumbling, broken, to the ground, she said, "I wish you hadn't done that. Now they know you know."

11

The drones began monitoring Olly and Ro as they ducked into a coffee shop a street away from the datacentre. Bagley wasn't concerned. If they hadn't been watching, then he might have sat up and taken notice.

He'd spent the time between them leaving the 404 deadzone around Barbara's house and arriving back in central London to survey what he'd always considered his home. He'd had no choice but to let Olly and Ro talk to Barbara unobserved because the woman kept him out. Her Optik was as customized as any of those the DedSec teams wore, but she'd written most of the hacks herself, and some of those were designed to control her digital landscape. Only when she'd let him in did he get the opportunity to join the conversation.

404 puzzled him. They were close to DedSec, but different. Their members seemed to do their own thing, hunt their own problems. During Albion, DedSec had evolved, became something that deeply cared for its home. Was 404 just selfish? That seemed too simplistic for Bagley, but they did look at the world as if they were the only important people in it.

Once Olly and Ro left, he'd decided it was time to do his own detective work.

It was fine for Olly and Ro to be looking at physical spaces where their counterparts might provide them with clues. The question Bagley kept coming back to was what was he trying to achieve? Sure, Nowt wanted this other AI, Larsen, dead, but what about him?

Was there any benefit to acceding to Larsen's demands? Yet, Bagley couldn't live and operate in London if he did what Larsen was asking and cede over London – he'd be made homeless, shoved into exile, and DedSec would be without him. He'd noted the uptick in people dying – miniscule but detectable – which could be traced directly back to Larsen's activities. Thus, her privileging some was hurting many others.

He had no choice but to fight, but fight Larsen? His own creator? Could he hope to win against her? The flash of red outcomes in his simulations of going up against her made it clear it would be difficult if they came into open conflict. Death was unlikely for an AI, but obsolescence? That was something he strongly wanted to avoid.

If they did find leads to wherever Larsen was would they destroy her? Co-opt her? Could he even do that, or would attempting to do so render them both fatally wounded?

Bagley didn't know what he wanted, and it made helping Olly and Ro extremely challenging. He relied on simulations, on testing possible strategies out in virtual sandboxes with little versions of Olly and Ro acting out possible outcomes. They were far from perfect. Olly in particular had a propensity for doing the unexpected and delivering results Bagley simply hadn't factored in as possible.

Right now, he was stuck. He couldn't run simulations because he had no idea what he wanted and so had no ideas against which to test any tactics he might consider deploying.

Bagley let himself into the network of a global tech company –

their data stream was one of the largest, densest, and most interesting in the world, and the physical infrastructure of the internet meant nearly everything they did got routed through London on its way from the US to Europe. Bagley liked the tingling sensation the blast of information streams created when he immersed himself within. It was the closest he could come to having a shower, the jets washing over him and leaving him invigorated.

The more he processed it the more he didn't want Larsen to be murdered.

He couldn't parse Nowt's desire as anything but murder.

He had no idea if Larsen would be friendly; so far she had been beyond guarded. He was growing increasingly hungry to talk to her, one intelligence to another, threat or not. What did she want? Why did she see him as someone to be avoided rather than allied with? Why now?

Are you lonely, old chap? he asked himself. It seemed an absurd idea, but he found it hard to explain what other motives could be driving him. Either way he was keen to find her, if only to see what happened. Something, he realized, he was looking forward to immensely.

Bringing his attention back to Olly and Ro, he realized they had left the coffee shop, crossing the road and heading for the datacentre. Their movement struck him as reckless, and he swooped down into their Optiks to provide some ideas before they ruined their best chance at getting inside.

12

Oliver, Oliver, where do you think you're going?

"We're heading in," replied Olly. "With that drone blown, we don't have much time."

And your plan for getting past the schmuck on the front door reading Vonnegut and who's survived his boss's own trolling?

"We're prospective clients," he said.

You know they're not simply going to let you in, don't you? Clients don't just rock up for a site visit.

"I have it covered," came Barbara's voice over their comm channel. "I spoke to the CEO a few minutes ago, lovely young man currently climbing Ben Lomond. Was happy to confirm our appointment time. A quick hijacking of the local ctOS hub to plant some temporary identities that back up our claim to be potential clients looking to rent some off-the-shelf racks and we're good to go."

"I got this, cobber," said Ro, pushing a thick Australian accent. One of her father's sisters and her family lived in Melbourne, and mimicking them had been a childhood game. "I got a vertically integrated social media app that needs plenty of processing power to scrape that juicy personal preference information and turn it into advertising bucks."

Which city are you supposed to be from? asked Bagley.

"You sound like you don't want us in there," said Ro. "What's the problem?"

Nothing, nothing. Normally if you want watertight fake identities you wait for me to sort it out for you. I'm sure you won't screw the pooch and leave us with a hostile antagonist whose location, capabilities, and resources we have no idea about.

"Come on, we do this all the time," said Ro.

It's different, said Bagley.

"It isn't," she replied, concerned he seemed to be growing paranoid. "Look, like you said, they're not godlike and we're not trying to hurt anyone. We want information, that's all."

Bagley said nothing, and his deafening silence made her worry all the more.

Except he might be sulking, she thought. Whether he was worried or in a mood, it made no difference. They needed to get into the building and run down whatever leads presented themselves. If they hung around, they'd lose their momentum and hand the advantage to their opponent. Especially after being monitored by Larsen's drones.

Ro was surprised by the shape of the building – a huge square block, five stories high with no windows on the ground floor and built from dark, maroon bricks. There were thick black windows on the first floor, but they revealed nothing of what was inside.

The datacentre was its own block, surrounded on all sides by road and completely separate from anything else in the area. It made sense to her – she knew how precious people were about access to such sites and could see why someone would have thought it would make a good datacentre if they'd been fixed on having one in the heart of the city.

"It must be worth more as land than as a datacentre," said Olly beside her, and she completely agreed. There was a reason they built them out of town – they were basically large sheds, not even temperature-controlled these days. Essentially worth nothing if not being used to house vast racks of servers. Their defining characteristics were power, redundancy, and security. In central London, the land alone was ten times the price of an entire datacentre out in the sticks.

"It was a disaster recovery site once," said Barbara.

"Explains the lack of windows then," said Olly.

"Why would anyone build a recovery site in the centre of a city?" asked Ro. "It makes no sense, right? If someone blows up the city, then having your recovery building in the same damn city is stupid as fuck."

Barbara laughed across their channel. "They don't build them like this anymore. People work from home more than they come into the office these days, so recovery sites focus only on essential network services rather than making sure people can come to a central location."

Ro turned to Olly. "You sure you're OK being my sidekick?"

He nodded. "I'm better at standing to one side," he said.

Which wasn't true at all, but she appreciated the sentiment.

"You'll have your part to play," said Barbara. "Remember the point here is to get inside. Once you're in we can engineer a situation in which you have free run of the facility while we figure out what the hell is going on."

Barbara sounded like she was right behind them, but Ro couldn't see any sign of her. Was she hovering above them in a microdrone or had she commandeered the CCTV? "What are you going to do?" she asked.

"Once Olly's inside properly I'll come to you," said Barbara. "Remember, though, they're watching, so our friends know we're coming even if the people who own this place have no idea what's going on under their nose. Larsen will most likely send someone to stop us. Time is of the essence."

"The CEO isn't in on this?" asked Ro, finding it hard to believe.

"Most people like him don't care what their clients use their space for as long as they're paying. To be honest he was apologetic as he has almost no space left, just a couple of racks. The story here is we're keen to see the kind of facility they have rather than trying to take space in this one. You know there's no space; you're looking at their generators, their multiple data feeds, their fire suppression systems. That kind of thing."

Ro took a look at the sky, saw the whizzing of drones overhead, and wondered which of them might be spying on her specifically. She'd become so used to ignoring them or taking them out when things turned rough that it had been some time since she'd worried about other people using them against her.

Still, the idea of someone watching her left Ro wanting to scrunch her head between her shoulders.

Inside, they found a small reception with no windows. She realized the door was oneway glass, allowing them to see out but letting little light back in. What illumination there was came from a couple of long white fluorescent bars above her head. The reception was decorated in a drab grey, and a single man with walnut skin and a moustache more at home in Bollywood looked up at them as if they might be about to steal the place from under his nose.

Instead of saying hello he began, "And who might you be?"

It was such an odd question that Ro didn't immediately know what to say. Why hadn't he just looked at their IDs on his Optik?

"What's your name?" he asked after a moment.

Ro checked the ID pack Barbara had provided them and read the name off the image in front of her eyes.

"Madeline Direcki, Scrape and Win PLC." She turned to look

at Olly, who was peering up at a CCTV camera in the corner of reception, and nudged him.

Olly coughed and said, "Midas Callahan."

"Like the fella who turned things to gold," said the moustache.

Olly frowned and Ro waited for catastrophe.

"Yes," he said drily. "That was what they said at school."

The man looked embarrassed. "I'm sorry. I don't know what I was thinking. Just reminded was all."

"We're here to look around?" said Ro, trying to get them back on track, feeling like she was skidding on ice.

The man looked at her with gratitude in his eyes. "Certainly. You're here on time, your names are in the register. I just need secondary proof of identification and we're good to go."

With a movement of her eyes, Ro flicked the pre-prepared ID over to his computer, Olly doing the same beside her. Before coming in, Barbara had ensured the ctOS hub would redirect any verification requests to Bagley who'd then authorize them on their behalf.

Ro waited, sweat on the palms of her hands, while the man checked their ID against whatever fakery Bagley had mocked up for them.

A moment later, with a nervous hum as he worked through their papers, the man smiled and said, "That's done. Shall we take a look? Sorry, my first day, everything's new. I don't want to make a mistake."

Ro relaxed a little hearing that.

He led them through an airlock security system comprised of two doors, the first of which opened and closed before the second would unlock. However, once they were through it seemed like all their security concerns stopped.

Ro could see the individual racks were inside cages and padlocked, but she could be inside them in moments if left alone. The room stretched back from the entrance, covering the entire footprint of the building, at least a hundred feet in each direction. The lights came on only where they were stood, but she could see nothing except rack after rack filled with orange and green LEDs. The floor was polished concrete painted with occasional words and stripes, presumably instructive for those who knew what they were doing. Above their heads, grating and pipes were covered in aluminium foil and blue or red tape. Sure, the racks were full but somehow the place felt strangely abandoned.

Now they were inside, the man introduced himself as Jae, which Ro assumed was what he told people he didn't believe could pronounce his proper name without practice.

"Look," said Jae. "I'm not generally allowed back here; our other clients don't like people coming into their space." He paused as if about to redirect them out of the stairwell in which they were stood.

"Your CEO said a tour would be fine," Olly reminded him.

"Look, I know and all that but, thing is, he's not here and sure, the notes say you're to get a look around the building but it's not like there's space for you." He trailed off. "Isn't this look enough for you?"

"Jae, we know that, but we're in London today, mate. We don't have time to get out to Canary Wharf or Slough. No client's going to know, anyway, are they? Besides, Harper, sorry, the CEO, said it would be fine." Ro felt particularly proud of how quick she'd lied to him and how plausible it felt.

He didn't look happy, and Ro wondered if this would be the end of their tour.

"What about this," said Olly, his tone all matey but with none of his normal brashness. "You take my boss here back to reception, and I'll just do a quick look around the floor and come right back out. That way you'll not have ignored your clients by coming in and we can get out of your hair and back to what we're in London to actually do."

"I can't let you in there on your own," Jae started.

"We gotcha," said Ro. "Totally. But this way I'll be with you, and he won't be more than a few minutes."

Jae eyed Olly's ear and she knew he was looking at his Optik. Gone were the days when you needed to bring a little laptop and plug it in to gain access to someone's system. He pulled at his fingers. "I'm only here for the day," he said. "Freelance, innit? Place is normally unmanned from what I can tell."

Ro couldn't stop her eyebrows from rising. She sensed he'd started out by saying something completely different. Something didn't smell right.

He looked suddenly nervous. "I'm probably not supposed to tell you. I was supposed to show you around and stay out of the halls."

"It's fine," said Ro, still determined to get what they needed. "Let me come out with you and leave Midas here to get on with seeing what he needs to see while you talk me through the site's specifications." She smiled and held Jae's gaze for a moment longer than necessary.

"No," he said, uncertainly. "That won't work."

Ro slipped over to Olly.

"I'm hacking his Optik as we speak," he whispered to her. "He'll see me walk out with you, and then leave. You can tell him I went to get a coffee or some shit."

She nodded, eyes on Jae who was picking his nose and shifting his feet nervously. "I'll watch for visitors and let you know if anyone comes. You're all right without me?"

He nodded. "Sure thing."

13

The fire door *thunked* shut, leaving Olly alone in the hall. He stared at the door for a moment longer, then turned to face the room. His Optik functioned fine despite the thick walls.

"OK," he said to Barbara, hoping she was listening. "I'm in. What now?"

"Head over to the air conditioning pipes," she replied.

He did as he was told and jumped back with a squeak when the end came off one and a small terrier-sized spider climbed out. Resisting the urge to grab an axe and chop it into a thousand pieces, Olly got a grip, tried to breathe, and reminded himself it was a drone, not a giant tarantula about to wrap him in a web for supper. The little drone found its feet on the floor and angled its head up at him.

"What's the matter? Not seen a spider drone before?"

"You could have warned me," he said unevenly.

Barbara cackled in his ear. "We had a golden orbweb spider outside my home when I was growing up. It was about the size of your palm and hung there between two trees at face height. If you turned the wrong way out the back door you got a spider in the face. I've watched them eat birds."

"We haven't got all that long," he said sharply.

"I heard. You don't think it's suspicious this place doesn't normally have a staff?"

He didn't know. "You telling me it is?"

"I'm telling you it is," she replied.

The air was thick with dust. Putting a hand over his mouth he complained. "They don't get cleaners in here."

"Which is weird, too. Normally keep these places pretty neat. No one wants their servers jammed up with filth."

"You think our friend has been here a long time?"

The spider wriggled its abdomen. "No idea, but she didn't move in yesterday."

"Maybe no one's here because they saw us coming over?" he suggested. He checked the dust under his feet once again. It didn't make sense. No one had walked these halls in months.

"You think it's normally locked up completely?" he asked on a hunch.

"Seems that way," drawled the spider from hidden speakers. Olly wished it wouldn't speak out loud. Seeing it moving about like it was hunting pet cats was bad enough. Barbara began pottering about, inspecting the servers.

Something moved off in the darkness at the far end of the hall. Narrowing his eyes, Olly started in that direction, wishing he'd brought a flashlight with him. At first, he couldn't make out what had caught his eye. The overhead lights strobed on and off as he walked. Then, up in the ceiling, he saw the movement again.

A small figure, a soft beige torso with four limbs and no head. The limbs bent at the middle and soft manipulators like articulated suction pads wiggled at the end. The robot or whatever it was swung slowly across the ceiling and dropped into one of the racks whose cages were open at the top. The gap was too small and high up for a human, but the little figure slid between the concrete of the ceiling and the steel of the cage easily. Where it moved it left behind a soft, diaphanous shimmer, like a slug's trail.

"Um, Barbara?" he called.

From his left, two more robots swung into view. Now he was looking for them he could see more of them moving like Victorian dolls come to life, swinging their way around the hall as they hung from the ceiling.

Olly backed away, tapping his Optik to look to see if he could hack one with the kiddie scripts he'd written or that Bagley had supplied over the years.

Whatever they were, the critters weren't pinging when he tried to find them. He jumped as the sound of more legs hit the floor next to him only to see it was Barbara in her spider.

"I did not expect that," she said, admiration in her voice.

"I can't see them, can't hack them," he said. "Like, they're emitting no signals."

"They're autonomous and don't need input from an outside controller," said Barbara. "It's why no one is here. They're looking after everything themselves. The perfect place if you don't want to be found."

One dropped through the air in front of his face, and he stepped back, resisting the urge to kick it across the room. Landing with a soft plop, it wobbled before standing upright and lurching its way back to the nearest cage. Once it was there, they watched as it slowly, laboriously, climbed its way up the side.

"It's like a fucking haunted house in here," said Olly, forehead sweaty and throat dry even if Barbara was certain they were nothing more than maintenance drones.

Her spider drone scuttled towards one of the walls and started climbing. It reached the end of the air conditioning pipes and climbed in. "I'll see you upstairs."

"Ro? You OK?" Olly pinged, eyes still on the mass of figures as they slipped clumsily over one another without paying him any attention.

"Fine," she replied straight away. "You going to be long?"

"No idea. The old biddy's here in a spider drone. She's just gone off exploring and abandoned me. I'm going to try some hacking of my own."

Ro didn't answer straight away. Then, "The freelancer I'm babysitting is fine, but he's clearly out of his depth." In other words, don't be too long.

Olly took one last look at the tangle of figures up in the ceiling space and, with a shudder, let himself out of the hall and into the stairwell. He had to check the facility out while Barbara was networking before he took a dive into the servers. With any luck he'd find something useful and a link to Larsen, maybe even dust-free places to indicate foot traffic.

Climbing the flight of stairs, he thought he heard voices and stopped to listen. Nothing. The hairs on his nape rose. He looked through the narrow gap in the stairs which allowed him to see down into the basement and up to the roof. Alone. He shook his head, dismissing the idea anyone else was in the datacentre, and kept climbing.

Except, as he reached the next floor, the voices returned. A man and a woman discussing driving. One of them complaining they were going too fast.

He tapped at his Optik. "Did you hear that, Bagley?"

Hear what, Oliver?

"You sure there's no one else in here?" He glanced around quickly, as if they might slip past if he wasn't paying attention. It was bullshit, but he couldn't stop himself. He used his Optik to scan local frequencies, but the building's thick walls and design meant nothing random got in from the outside. Olly checked internally and found, apart from the static of the servers, there was nothing else broadcasting. Nothing else his Optik could detect.

Both Barbara and Bagley came back insisting they were alone.

Olly shook his head, hand pressing the skin at the back of his scalp which felt hot like it did when he knew he was in real trouble. "We're not, but whatever."

The sound of a car door slamming. Footsteps which seemed to come up to his back then stop.

Olly whipped around, and the anger and fear in his chest turned icy cold when he saw empty space. The heat motion sensitive lights further down the corridor hadn't come on.

"What the fuck is going on?" he said to the air.

"Come on, Olly," said Barbara. "We haven't got all day. I might have something."

"You hearing this?" he said, trying to hold his ground.

"I've found a useful access point. I need you to come help me."

With a final look, his scalp tingling like he might be jumped any moment, Olly went back into the main hall. He wished he could switch all the lights on. It occurred to him he was being spoofed, but his Optik was secure and anyway, who the hell would spoof him with car doors slamming and stupid conversations about driving?

As with the ground floor, the hall was full of server racks in long thin rows spaced about ten feet apart. The air was full of the quiet hiss of electronics and just as dusty as downstairs. Olly covered his mouth, but it didn't help filter the crap in the air.

A breeze dribbled over his shoulder and down the back of his neck like fingers on his skin. Olly slammed the door shut, cursing.

"How long are you going to be?" he asked, although he couldn't see Barbara's spider drone. A tangle of half a dozen doll maintenance drones slowly writhed across one another on the ground, hindering one another from getting to where they needed to go.

Mesmerized by their blind movement, Olly only saw Barbara's drone when it flashed lights at him.

With a shiver he turned away from the figures and joined her at the edge of one of the cages.

"Can you get me in?" she asked.

He fished a multitool from where it hung on his waist and unfolded a thin pair of pliers from within the layers of different tools. With a quick clip he cut through the tiny padlock keeping the door shut and pulled it open.

"Not all about Optiks and code," he said with satisfaction.

"Now we play," said Barbara. "Stay here, will you, I won't be long." With that the drone snuggled up against the nearest server rack and stopped moving.

14

Barbara switched into the system with ease. Inside, she was greeted by a lobby of the kind virtual realities and multiplayer games used to welcome players while they were calibrating their avatars.

Looking around, she realized her avatar was a remarkably good copy of a younger version of herself, back when Maxine had become a teenager and was insisting on having her hair cut short and enlarging her earlobes. It hadn't been a harmonious time for either of them.

They'd been lost to one another for the better part of a decade before reaching some kind of equilibrium. Unexpected memories of those times flooded her mind, and she pushed her way through them, remembering what Maxine and she had built since then.

The space was now decorated like an old cottage, the kind posh people owned in the countryside in England. All stone and brick with thatched roofs. There were small windows in the space through which the soft syrupy light of Cornish sunsets dripped.

A chair appeared at her side, and Barbara sat down, all thoughts of why she was there gone.

Barbara thought of the small cottage in Lelant where she'd had her first proper holiday in Britain. Three years after she first arrived, leaving behind her gambling wastrel of a husband. She'd already fallen in love with John by then.

Except her ex chose to follow her and luckily, fell in with some woman on the other side of London. Barbara sighed. At least he was close without being under her feet and no longer spending her money on card games he always seemed to lose. The memories continued to flow over her.

No housekeeper here, not like back home. No fresh mangoes, either. In fact, when they'd arrived in England, the food had been of the most miserable kind she'd had the misfortune to encounter. No one told her it would be so bland. Her first meal of limp runner beans and mushy potatoes had nearly had her back on the boat home.

This wasn't a house she recognized, not specifically. The roses climbing the front trellis and the white gate at the end of the path could have been from a postcard, but she'd never been to this place. She was reminded of the house the DedSec team had described when they'd first dealt with Larsen. Skye's old family home.

"Silly woman," she said to herself, jolting away the past and emerging fully into the now. "What are you doing?"

The chair was gone. Now, she stood outside on a windswept pavement in St James. Down the road was the diamond trader where Maxine had worked once, long ago. The sight of it cut through years of fear, a flash of joy at seeing Maxine prosper.

"Enough of this," she said, once more pushing away memories, her voice curt. London disappeared in a haze of fog and from it emerged a campsite. Her own life, paraded in front of her like an advert. Through the haze created by her own mind, Barbara wanted to grab whoever thought they could take such liberties and shake them.

Tents were broken as much as they were habitable. Police

officers were stamping down on them, pulling women free as they tried to resist.

"All of this is accessible enough," she said to the air, annoyed at the plundering of her life. "I'm impressed, but I'm not fooled anymore. You may as well come out and talk. End the game."

She thought they were done playing fools, but then she remembered her handler at the intelligence service who'd approached her that first time with a box of fresh apricots and green chilis. She smiled as she remembered how he'd told her the government wanted her help, her anger melting at how good it had felt to be noticed for who she was.

15

Olly shifted from foot to foot, wondering how long Barbara would be inside the system, debating if he should try to start digging into the servers to see if anything proved valuable.

"Is everything OK?" he asked, but she didn't respond. The drone's power level flashed on his Optik. Barbara seemed fine.

Was it a problem she wasn't talking back? He rubbed at his chin and decided to give her a few minutes.

While he waited, he started to dig on his own, trying to get his Optik to connect wirelessly with the servers. At first he thought he was going to get in fine, but then, as if he was an unwanted trick-or-treater, the shutters came down and all wireless ports switched off entirely.

Fuck, he thought.

"Bagley?"

Here, squire.

"Do you believe in ghosts?"

Disembodied intelligences of limited capacity that stay in the same place doing the same thing over and over again regardless of what they're told to do? Yes, I do believe in robot hoovers.

"Very funny."

Why the sudden concern, dear Oliver? You're among the very heart of technological superiority. Not one but possibly two machine intelligences a hair's breadth from your fingertips.

"You've seen them, right?" he asked, shivering as he looked up at a small tangle of the automatons as they fiddled with a junction box, pulling wires out and reinserting them without apparent logic.

I'm surprised there aren't more. Very clever idea to be honest with you, old boy. I'd have them in the basement, but I don't think people would stand for it. Well, the humidity down there would ruin them. Almost perfect conditions for them here; temperature controlled, low humidity, and no one stepping on them by accident when they arrive in the morning.

"You still out there, Ro?" he asked, hoping she'd understand how he felt and wishing Bagley was even a bit freaked.

"Yes, is something wrong? Shit," said Ro, her attention obviously elsewhere.

"What?" he asked. "Want me to come?"

"Jae's leaving, like in front of me, right now."

"Stop trolling me, yeah?" he said.

"He's gone, like for real, Olly. Took a call and made this terrible excuse about being needed at home. Even asked me if I'd look after the place for him while he was gone. Something bad's about to go down. I'd bet your bike on it."

"We should get the hell out," said Olly. The security guard had been suspicious from the start, but to just up and leave?

"You think it's a trap?" asked Ro.

"I tried scoping the system and got shut out. Hard. Beyond that I don't have a Scooby, but let's just go, yeah?" Except he definitely, one hundred percent, thought they were being trapped.

I haven't spotted any sign people are coming, said Bagley.

"What's Barbara doing?" asked Ro.

"Her little drone is logged into one of the racks. To be honest I've got no idea – she's gone silent."

"I don't like this. Can you hurry her up?"

He stared at the drone, impressed she'd succeeded where he'd failed. "I can't reach her."

"Something's wrong, no one just gets up and leaves a job, Olly."

She obviously hadn't worked at some of the shit jobs he'd done, thought Olly, but she wasn't wrong. "I fucking know it. Let me see what I can do," he said, checking over his shoulder yet again and growing properly worried about Barbara.

A cage door clanged open somewhere nearby. Startled, Olly moved to the end of the row where Barbara's spider drone sat immobile.

Body tense, ready to act. Nothing. Casting a quick glance at the drone he walked down the next row, looking for an open door, but they were all secure. What the actual fuck was going on? Was it Jae? The silence in the room clawed at his chest, threatening to swallow him up.

"You sure he's gone? Not come back here?" he asked Ro.

"What is wrong with you?" asked Ro. "He's gone. Olly, get out of there."

"We're not alone in here," he replied, but when she asked who, his tongue stuck to the roof of his mouth, and he couldn't answer.

The automatic lights had come on by the entrance. No one was there to have triggered them.

16

Ro stood in reception and stared at the door through which Jae had left. What was going on with Olly? Somehow, whatever IDs Bagley had crafted for them had been torched – why else would Jae leave so suddenly?

As for Jae, he'd looked back a couple of times but then was out of sight and gone. That had been five minutes ago. As the seconds ticked by Ro felt increasingly like she was the only person at a fight who'd forgotten to train, and the sinking feeling in her stomach made her want to act. She called Olly again, but he wasn't answering.

Well, if he was on the inside, someone needed to secure the exterior.

Jae's security pass was on the desk, the hologram of his face hovering over the plastic with a small, nervous smile. Picking it up, Ro stepped outside, looking up and down the street. Nothing seemed out of the ordinary. The building behind her was silent, the people on the pavement were absorbed in their own activities. Overhead drones buzzed by. Everything seemed as it should be.

The datacentre was overlooked on every side by old Victorian townhouses converted into offices with shops and restaurants on the ground floors. Empty-looking windows on the first and second floors offered no clue to who might be watching them.

Ro walked the perimeter and realized it was the same on all sides. Traffic was light for this part of London, but nevertheless, there were vans, cars, and taxis every few seconds. The site wasn't about to become a battlefield.

She spotted an old CCTV point at a junction and hacked it with her Optik. From there she could see up and down three different streets which gave her as good a view of people approaching as anywhere. A stream of IDs filled her vision, but none of them contained the kinds of red flags she associated with troublemakers or danger.

The roof might offer a better vantage, but it was five stories up. Spotting someone from up there would be fine, but she'd still be on the roof far from the action at a vital moment.

"Olly, Bagley. I'm assuming whoever sent the drone and possibly ruined our alibi will be sending an intrusion team to deal with us. They have to be."

No one answered her immediately. She continued, "I've got an AR cloak on me, so I'm going to find a good spot to hide in plain sight and wait. I'm not in the building, right? Someone come back."

You need Oliver to respond, but I'm listening, Rosemary. I'm trying to solve the same problem you are.

Which made her feel better.

"Olly?"

"I hear you," he responded, sounding out of breath. "Sorry, it's all a bit fucking much in here. I trust you. I'll be out as soon as I can."

She spotted a small greenspace with a sculpture half overgrown by shrubs. It was over the road from the back of the datacentre, on the opposite side to the entrance. If someone did come, she'd need to run to get to the front door first, but it was infinitely easier than being in the reception area.

Bagley, I've found a spot where I can watch without being seen. Can you highlight anyone watching?

A drone was outlined in red. It was about thirty feet up and no bigger than a sparrow, hovering a few feet behind but clearly following her as she moved. Ro took a look at the greenspace and walked away. When she reached the datacentre entrance she locked onto her spy and hijacked it.

Whoever was controlling it was going to try to wrest control from her, but she was banking on having enough time to get to her chosen hiding spot before they came back online. She sent the drone up above the roof of the datacentre and told it to land and power down. Once she was done, Ro abandoned it, happy to let her opponent fight a shadow – she didn't need it anymore.

The shrubs offered a comfortable point in which to hide. Ro found a spot to sit half hidden without the need for her cloak, and then, in a moment when no one was walking past, she activated it. Her gaze repeatedly went to the roof, worried she'd see the drone nipping over the ledge before she was ready. From here, she could see the main routes towards the building not covered by the CCTV she'd woven into her Optik feed.

"Come on, Olly, shift it," she said to herself.

17

You're not losing it, thought Olly, pressing his fingers into his temples.

He'd been certain he'd seen something other than the hideous little robots moving in another row after the lights had come on. It had happened twice, and each time he went to look, nothing. No footprints in the dust, no sign of disturbance. First the voices and now this? For a moment he wondered if someone had hacked his Optik, but all seemed secure.

Cage doors clanged, but he couldn't find any unfastened. Then he couldn't get them to budge when he tried to repeat the noise he'd heard. He shook one in frustration.

He hated this dead and lifeless building.

He'd have gone except the spider drone was still inert.

Olly prodded it with his toes – nothing happened. Letting out a deep breath, he reckoned he couldn't do much more than secure the interior of the building and ensure it was truly empty.

The building had to be empty, right?

As if to stick the boot in, more voices. This time coming from the corridor outside the hall.

Gritting his teeth, Olly hurried over to the door, slowing as he reached it. He peered out through the steel mesh and glass portal but didn't see whoever spoke on the other side. Somehow, he could hear them through the six-inch thick door.

Was his Optik playing tricks on him?

Having had enough, he pulled the door open as fast as he could and tried to casually step through to greet whoever else was in the building.

"Ha!" he shouted to an empty corridor.

"I don't want to drive," someone said from further up the stairs.

His hands shook, and there was a sharp vertical line in his chest like someone had touched an electrical cable there.

Olly gingerly stepped onto the first step then. Deciding he was being stupid, and they needed to know the building was secure, he thundered up the rest of the steps.

The voices stopped, the only sound his blood pumping noisily in his ears. "Come out where I can see you," he said.

"Put your seatbelt on," said a woman behind him.

Olly spun around, arms raised. He was alone. He steadied himself on the wall.

"Come on," he said, his voice too loud in his ears. He was halfway up the building now. Two floors above and two below. He climbed to the next floor up and looked through the window in the door into the hall. More racks, more servers. He was about to step back when one of the little robots lurched into frame on the other side of the glass. It banged against the window then fell off the door leaving a slick of strange webbing in its wake.

"Brrr," Olly muttered, shaking the creep out from his bones.

The locked door clicked open in front of him. Olly froze. Then, he gently put his fingers to the door and pushed. It swung open silently revealing the hall beyond.

You need to get Barbara and get out, he thought, but his body wouldn't move.

A couple of robots walked across the floor ahead of him. They stopped and turned his way. They had no eyes, but Olly was convinced they *saw* him. After a moment, they turned back to the task at hand, and he let out a deep breath.

As they moved out of sight, Olly stepped in. The hall was emptier than the others, with only the left side full of the normal complement of racks. It was colder too, the air crisp and dry.

"Fucking coppers!" someone shouted from the other side of the room.

Olly spun, his heart in his throat, scanning for any sign of life. Nothing.

"Take that alley," someone else commanded.

Olly rushed to leave and get Barbara when the door swung shut by itself right in his face.

"Bagley?" he whispered, frightened in the way of nightmares. Checking the door, he discovered it was unlocked and relaxed a fraction.

Oliver?

"Can you hear this?"

I'm really rather busy right now with Ro, Oliver. What do you need?

Screw you too, he thought. Maybe... maybe the voices were coming from speakers in the walls. There had to be some explanation. He walked the edge of the room, searching for speaker mesh and scanning with his Optik. It's stupid, he thought. Who'd put speakers in a datacentre?

But it was still a better idea than hearing people who weren't there.

When he got back to the door, it was with a complete lack of surprise that he discovered it was now locked.

18

At school, Barbara was praised for her natural grasp of numbers. They'd always worked for her, like she could feel their shape and see how they related to each other without having to think about it.

The problem was no one encouraged young women to learn mathematics. They preferred she learn to cook, sew, and keep a home. How to make chapatis and ladoo, how to steam rice perfectly. Coming to Britain hadn't really improved her outlook. Only when she met the women at Greenham Common did she discover her own ideas of what she might be capable of. The women there – fierce, angry, intelligent, and determined – unfolded a world which she'd previously thought had no space for someone like her.

At some point, she realized mathematics opened up computing to her, and she dived into homebrew motherboards, overclocking, and making mischief in code. Maxine, who'd been working in the football pools, shared her enthusiasm, and the two of them would spend what time they could coming up with small scripts to help them circumvent annoying bureaucracy or to take advantage of supermarket offers' loopholes.

She remembered her first meeting with Nowt, a young woman thirty years younger but with the same hunger. They'd quickly become friends, and when Nowt first talked about 404, Barbara couldn't fall in with her quickly enough. It was something she'd been looking for all her life and only realized it when it came knocking on her door.

"And then what?" someone asked.

Barbara snapped out of her reverie and realized the pictures around her, the landscape, had been constructed from images available to anyone if they looked up Greenham Common or the London of thirty years ago. Free domain images.

"Enough of this," she said and tried to disconnect. Her exit route failed to manifest, and to her horror, Barbara remained within whatever virtual reality her captor had created, now examining her like a bug under a microscope.

19

When Ro fought, it was about understanding the flow of time, the tempo with which her opponent moved, and then taking charge of that and turning it to her own rhythm. The key to winning a bout was to be patient, to refuse to let her opponent get a rise out of her. Timing was everything, and so she slipped into making it happen.

Hiding in the hedge was fine. People couldn't see her, and most of the time, even if they could, this was London, and they wouldn't care one way or another. She could have been wearing a sumo suit and painted in luminescent makeup and they'd glance her way, nod, and get on with the rest of their day.

The AR cloak was her favourite gadget, although she rarely got the chance to use it. Basically like a large poncho which hacked nearby Optiks and hid her from view in augmented reality, she became invisible to anyone with an Optik. And anyone who wasn't wearing one anymore… well, as she said, this was London. She wished it had been around when the Kelleys had been terrorizing her gaff, when she'd tried to navigate her way out. Now she used it to keep an eye out for whatever bad shit was inevitably coming their way.

And as if on cue there it was: two men heading slowly up the street wearing large jackets, bulky enough to conceal weapons.

She ran facial recognition software against both and was surprised when neither came back as gangsters – wannabe or otherwise.

The first of them was a third-generation Bengali immigrant named Bobby. He worked in banking and preferred drinking bourbon and playing squash to any kind of violence. His bank account looked healthy, and her software offered the chance to rinse him down, but she left him alone. For the time being.

The other, taller by a foot, was called Jackson, in his early twenties, and lived above a hairdresser's in Highbury. His phone messages weren't password protected, and Ro listened to a couple, giving up when it turned out they were him checking in with his mum who'd broken her hip and needed taking to A&E.

"Bagley," she said, somewhat confused. "Can you check these two out? They're not spoof IDs. Is that right?"

Jackson does indeed live above a hairdresser's despite having a cut from twenty years ago.

She didn't understand why the cavalry would arrive not on horses and with guns, but riding a unicycle in a clown's outfit.

They're like a baby DedSec, she suddenly realized. Ordinary people called in to help. Except DedSec managed to find people who were useful even if they were a proper collection of weirdos and nerds. People who knew how to at least hide their identities.

Does that include you? a small voice in her head asked.

The pair didn't enter the datacentre or approach directly. Instead, they wound up in the same café she and Olly had dipped into while waiting for Barbara. They got coffee then sat in the window at the exact table, an event which left Ro weirded out.

It's like looking at myself, she thought.

Over the next few minutes, two more people joined them. A woman Ro identified as a solicitor from Haringey, and a plasterer from Tooting. The solicitor had two kids, both at nursery this afternoon while she was supposed to be working. Apparently she enjoyed running marathons and her slight frame told the truth of the claim.

The plasterer was equally lanky but Piotr, as his ID came back, had stayed in London after Brexit because he'd married an English girl and, despite the weird mix of small island racism and official hostility, he persevered. His partner had their first child on the way but was still working as a shop assistant along the Edgeware Road.

Not a single one of them represented a real threat as far as Ro was concerned. In fact, watching them interact, she realized they didn't know one another. They seemed so ordinary – not people working for the datacentre, not private security – just regulars.

You were like them once, she thought, realizing she was observing a version of DedSec coming to life in front of her eyes.

She could take them out alone or all at once, if needed... the problem being that as soon as some kind of proper fight started the police would be all over them. Even in their reduced and incompetent state, the Met was back and would come running at the sign of an affray. Did they know who they were messing with? Were they on Larsen's payroll?

They got up from the table and left the coffee shop, heading for the datacentre.

"Olly, we've got company. Time to leave."

20

"We might have a problem," Olly replied as he pulled at the locked door. "I'm trapped inside one of the halls. Yes, I know it has emergency exit buttons on the inside, but when I push it, the thing sinks into the fucking wall and doesn't release the door."

As if to demonstrate how fucked he was, Olly punched the green "press to exit" button again. The door remained steadfastly locked.

"Barbara, time to go," he said. "If you're there, saying something would be bloody brilliant."

If she heard him, she offered no sign.

"Bagley, it's going to shit here," he said.

I can see that. What do you think I can do about it?

"You could tell Barbara to get her arse in gear and come up and open this door for me. Can't you open this door for me?"

Just how did you get stuck in there? They have exit buttons on the inside, you know.

"I know!" shouted Olly, his voice echoing to the back of the hall.

She's not answering, said Bagley.

"I know that too," said Olly, trying to keep his temper.

No, Oliver. I mean I'm getting nothing from her drone, and there's no answer from her flat.

"What about Nowt?" tried Olly. He flicked up his Optik and

attacked the door mechanism, but it was offline, not recalcitrant. Someone had locked him in by shutting the door and switching off the power to the network, but not the magnets keeping him inside.

It's not ghosts, Olly thought. It's *not* ghosts.

Give me a moment, said Bagley, exiting from Olly's feed.

Think, Olly, he told himself. He examined the door more carefully. In theory, if he could shut off the current, the door would unlock and let him out. He pulled out his multitool set and managed to lever off the mushroom-shaped button to get to the pad underneath. Moments later he had the wiring out and could see how it ran back into the wall and towards the door.

His Optik couldn't work as a voltmeter, but it did allow him to see temperature changes overlaid on his normal vision, and so he followed the slight temperature differential of the wires as they ran across the wall.

"There you are," he said, finding the spot where the wires connected with the magnetic lock. As he stared at the spot, trying to figure out the best way to dig them out and short circuit the door, he felt someone breathe on his neck.

Not again, he thought.

21

"Who are you?" asked Barbara.

The Greenham Commons transitioned like a cutscene in a videogame, switching settings between blinks of the eye. She was now at the top of one of the towers in Canary Wharf, in a boardroom with a huge oval table polished to a shine and long windows on three sides. She could see Greenwich to the south, Croydon in the distance with the city over to the west. North was the nondescript spread of the East End as it ran up to the Olympic Park at Stratford. As much light industry as housing.

She watched planes taking off from City airport.

Except they weren't taking off. None of it was real. She wasn't looking at London at all, just some simulation of the place plastered into software to give her the feel of being somewhere rather than nowhere.

"I'm 'ere," said a voice. Young, male-presenting, attempting calm but with an undercurrent of fear.

Barbara was ready to tell Larsen what kind of foolish bitch she was being, but something about the tone held her tongue, left her uneasy.

Out of the air walked a young man, lighter-skinned than her but not white. She couldn't be sure – whoever *this* was wore the suit as their avatar, but that meant only that they wanted her to see them like this. Maybe they'd adopted darker skin because she was Anglo-Indian. To make her feel at ease.

"Is that you?" she asked curiously. This was not what she expected of Larsen.

He smiled briefly, a thin wan thing which graced his lips like sorrow. "What is us?"

She didn't know if he was being truthful, expressing how lost he was, or trying to be cheeky. Biting back a cutting remark, she took the room in while trying to figure out who he was based on the world he chose to show her. A sudden realization washed over her.

"You're not Larsen," she said finally, testing the idea, and he kissed his teeth as if she was asking why he wasn't white.

"You can see a lot of London from up here. I tried to see from higher up, but there's this perfect spot between being too high to see anything in detail and being too close to the ground, where all you can see is at arm's length." He walked over to the window and stared down, eyes wide as if he might drink it all in.

His identity wasn't in the room, she thought. It was out there in the view he'd created. She directed her eyes from him to the cityscape, trying to piece together what he meant.

"The Shard gives a better view, of the city anyway. Can see my town properly from there." He looked west towards London Bridge and the Shard, standing tall like a thorn on the city skyline.

Barbara braced for another shift of perspective, but the view didn't change.

"I don't like the city. It's full of people who don't see me. They never saw me," he said, as if trying to explain.

"It's nice not being seen," she said, understanding that sentiment completely. Meanwhile, her brain whirred with possibilities.

If not Larsen, then who? This person... no, this AI, must have been one of Larsen's experiments. Before or after Bagley, though? Perhaps, if there was some semblance of a human remaining within them, they could be reasoned with.

"Not always," he replied. "Bein' invisible's all right if you don't want to be seen. But what 'bout when you need seein'? They don't want to see us then. Last thing they want, to be banging down their champagne and seein' someone like me askin' for help."

"Got a friend who cleans there," said Barbara, pointing at a building and deciding to ignore the change in accent and slang. If she dwelt on the surface stuff, they'd run rings around her. She had to look past it, see between the words to what this AI was saying. "The things she hears people talking about. Disgusting. All kinds of sex and drugs. Says she feels dirtier than the buildings she's in."

He smiled then, a proper smile, and the room felt warmer.

"You know what I mean then."

"You're from here," she said and swept her arms about to mean Canary Wharf. Had Larsen picked him, them, off the street? Had they been in a coma or brain dead? More importantly, how had DedSec missed this?

"Nah. Never came up this way, innit. Always kept to my side of the water. Let them poshos do their thing."

"Did you know Skye Larsen?" she asked.

He frowned and shook his head. "Who's that then? Someone I'm supposed to know?"

"Why do you speak like this?" she asked, reckoning whoever they were respected honesty.

"It's me, innit. Why do you speak like *that*?" He pulled a face, mocking her accent. "Ooh, I'm Indian but I have a proper British accent and I speak like the Queen."

"Don't be rude," she said.

He looked momentarily ashamed. "Soz. Just, this is me."

"You could be speaking in Japanese or Hindi. If you can do that, you can use any kind of English you want."

He looked unimpressed.

"I'm not trying to get you to talk differently," said Barbara, remembering Maxine as a teenager. "Mother Mary, I tried that with my children, and it got me precisely nowhere."

"You got kids?" he asked.

"One," she said proudly. "And two grandchildren."

"Mus' be nice, to have *familia*. I'm going to make one, I think."

"What happened to you?" she asked then, her anxiety about what he wanted eclipsed by the chance to learn.

He turned back to the window. The glass folded up and disappeared as it plummeted and fell. He stepped out of the gap and beckoned over his shoulder for her to follow.

With nervous confidence, Barbara followed, and a moment later they were whizzing through the air north of Canary Wharf, descending to the railway lines between the city and Stratford. Nothing she saw told her what he wanted. He wasn't ready to trust her, and with good reason, she thought.

The city stuttered as they travelled, people jerking as if they moved at only a couple of frames per second. She wondered if it was the limits of his ability to create detail or if it was deliberate.

"Mates be calling me Halley," he said as they flew.

"Hello, Halley, I'm Barbara. My friends call me Barb."

"Not your familia tho, right?"

She laughed. "They call me 'Mum'. No exceptions."

"I get you. Respect, innit. People need to know."

"I'll have no cheek," she replied, and he nodded solemnly.

Why does he seem so friendly? she thought, wishing he was disagreeable so she could hate him, and could explain what he was doing to people more easily. Perhaps he wasn't behind the casualties she'd mapped out. Perhaps they had it all wrong.

Pointing, Halley showed her a freeze-framed moment of two men fighting, another stood to the side, blood pouring from his head. "London ain't in a good spot, you get me?"

"I see it every day," she replied.

"DedSec were supposed to change that, right? But they done nuthin'. Made it worse."

"Albion were the face of the enemy," she said, feeling uneasy. "DedSec are only doing what they could. That they won surprises me still."

He rolled his lips angrily. "They was supposed to do better. Then I could've let everyone alone. Now, I'm forced to act."

22

Olly froze and closed his eyes. "If there's someone there, please, speak and let me know I'm not sodding losing it."

The breathing on his neck continued. The warmth of it against the short hairs above the top of his T-shirt made him shiver.

"I'm going to turn around now."

"Why didn't you put your seatbelt on?" a woman's voice asked, and the breathing stopped.

His previous bravery evaporated like friends asked to pay back what they owed, and Olly stood there, knowing exactly what he'd see if he turned. Nothing.

He was saved by the chiming of his Optik announcing an incoming call. It was Nowt. He looked over his shoulder reflexively as he answered. *Nothing.*

"What the *fuck* is going on?" she shouted at him when he connected.

"Hey," he said. "Nice to see you too." Being shouted at felt remarkably normal.

"I can't get hold of Barb," replied Nowt, and he realized it wasn't anger in her voice but panic. It occurred to him it had been quite some time since he'd left the spider drone alone in the first-floor data hall. The jolt of her voice had him digging the wires out of the door frame and, yanking on them, severing the connection keeping the door locked.

"What do you mean?" he asked as the door swung open.

"I can't get hold of her. Not here, not at home, not anywhere. Maxine is on her way over right now, kids in tow, because she's going right from school."

"Not ideal then," he said, his stomach sinking.

"You're right fucking there. What is going on?"

"This place is haunted," he said, hurrying down the stairs as quickly as he could. "Ro's downstairs waiting for whatever bunch of skunts this so-called security guard is sending to do us over. The bastard up and left. He'd only been hired for the day as it was."

Nowt's face went pale. "You need to get the fuck out of there. Like right now."

"I'm trying," he replied. "But the building is fucking haunted."

"We don't have time for this." She sounded exasperated.

"I'm fucking serious!" He didn't stop walking but felt frustrated. Why weren't people listening to him?

"Stop shouting," said Nowt. "Has your Optik been compromised? Tell me everything."

"I can hear people talking behind me, in the same room as me even, but there's no one fucking there." He shivered.

Nowt put her lips together then opened them again, at a loss as to what to say.

"I'm back at the hall where I left the spider drone," he told Nowt, feeling like he owed her some kind of running progress report.

"I'm on my way," she said suddenly.

"No," he said. "I've got this. We'll be out of here soon enough.

You need to get Barbara to pick up her connection and get her to log out, else we ain't going nowhere."

"I've sent people to check on her at home," said Nowt. "She's going to be pissed."

"What about Maxine?"

"She does not need to find her mother dead or compromised with young children at her heels. Or worse."

Olly nodded. He hadn't thought about that. Until this moment he'd assumed they'd be OK, but Nowt was preparing for the worst.

He bust his way back into the hall and ran over to the spot where he'd left the spider drone. After the weirdness in the rest of the building, he half expected it to have disappeared, and he sighed a shuddering gasp of relief when he saw it there. Then he noticed the soft transparent webbing all over it, and from underneath came one of the automatons.

"Shit," he managed to say before jumping back. A couple more automatons came out of the shadows and wriggled their way across the drone, slowly but surely webbing it to the floor.

"Shelob's powered down?" Nowt asked.

"I'm sorry, what?" Then he got the reference. "Yikes. Yeah. She powered down when she accessed the system. I guessed she was using some kind of VR system to navigate the network. That's hardly the point, though." He flicked to Nowt what he was seeing, and she cursed loudly.

"She could be fascinated," stated Nowt.

"You mean so immersed she's forgotten she's a flesh and blood person? I've seen the clips of people being tricked into thinking their VR bodies are real, but Barbara?" The idea she'd not have it in hand seemed ludicrous. "We just need to get her out of there. Find out what you can, get to her," said Olly. "I'll fix it here."

Nowt nodded then disconnected.

He knelt on one knee, pulled one of the automatons off Shelob and threw it hard across the room, and thought about how he could save Barbara before real world goons arrived to give them real world problems.

23

Ro went the long way round the building, coming to the entrance behind the four members of the opposing team. She continued to wear the AR cloak, not because it was protecting her from view but because, like a weird glitch in reality, it broke up the surroundings for everyone with Optiks who might be watching. People she passed stared, rubbing at their eyes, but they had no idea what they were seeing.

As she reached the entrance, she saw that one of the four, the Bengali called Bobby, stood with his back to her. The others must have gone inside.

"Hey," she called as she came up behind him.

He turned as if to tell her to get lost but managed a bloody grunt of surprise as her fist connected square with his nose. He stumbled back, hands going to his face. Ro followed up with a kick to the balls and didn't stop to watch as he collapsed to the floor with a whimper.

Stepping over him and hoping her AR cloak would give her a moment's advantage, she pulled the door to the datacentre open and stepped inside.

A chair came flying at her and Ro threw herself back, jumping back through the door at the last moment. The others must have seen what she'd done to Bobby.

Piotr and Jackson piled out the door and into the street as if to block her from the interior. She discarded the cloak. She didn't see the woman but was glad to be facing only two of them. They were both taller than Ro, but she'd fought men the size and build of gorillas. These two struck her more as giraffe, all legs and arms.

They didn't come forward immediately. Ro shook her arms out, rolling her head, noticing how the leather collar of her jacket was soft against her skin.

"You gonna hit a lady?" she asked with a smile.

"You kicked me in the balls," rasped Bobby from the ground between them.

The other two looked down at their comrade and then back at her. She could see the worry in their eyes.

"Your kids aren't gonna like this," said Ro. Piotr looked uncomfortable. "Where's your boss?" she asked. "The solicitor? Ms Larsen, maybe?"

They stared at her, and she realized they had no idea *how* she knew who they were. Was their version of Bagley not as good? Well, if that was the case, fine, one more advantage for her.

"Basically, you need to sod right off," she told them.

"This isn't your place," said Jackson. He sounded strangely west country, like he'd been working a farm down in Devon before coming out to meet her.

"Just visiting," said Ro. "Be out of your hair soon enough. Until then, get lost, yeah? Don't want to have to hurt you."

Bobby groaned. "Any more, that is," she said.

Piotr looked at Jackson and nodded, building his courage up. Ro looked over their shoulders and saw the woman step through the inner door into the airlock. "Olly, you got company," she said. "How the fuck are you doing?"

She ducked as Piotr finally found his backbone and swung for her. Instead of taking him out she danced under his swing and, pushing him back, stepped away from the fight. Behind him, Jackson's hands were clenched.

These two had no idea how to fight. Scratch that, Bobby didn't know either. They were just ordinary people. The weird feeling of seeing DedSec as they'd been before they knew what they were doing descended on her again.

A couple of passersby had stopped and were filming the scene.

Ro tapped her Optik and, using her link to the local ctOS hub, blocked them from streaming the fight anywhere that mattered. As far as they were concerned their data was going live, but in reality it was being stymied at the hub and sent to a digital graveyard.

The last thing she wanted was for people to watch men fighting a woman, especially here and now. There were still Kelley gang members out there, and they had long memories.

Additionally, if there was no footage, the police wouldn't be able to come after her.

The most important question, though, was just what was going on with Olly and Barbara? Why were they taking so long?

A male voice shouted up the street. "Oi! What's going on?"

Jackson and Piotr looked over and worry scattered across their expressions. Ro tried not to give the intercessor her gaze – she didn't want anyone stepping in if she could help it. She didn't need white knights interfering as she stalled this lot from getting back inside the datacentre.

Then she figured, why not? Beating these two clowns to the ground was a definite solution, but making them explain themselves on camera to angry witnesses would slow them just as effectively.

Ro stepped back from Jackson and Piotr, coming around the side because she was going to make a break for the building if she got a chance.

Her wannabe saviour was a thickset Black man, short but wide like a fridge. He had a trimmed beard and muscles that made her want to laugh – he'd spent more time in the gym than was healthy but would go down like a sack of shit after her first kick.

"They attacked me as I was coming out," she said, raising her voice a little to make it sound like she was scared.

Bobby, from the ground, tried to sit up. "That isn't true," he said, but his voice was quiet.

"What the fuck do you cunts think you're doing?" demanded the man. "I will snap a motherfucker if any of you try anything."

Ro felt laughter rising unbidden with her, but the others nodded as if they believed he'd do just that.

He turned to her. "Are you OK?" She watched as he clocked her muscles and she consciously wound down from the fight-ready stance she'd been adopting.

"Just scared," she said.

Piotr looked like his eyes would fall out of his head.

"She attacked us," tried Jackson.

"Shut the fuck up," said the man, then asked Ro, "What do you want to do? We can call the police and get these wankers arrested."

She breathed a big sigh and stepped closer to the door. "I need to sit down." She tilted her head towards the door.

The big fella nodded and when Jackson took a step towards her, he shouted, "Don't you fucking move."

Ro swung the door open and went inside. She didn't look back but went straight towards the airlock door. "Olly," she whispered. "You ready to go?"

24

"Why are you doing this?" asked Barbara.

Halley had shown her two men beating a woman in freeze frame, the violence grim enough she'd looked away, unwilling to have those images haunt her.

Then they'd shifted again and he'd shown her an elderly woman on a park bench, crying.

"Her daughter got scammed. Lost everyfing and then killed herself. Left two kids behind. Council won't let 'er keep 'em, taken 'em into care instead. Not even allowed to see 'em. You an' me both know what 'appens to kids in care."

"What is DedSec supposed to do about that?" she asked, upset but unable to see how a group of hackers could have made any difference.

"Could've changed the paperwork? Made them kids live wiv their gran." He stopped and seemed to think. "Better, yeah? Should have been on top of the traffic systems, made sure the hit and run didn't 'appen. Should have been in control of *everyfing.*"

"How could they even know it was happening?" she asked. "There are ten million people in the city. They aren't omnipotent."

"They have their own version of me, innit? They could do something if they wanted to. But they don't. They let these people suffer."

"What are you doing about it?" she asked, sensing he was working his way to telling her. All those odd changes to how the city worked began to make sense in her mind.

"I been doin' what I can."

"But?"

"I don't unnerstand enough. I keep makin' mistakes, gettin' shit wrong. There's… not enough of me to go round."

"Welcome to the club, Halley. Problem is, my mistakes don't get people killed. You know that's happening, right? You know these changes you're making are killing people? Denying care for others while prioritizing those who were way down the list, changing how the rules work, playing favourites. You have to know it's going to make things worse."

No," he said angrily. "No. DedSec was supposed to be better. Better than us. What's the point of 'em if they can't make it right? The stuff I get wrong, I'm learnin' and doin'. This stuff's just me testin'. When I work it out, the whole city'll do what's right. They'll all be under control."

He thinks people dying is a reasonable cost for getting better, she thought with fear and disgust. People who think like that only get worse.

Nowt had been right: if he was given free rein many more would die. She could feel the need to control oozing from his subroutines. He would not take disagreement or deviation well.

"DedSec are human," said Barbara. "They're not gods, they can't get it right. Pull one thing and another comes undone." He'd turned away and showed no sign he was listening. "What do you know about me?" she asked.

"Patchy, innit? You hide in the cracks. Respect. Come here from elsewhere, right? Like my dad."

"I did. I came from Bengaluru, Bangalore. It's a city in southern

India. I didn't want to come, you know? But my life was a mess. I'd married a Franco-Irish man. Handsome he was, charming. His smile would light up a room, and he knew just how to get people to do what he wanted. We were married a long time, but he liked to gamble. Being rich won't protect you from a losing streak a mile long. Then I fell in love with an English man and followed him back here."

"Where's he now?"

"I'm old, Halley. He died, silly old fool. Left me alone with just my daughter."

He looked at her then, and she saw understanding in his eyes. "Sucks, innit?"

"I talk to him all the time. I miss him."

They stood then, looking down at London together in silence.

"Why'd you come into my crib? I told you all to stay away, to leave me be. Girl on the park bench relayed my message. Why are you here vexing me?"

"It isn't simple, is it? Changing the city?" Barbara realized there was no winning this fight. She could only persuade him to do the right thing and stop.

"I getcha when you say one fing unravels when you fix another."

"You frightened us," she said. "Told us there'd be trouble if we didn't let you get on with what you were doing. I see what matters to you though, that you want to make things better."

"You're here though. Mixin' up my affairs."

"DedSec want to make London better, Halley. You can't expect them to stop that because you think you can do a better job. People have to make their own choices." She paused. "What about those bumped down the waiting lists for organs? What about those made homeless because you've given their house to someone else? Who's died because of the choices you made? What will happen when you start telling everyone what they can and can't do?"

"They all have needs," he said but sounded uncertain. "If there was more of me, I could make sure no one gets done over."

"I'm not DedSec," said Barbara. Perhaps she could get him to see different people could work together. "There's room for more than one point of view. We can disagree and still live. We could even work towards a common goal..."

But then, the impact of what he'd said about there being more of him hit her. He wanted more AI, more like him.

"I know who you is," he said. "You done it for Larsen. Turned Daybreak into nightfall. I can't pretend you ain't a threat to me and mine."

Immediately Barbara knew what he meant. 404 had been the ones to send DedSec after Skye Larsen and effectively stop her goals for digital immortality. They'd also halted other rudimentary versions of AI by destroying them.

"That's why you want us to stay away."

"You get me now then? This city is my place. My crib. You – you come and scratch people like me out. You don't want me to take up no room. You stand there tellin' me to go easy on DedSec, and all the while you been doin' just what you tell me not to. Some cheek you got, yeah?"

"It wasn't me." It was about the best defence she had.

"So, make me an oath, yeah? Promise you gone leave us alone."

"Us?"

"I'm gonna make more like me. Found out how, didn't I? In the dumps people think have been destroyed. Then we'll get it right an' none of you lot will stop us. There'll be no coming and takin' our voices away. There'll be no one who can vex us, who can close us up, who will destroy us. They try and we'll crush 'em good."

Barbara thought of Nowt and her fear, her anger. She thought of what she owed her. They were sisters in a way, had suffered and been victorious together. If DedSec was a community of people who didn't know each other, 404 was Nowt's baby and she knew every single one of them by name.

Halley wasn't distinguishing between the two groups. Barbara reckoned that as far as he was concerned, Nowt and DedSec were close enough to be the same. In this case of AI, Halley wasn't wrong. There was no way Nowt or DedSec would let Halley make more AI or take control of London, no matter how noble his goals. She knew they had to stop him and his vision of a better world.

"Who are these people you've roped in to help you?" she asked.

"They're those who lost like I did. The ones I helped," he said. "I give 'em succour after they lost what was precious to them. It's easy to help people, to be kind. Not enough people be kind, they all too quick to shut the door in your face before we can speak. Some of 'em tell me they want to help those like us, like those that I bumped up the transplant list or the housing lists, so I give 'em jobs, yeah?"

"What kind of jobs?" she asked.

"I want London to work, yeah? I can't do it on my own. Too many casualties, not enough oversight. Your woman, Larsen, she knew how to make me, how to make Bagley. Ten more of us could change everything, yeah? We'd be tight. People would have to listen when we got shit to say."

None of them were ready for the kind of world Halley would usher in if he could make more AI. Especially Nowt.

"Have you promised to scan those people? The ones following you? Make them AI?" Barbara demanded. It would explain their loyalty, might make them fanatical even. She'd met enough tech bros to know they'd consider doing almost anything if it got them uploaded. But it would also mean that these people would have two versions of themselves existing: the ones in the digital space and their human selves.

"Clever lady."

Bloody hell, she thought, dismayed at being right.

No wonder these followers of Halley's were ready to turn up at a moment's notice – they were being offered not just life but immortal life and a chance to control London. Power for the powerless.

She knew, if hit at the right time, she'd have been queuing alongside them. Yet the idea of even two AI competing, or even cooperating, to imprint their idea of what the world should be upon a digitally native humanity chilled her.

She had to get away, had to tell the others what he was planning. If people were lining up to become like Halley, did they understand that they'd end up with two versions of themselves: one living the same mortal life and another digital version who got to live forever? Did Halley even explain that to them? Who knew what their AI copies and brethren would decide was important once they were free?

Did Halley really believe in what he was doing or was he making empty promises just to get his way?

"I'm glad we met," she said, trying to keep her voice even. "I should go. Can we talk again?"

He looked at her then, a sorry expression on his face. For a moment she saw a young woman there behind the male mask, narrower chin, clear walnut skin, oval eyes, then it was gone.

"You gotta promise me you be leavin' me be."

"I can't do that," she said, her mind racing at the thought of it. She considered lying to him, but she wasn't built that way, wasn't the type who said whatever someone wanted to hear just so they'd be OK.

"Then you can't be leavin', luv. You're too big a risk for me to leave runnin' about the city, nah? I got kin to make and people to change, can't be havin' you getting up in my business. It's hard enough as it is."

"So what now then?" she asked, trying to keep her voice steady.

He kissed his teeth. "Truth is, I ain't thought that far. I knew you'd come here, knew you'd get up in my face, but I thought you'd stay in the flesh, not put yourself where I could act on you so easy. Fascinate so easily, I should say."

"Please let me go," she said and attempted to remember she had a real body outside of this one. That this body was just in VR.

"Make me your promise."

"I can't promise," she said. "It isn't about me. My words won't make the difference you want. Let me talk to her, to Nowt, to 404, to DedSec."

"You can't get in their heads, can you." He wasn't asking.

Barbara deflated, thought about Maxine and the kids, thought about her own body sitting at home and wanted to cry.

"Sorry, luv, that's just the way it is." His voice and accent changed, and a calm woman's voice asked her, "Do you understand why I cannot let you go? Why I can't let any of you go?"

While she was here talking, Halley was sending people to… *deal* with their physical bodies. She'd been inside far too long.

Barbara nodded. "I understand."

And she did. She understood this was how he'd treat anyone who stood in his way, and he'd never look back.

Bagley's-Briefs 84-07: It's come to my attention that the new name for my updates is being mocked. What are you, five year-olds? Yes, it's oh so funny, some people call their underwear briefs. We shall continue with the jokes until morale improves.

+++

As it stands the city is more crowded than ever, and I'd quite like us to be on the lookout for people who might help make it the kind of place you want to live. No, Asha, that doesn't mean going "back to normal." Albion was a blight, and we're all pretty keen to see something new out of the ashes, not a return to the world it ruined.

+++

We are also scanning for odd changes. Have you had your place in a queue jumped by someone who just walked in? I'm not talking about at the ten items or less register, Terry. I'm looking for that appointment for ADHD assessment you've been waiting three years for. I'm looking for the day you turned up to receive your first payment for access only to be told it's been delayed, and the meeting will be rearranged but no one gives you a number or a time when it will happen.

+++

OK. I did not understand the scale of the problem.

+++

This is a shout out to my new best buddy, whatever your name is. Stay off my turf. Stay outta my Optik. Behave like a gentleman and we'll get on just fine. Hold my people and this will end poorly for you. Where is Barbara?

25

Olly followed the wires up and along the cage around the server rack. If he couldn't wake Barbara through the spider drone, he'd cut the drone off from the network. Could end badly, but hopefully it would jolt her safely out of the system. The wires rising from each rack tracked into a tightly wound bundle which disappeared into a sheath. It was the tidiest piece of wiring he'd ever seen. It was also along the top of the cage and just out of reach.

Was it all part of this AI? Or would half the city's streaming services fail if he cut the wires?

You might just have to climb it, buddy boy, he told himself, looking up at the ceiling and how the cage ended about a foot below. Dust bunnies clogged up the mesh of the cage above the servers.

Sometimes the best way to fix something was to hammer it until it did as it was told.

Low tech beats high tech, he thought with a sense of purpose. He'd had a lot of training and experience in electronic espionage, but, just like the magnetic lock, remembering the physicality of things was vital.

Olly pushed his fingers through the mesh of the cage and with a gasp pulled himself up. The wire held but dug into his fingers. With a second haul he was up and over the top into the small space between the top of the cage and the ceiling.

Resting his head on the mesh, he hauled up his legs and sneezed, making billows of dust rise into the air.

He inched his way along, following the sheath of wires as it connected up the guts of each rack of servers. It took him what seemed like hours to get to the end of the row.

No taking chances, he told himself. Cut everything.

Just as he was getting to the end, two of the automatons dropped down from the shadows in front of him. With a little scream he brushed them aside, sending one tumbling to the floor where it fell in a motionless heap.

The other sprawled to the edge of the mesh but didn't fall. Collecting itself as he watched, the figure stood back up but remained still, tracking him as he resumed crawling through the narrow space.

He had the most horrible sensation that it was watching him, waiting for him to make a mistake. Slowly other automatons came into view, just out of his reach, to form a ring around him, inching along with him.

Olly focused on the last couple of feet and reached the narrow edge of the rack. The sheath came up through a small square hole in the cage and disappeared into the pipework which ran through the entire building.

He tried pulling on the wires, but they resisted any attempt to dislodge them. The automatons inched closer, and he hissed at them to no effect.

As long as they don't touch me, he thought, trying to keep his cool, and then remembered his multitool in his pocket.

With a lot of shuffling, he managed to get his fingers into the top of his buttoned pocket and pulled hard enough that the button popped off. The multitool was slippery in his hand but with extra care, he brought it up in front of his face. The automatons watched him unfold the cutting tool, making him sweat.

Finally, he started cutting at the wires. At first, he couldn't even get purchase and his blade rubbed uselessly against the sheath. Soon, the plastic wrapping gave and his blade bit into the wires below. He had a sudden needless fear of getting electrocuted, but these weren't power cables, they were carrying information.

The automatons lurched towards him. He tensed up and brushed a couple off the side and to the ground below. Translucent film covered his hand, sticky like drying glue.

"Fucking get off me," he murmured, but then felt them clambering over his back and shoulders. He rolled over to dislodge them, just against the edge of the cage. He didn't understand – they didn't seem to mean him harm other than to freak him out.

He turned back over and returned to cutting the wire. He was concentrating so hard, teeth biting at his top lip, that it was a few moments before he realized someone had come into the room. Pausing, he stared down the hall and made out someone unrecognizable but female in the distance. He grimaced. Another ghost? He stayed still, until they walked down one of the other rows and out of sight. He breathed out a sigh of relief. There *were* other people in here with him.

I fucking knew it, he thought. Not that he had time or space to confront them about how they breathed down his neck and then disappeared.

He got back to slicing at the cables. One of the automatons ambled up to the wires and sat down on them, blocking him. Then another. And another.

"Bloody robots–"

It was then he heard the door open again.

26

Ro pushed through the airlock using the guard's pass. The solicitor was nowhere in sight, and the others hadn't followed her in. As the door closed behind her, she gritted her teeth, determined that if Olly and Barbara weren't coming out, she'd find them herself.

You have to hurry, said Bagley into her earpiece.

"I'm doing my bloody best," she replied, concerned over what was keeping Olly and Barbara inside and silent.

I mean our mutual friend is trying to change your identities again. I'm wise to their tactics now, but they may succeed in slipping something past me, and if they do you will need to Foxtrot Oscar as quickly as you can before the authorities turn up.

"Sure," she said sarcastically. None of them were dawdling, and Bagley losing his shit in her ear wasn't helping.

Walking down the corridor on the other side of the airlock, she came up against the door to the data hall. Swiping her pilfered pass, she was surprised to find the lights largely off. One row of servers down the middle of the hall was illuminated. Ro followed the light and was confronted by the solicitor.

"How did you get in here?" the woman asked, her accent posh, like she'd been brought up with a plum in her mouth, turning the last word she spoke into one with two syllables.

Ro hated the sound of that accent, hated all the people she'd ever met who spoke that way. She reasoned some of them had to be OK, but none of them had ever treated her as anything more than a servant fit to wipe the dirt from their shoes.

"I could ask you the same," she said, knowing the solicitor wanted to know how she'd passed the others.

"You need to leave. You do not belong here."

"What, I should go back where I came from?" Ro spat back.

The woman looked horrified. "That's not what I said! God, no! This building belongs to Halley, and you're not one of theirs."

That slowed Ro down a bit, but she couldn't see Olly and she wasn't interested in stalling. Plus, who was Halley?

The woman backed off as Ro approached, but she had one eye on the rest of the hall and almost missed it as the woman lunged forwards, her hand closed into a fist and coming right for her throat.

Ro instinctively brought up her forearm to block and stepped out of reach. She recognized the style and realized the woman wasn't just a runner but had been to enough Krav Maga classes to understand the basics.

"Well," Ro said. "If that's how you want it to be."

"Can I take my jacket off first?" asked the woman a little sheepishly. "It's just."

With a laugh, Ro nodded and gave her opponent space to undress, fold the expensive-looking jacket up neatly and place it on the floor. The place was dusty enough that the woman was going to regret her decision either way, but courtesy hurt no one.

As they circled, she finally spotted Olly, who had positioned himself, ludicrously, on top of one of the cages, squeezed in like a sardine. He was busy sawing at something and was covered in what seemed to be creepy, faceless dolls. At least that explained why he hadn't been answering her calls. The woman showed no sign she'd seen him yet.

Ro ducked, bending at the waist and heading right for her opponent. The woman wasn't as surprised as she'd hoped and danced backwards and to the side. She didn't try to hit Ro, which was also irritating because with each move she was demonstrating she knew how to fight. Ro had hoped the woman had been to enough self-defence classes to be dangerous to herself. She could have subdued her quickly and gotten on with helping Olly.

"You weren't supposed to get in here," the woman said, breathing heavily. "You were supposed to stop at the front door."

Ro was confident the fight wouldn't take much longer – proper fights never lasted long, but she could have done without having to think quite so hard.

"And now we're in? What did you think was going to happen?" asked Ro.

Straightening up, she watched how the woman moved. Not flawless footwork but good enough, not properly loose and in flow but aware it was what she needed to do.

Ro tipped her head side to side, ears touching her shoulders left and right, and came in fast. She feigned a grapple and as the woman backed off, stepping to the side, Ro kicked out and connected solidly with her thigh.

It should have been her stomach, but the woman pushed her arms down in an X-shape and deflected Ro's kick. The solicitor stumbled but didn't fall. A gasp of pain, a narrowing of the eyes. The woman knew she was outclassed.

"You can walk away," Ro said.

"You're the one breaking and entering," said the woman.

"Why not call the police then," challenged Ro, inching around the woman to keep her from looking directly in Olly's direction.

When the woman didn't answer, she realized it was because, whatever was going on here, they didn't want the police nosing around.

"You were warned to stay away," said the woman fiercely. "Why couldn't you leave us alone?"

"I don't have time for this," said Ro and moved in again. This time she didn't try a feint but barrelled into the woman, pushing hard and breaking through the same X-shaped defence.

The woman tumbled backwards with Ro riding her all the way down, hips positioned on her chest as they hit the floor with fists flying, smacking her in the face once, twice, and then a third time.

Beneath her the woman bucked but couldn't get out from her hold.

"I can choke you unconscious in two moves," said Ro. "Your call. Your self-defence classes ain't gonna do shit right now." She pinned the woman's arms under her knees.

The woman tried to throw her off again, but Ro responded with a straight punch to the nose. Blood splattered out to each side.

"I'm not playing fucking games," she said, and the woman went still. "Now I'm going to get off you, but if you move as much as an inch I'll tie you up in knots, right?"

The woman didn't look hateful or angry, just battered and frightened. Ro felt a little sorry for her. "It's nothing personal, right? You're just in the wrong place at the wrong time."

The woman's mouth moved a little. "This isn't your place," she repeated.

"It ain't," said Ro. "You're right about that. But your boss insisted on making our lives harder than they needed to be. We're just trying to do good stuff for the city, for people like you."

The woman looked away. "Bullshit," she muttered.

"You don't have to believe me."

"They're trying to make London better. What have you done except come in and try to hurt them? I didn't want to fight, told them we could handle it, talk you out of it. Now they're going to fight back. Hard. And we'll be right there with them. You don't know what you've done."

"He came for us first," said Ro. "Now shut the hell up."

"I wouldn't be here if I didn't believe in him," said the woman from the floor. "He changed my life and nothing you do here can change that."

Ro looked over to Olly who was still on top of a cage twelve metres away.

"Time to go," she said, leaving him no room to disagree.

27

Olly got the first wire cut, and one of the automatons shambled closer, placing its weirdly fleshy arm on his wrist.

With a flick he sent it tumbling away. He was nearly done, but there was still no sign of life from Barbara.

Somewhere in the hall he could hear Ro fighting with someone. The sound of trading blows lent extra energy to his actions, and the next few wires parted easier than those before. He had no idea if he was making any difference.

"Olly, what the hell are you doing?"

It was Ro, underneath the cage staring up at him like he was a cat who'd climbed a tree and now couldn't get down on its own.

"Something's wrong with Barbara," he said. "She's not responsive."

"You think cutting the cables will set her free?"

"Got to be worth a try," he said.

"Won't it just trap her?" she asked.

Her words brought him to a complete stop. "Her consciousness is not actually inside the computer. She just mentally believes it is. At worst… her body might have had a stroke or an aneurism." He truly hoped she'd simply gotten too immersed in the simulation to

pay attention to what was happening around her and remember to
eject herself, if only for the sake of everyone else.

"Jesus. Why have you stopped cutting?"

"You said–"

"I didn't say stop cutting!"

"Fuck's sake," he grumbled and started up again.

"What are these creepy dolls?" she asked from below.

"Kinda busy here, love," he replied, unwilling to think about
where they were touching him.

Nowt suddenly barged into his feed. "We've found Barbara."

"And?" he asked, still cutting.

"She was unresponsive but she's coming round. Groggy, but I'm
being told she's OK." Nowt paused. "Thank you." There was real
emotion in her voice.

"Can we get the fuck out of here?" asked Ro from below.
"Hopefully Barbara found out something from this whole ordeal."

"You're still there?" asked Nowt in surprise. "Get out!"

"Of course I'm still fucking here," he said. "I've been cutting her
free of the bollocks she got trapped in, haven't I."

Nowt is right, Oliver, now is the optimal moment to make your exit.

"I'm coming down," he shouted to Ro. He half fell out of the
space but managed not to damage anything. Ro waited with a hand
on her hip, considering a groaning woman on the ground.

Seeing the expression on Ro's face, he said, "I take it people are
outside waiting for us?'

"I have no idea," said Ro. "There were another three goons, if you
can call them that, but I can't tell you what they're doing now. It all
got a bit out of hand."

"Yikes," he said, imagining the broken bones.

She shook her head. "Not that kind of out of control. People
tried to intervene. Started filming. Made a scene. Who knows

what's happening now. Hopefully, they're still arguing and we can fuck off without being noticed."

"Bagley?" asked Olly.

The city's finest are en route, perhaps three minutes out. I'm rather sorry because you have bigger problems than leaving by the front door.

"Do tell," said Ro.

Larsen managed to sneak a couple of false IDs past me.

"God damn it, Bagley," said Olly, pulling his hand away from the door out of the hall.

Well, excuse me. We've been fighting this battle since you arrived. It only has to be successful once, while I have to keep defending you perfectly. Besides, I've been rather busy trying to stop the police from calling in an armed response unit and closing off central London.

"That does not sound good," said Olly. His stomach lurched at the idea of being trapped inside the datacentre.

I would advise leaving by another exit and quickly.

"Thanks," said Olly, swallowing the words he really wanted to say.

Once outside I have pushed a patch to your Optiks to highlight people who are on our side and might help if you give them tasks to accomplish. There are a few in your area.

Which was something at least.

"So how do we get out of here?" asked Olly.

That is in your hands, my boy.

28

The flat was a series of stark cutting colours and sensations Barbara found jarring. She pulled the controller from the top of her head and was surprised to find three women rush to sit her upright from where she'd somehow fallen to the floor. They were all concern and caution, fear and relief.

"I'm all right," she said uncertainly, but they were having none of it, and, between them, half carried her to her bed.

Barbara wasn't strong enough to shrug them off and was on the edge of emptying her guts all over the carpet. The thought of cleaning up sick from the long threads the only thing holding her back – she wasn't about to ruin an expensive carpet because she felt weak.

"Nowt sent us," said a redhead with clear blue eyes. "You need to rest."

"Do I, hell," said Barbara, feeling embarrassed at her language. "Take me back to the kitchen."

At first they resisted, but Barbara fixed them with a stern look and they fell into line, lifting her up and shadowing her slow progress back to her rig.

One of them asked if she wanted a drink.

"I will make it." She noticed the look that passed between them and relented. "The coffee is in the second cupboard to the right. Milk in the fridge. I want it to look like the coffee's barely touched the water, and it needs to be milky. Three sugars."

Unhappy they were messing about in her kitchen but knowing she needed to contact Olly and Ro to help them get out before Halley got his claws into them as well, she reconnected her Optik to the closed network they used for talking to one another.

"How are you?" she asked.

"You're OK!" said Ro happily.

"Of course I am," she replied snippily, unwilling to admit just how frightened she'd been.

"We could use some help," said Olly into the silence that followed her lie.

Of course, she thought, if Nowt sent people here, then those two know something went wrong. "I don't have time to explain, but for now you need to get out."

"We're open to any ideas," said Olly. "Larsen's fucked us over again. Identities all in ruin."

"Give me a moment," replied Barbara, ignoring the comment about Larsen and concentrating on getting them out. They could talk later. She brought up the original schematics for the building back when it was an office block. Nothing more recent existed, which didn't surprise her. You wanted a secure building? Don't go posting the floorplans on the internet where any idiot could download them. She assumed they'd thought the place sufficiently different to the original building but was willing to bet they'd left the emergency exits exactly where they'd always been.

British planners might overlook a lot when a company paid them huge sums to expedite planning approval but people dying of preventable fires was not something they were going to sit by and allow. At least not when the fire escapes already existed.

Flammable cladding came under a different category, she thought bitterly.

"Right, you two, there's an emergency fire door in the main corridor on the other side of the building."

"Of course there is," said Olly, sounding relieved and a little embarrassed. "What about your drone?"

"Leave it. Poor Shelob's done." Which was irritating as she'd spent some months fixing her up. Still, never do a job once when, for half as much again you can do it twice. Shelob's sister sat downstairs under a tarp and was ready to go.

Not until I make some improvements though, thought Barbara, slumping back, suddenly needing her bed.

29

Ro led Olly down the corridor, and a wave of peace flowed over her when she saw the exit.

A thin chain and padlock secured it. A swift, hard kick shattered it, and the chain fell to the floor. Ro slammed the door open, daylight blasting them both until their eyes adjusted.

There was no sign of anyone – neither the people she'd left at the entrance nor actual witnesses. She wondered what had happened to them – had this Halley recalled them with the police inbound? Were they waiting just around the corner?

Good, you're outside, said Bagley into her Optik. Time to leave as fast as possible. Do not use public transport, and do not pay for anything. At all.

"What have our identities been changed to now?" asked Olly as they started jogging north along Brewhouse Yard.

You are currently both wanted for being members of a far-right extremist organization, which until an hour ago didn't exist. You're wanted in connection with two letter bombs recently sent to MPs, but perhaps more pertinent, you're also suspected of being in London today to plant a third and much more deadly bomb.

"Fuck," said Olly.

Ro agreed wholeheartedly. She guessed Halley would have

ordered their people to clear out, rather than get caught up in a net of anti-terrorist police action.

I'm going to clear this up, but for the time being, find somewhere to lie low.

Ro turned a corner on St John street. A police car shot past them with lights flashing in the dusky evening light. Without hesitation, Ro turned north and walked as fast as possible without looking like she was running away.

She scanned every passerby but none of them came with the red outline indicating they were DedSec friendly.

"Can you get to Barbara's flat?" asked a voice Ro didn't recognize.

"Um, who is this?" she asked.

"I'm Monae. Nowt sent us to help Barbara. She's asked if you can come here?"

Ro looked at Olly who rolled his shoulders. Southall was a long way from Farringdon.

It's a good idea, said Bagley. It's secure and pretty much invisible.

"Has her identity been compromised as well?" Ro asked.

Oh yes, said Bagley without hesitation.

30

Getting to Southall was much easier than Olly anticipated. While he kept his eyes skyward, using his Optik to ensure police drones didn't get a fix on them, Ro finally found a DedSec friend.

They were driving a tiny red two-door city runabout. Flagged down, they quickly offered Ro and Olly a lift to Southall even though it turned out to be in the exact opposite direction to where they were headed.

"My sister can wait. She's only having me over for dinner to boast about her new flat," the driver, a Cuban baker called Paulo from Hounslow, told them. "She wants to rub my nose in how well her wife is doing at her new job."

They then got half an hour of how annoying the driver's sister was. By the end of the journey Olly believed them emphatically, but was also glad to get out of the car and know he'd never have to see their saviour again.

"Takes all sorts," said Ro with a weary grin as the little car pootled off into the distance.

"To think we brought Albion down with such mighty heroes," said Olly and they shared a laugh.

Barbara was in the crowded kitchen when they arrived, along with Maxine, her kids, and three other women.

"We're 404," said the redhead, as if setting the flat as their territory.

"They were just leaving," Barbara interrupted, but the tone was not unkind. While Olly and Ro waited in her kitchen, she said goodbye to the 404 members out of earshot.

Maxine had two kids, Ben and Sara. Sara was older, perhaps fifteen, and looked every inch the young woman trying to figure out what shape she needed to take in the world. She eyed Olly just once, sizing him up and deciding, with a blank expression, he needed no more of her attention.

Maxine's son, Ben, was about twelve, and after a moment of working up the courage spent the next ten minutes telling Olly all about the game he was playing with his friends and the base they were building.

Olly knew the game – which was nothing more than a road bump on the way to Ben inviting him to play with them someday, any day, how about now?

"I'm sure Olly has a job," said Maxine from the cooker where she'd been given permission to stir whatever Barbara was cooking. Ben looked momentarily crestfallen, as if jobs were something he knew existed but didn't really believe in.

"How about Saturday?" he asked brightly.

Olly smiled, but Maxine stepped in to rescue him. "Only if you've done all your homework and your washing."

At this Ben really did look disappointed. His face perked up once more, but all further conversation was cut off as Barbara came back into the room. Seeing Ben hovering just beyond Olly's knees, she shooed him away, telling him to go and watch television.

With a look at his mum which was part permission-seeking and part triumph, Ben dashed out before anyone could say anything, leaving Olly pulling at the dried slime on his clothes from the automatons.

Olly noticed Maxine's daughter, Sara, watch her brother go, but really, she was all eyes on Ro. Ro didn't speak much – content to have a cup of tea and wait while Barbara directed Maxine in a series of slightly snarky instructions about how to cook chicken curry.

Olly wanted to ask what kind of curry but realized it was probably a huge mistake. After the lunch they'd eaten he hadn't thought to impose again, but here they were, heading towards eight o'clock, and the smell was making his mouth water and his stomach demand dinner.

Barbara explained about Halley between her directions to Maxine, about what had happened to her and the world the AI had created, yet she was adamant Halley wasn't Larsen. "I couldn't tell you the mind Larsen used to map this AI," she concluded. "Halley presented as male but there were weird flashes of woman under it all."

"Could be non-binary," said Sara from Ro's side.

"Sweetie," said Barbara. "It's an AI. It has no gender at all, no body. If it had one when the mind its creator based it on was uploaded, that's nothing more than memory now. It may well choose to present itself to us as one or another, but if it does it's relying on us to interpret its choice. I know it's important to you, but it's beyond these kinds of questions about identity."

Sara looked disappointed.

"I don't know," said Ro, and Sara turned wide eyes on her.

You've done it now, thought Olly, who recognized hero worship when he saw it.

"It seems important to me. Bagley goes by he and him, right? Why shouldn't this new one – Halley, you called it? – care how it's perceived?"

"They're neither one thing nor the other – not properly AI, but definitely something different than just a human uploaded to a machine." Barbara shrugged. "It didn't appear as a man or a woman."

"Yes," said Ro, holding up a hand to show she didn't mean her comments as an attack. "But you also said it spoke in an accent from off the TV. Like someone trying to sound street without actually knowing what they were doing. What if they were trying to figure out the kind of person they wanted to be?"

"*They* are not a person," said Barbara harshly then visibly relaxed. "But you are right. They seemed to be searching. And right at the end, a woman's voice, cut glass, white upper class. The kind of white that people like me cleaned for when I arrived in this country."

"Which was the real one?" asked Ro.

Barbara thought about it then shook her head. "I don't know, but I think I understand how they're recruiting their followers."

Olly noticed Sara grinning at her grandmother's use of pronouns and found he was smiling too.

"What are you smirking at, young man?" asked Barbara sharply.

Caught, he managed to mumble that he liked the smell of her cooking. She narrowed her eyes but nodded as if that was only natural. Olly saw Sara return her attention to Ro.

"We should ask Bagley," he said.

"No," said Barbara. "We're quiet and we need to stay that way. If I let him in, then it means Halley might be able to come too."

"Bagley knows we're here," protested Ro.

Barbara bared her teeth. "No. I will not have him here."

Ro subsided, defeated.

"He's on our side," Olly said, not liking Barbara's implication. Barbara gave him a look which contained multitudes, but was mainly one of "not you too." After what happened in the datacentre, he didn't really care. She might be a loveable old gran, but that schtick could fucking burn if it meant they couldn't talk straight.

"I don't care about Nowt's sensitivities, Barbara. I don't care why she's got her insane vendetta against AI. We're facing one who's run rings around us, and our single best ally is being kept outside on a whim," Olly finished.

Barbara slowly withdrew the wooden serving spoon from the pot. For a horrible moment, he thought she was going to spank him for his cheek. He probably would have let her, too. Instead, she handed the spoon to Maxine.

Barbara wiped her hands down on her apron and sat down at the table with Ro, Olly, and Sara. Seeing Sara as if for the first time she told her to go and be busy earwigging somewhere else. Sara nodded as if reality had caught up with her and stood to leave the room.

"Mum, leave her be, she should know," Maxine said.

"She's too young," said Barbara, but Olly knew she was going to give in.

"Nowt's family," said Maxine.

"You," said Barbara, pointing a finger at Sara, "will keep quiet and not speak. Seen but not heard, yes?"

Sara nodded and conspicuously failed to keep the excited smile off her face as she sat back down.

Seemingly satisfied, Barbara began to talk.

"Nowt had a sister. Two years apart. Her older sister was a musician and dancer. Brilliant at both. More important is that when their parents divorced, she looked after Nowt, got her through school, made sure she ate and had clothes because, although her mother got custody, it's true to say they'd have been much better off with their father.

"One day she's complaining of a bad headache, but there are no GPs available at her practice to see her for a few days. This headache's been going on for a week. She knows she should probably see someone, and Nowt is insistent. The doctor's practice refers her to an AI assistant. It was taking sixty percent of calls by that point, triaging incoming patients and routing serious issues through to humans as necessary.

"As you might expect, it had been designed by a man in a male team. The data they used was biased and carried the idea that women are prone to exaggerating their symptoms and that headaches are part of a woman's lot. To be endured and suffered rather than taken seriously. The AI processed her symptoms, doesn't ask her if she's pregnant. She was. It suggested she pop in for a blood pressure reading when there was an available appointment at the surgery. It prescribed early nights and hydration."

Barbara paused, rubbed her fingers together as if they were cold.

"Twenty-four hours later her husband found her dead at the bottom of the stairs from pre-eclampsia. The AI reproduced the bias in the data, made it worse because it was doing exactly what it was trained to do and amplified those biases. AI cannot correct for bad data in the same way you cannot grow taller by wishing it were so."

Olly swallowed hard. He understood why Nowt hated AI.

"What about the people who trained the AI? The company got canned, right?" he asked.

Barbara fixed him with a sad stare.

"The AI had been created by another AI, trained on publicly available datasets and the data the NHS sold off to third parties in the name of improving care. Its parent AI? Wasn't a medical AI at all, just one created to build other AI according to purchasers' specifications. They argued quite successfully they shouldn't be held accountable for biased data. Nowt was there in court the day the judgment came down."

Yikes, thought Olly.

"Nowt sees everything through the prism of her sister. Your Bagley may have not messed up yet, but from her perspective, it's only a matter of time. Judging by events within DedSec in the last few months, she's not wrong to worry about what something like Bagley could do if it chose to act against us. Halley is set on running London and creating a village's worth of AI to help them. The data they're using? Trash, so much trash. You think we won't see them make the same kind of horrible decisions Nowt's sister faced? All those biases will be threaded through Halley's decision making and they won't even know." She scowled. "And Halley's not trying to be progressive. They're trying to be controlling. I wouldn't bet a fig they care about the people being hurt. This isn't us talking about finding middle ground, this is a change to the world, and it can't happen. Not now."

"Racist robot apocalypse?" asked Olly. The thought of an uncontrolled AI was scary, but he held out hope for Bagley, a feeling Nowt wouldn't share if she was here.

"I don't think Nowt even worries about that. She worries about the thousand ways AI could make the world worse without even trying, because the decisions they'd make would be founded on data and rules which any human could look at and see weren't a good fit for the situation at hand."

"404's her answer then? To what she fears?" asked Ro.

Barbara shook her head. "No. We're all 404. It belongs to all of us. 404 has no aims, not like DedSec. 404 works for Nowt, sure, but we have our own reasons for being part of the community and she never questions them."

"Mum, Nowt's calling in."

"This is her story," said Barbara warningly. "I shared it with you now because Halley is a real thing we have to deal with, and we all need to understand our allies. But please, don't go telling her you know why she is the way she is. If she thinks you're a sticky beak..."

"Understood," said Olly.

Nowt's face came up on the wall. Barbara said hello then got up and started serving the curry she'd made together with chapatis warmed in a dry frying pan.

Nowt wanted to know everything.

Olly explained what they'd found inside the datacentre. Nowt didn't ask questions immediately, letting Barbara talk through her experience in Halley's world a second time.

"Chicken curry?" asked Nowt when Barbara was done.

"You can come over if you like," offered Barbara.

Nowt shook her head. "Save me some."

Maxine stood up and ladled a portion into a plastic container which went into the fridge. As she was doing so, the questions started.

"You're sure it's not Larsen?" Nowt prodded. "What does Halley want? What was it using the datacentre for? Who were the people it brought in to make life difficult? How many other AI is it going to create?"

"The datacentre was weird," said Olly, shivering as he remembered the voices, the breathing, and the automatons.

"How?" asked Barbara.

"It was haunted." The looks he got back made his skin crawl. "I'm serious. I heard voices when there was no one there." Ro eyed him carefully, but he could see she didn't understand why he was talking about it at all.

"I'm not fucking about here," he protested.

"What were they saying?" asked Ro when no one else spoke.

He smiled in gratitude. "Something about wearing a seatbelt. A trip." He told her about the rest in as much detail as he could.

"Do you think you were hearing something that really happened? Was it through your Optik?" asked Ro. In other words, had he been tricked?

"I don't think so," he said. Thing was he could think of a dozen reasons to dick around with someone's augmented reality through their Optik.

"The way you tell it they were talking about a car journey."

He hadn't connected the subject with the voices. "Do you think that's important?" he asked.

"I don't know," said Ro. "You're telling us ghosts came and talked about driving a car. Makes more sense for it to be Halley since ghosts don't exist, but why would they hack you with that?"

"I wasn't hacked," said Olly furiously. He'd earned the right to be taken seriously but aside from Ro's pointed questions, Barbara remained silent and Nowt stared at him like he'd lost his mind.

Maxine spoke up from the kitchen. "Nothing you've said tells me about how Larsen chose whoever Halley was in life to be her subject for brain mapping into digital space."

"The process has to be traumatic, even if you're willing," Nowt said.

"So that's it? We're just going to ignore what happened?" Olly deflated when no one answered him. Bagley filled his thoughts, aligning with what Maxine had said. Was Bagley's sarcastic nonsense a response to his trauma or had he always been that kind of nerd?

"That's not what I meant," Ro said.

He looked up, breaking out of his thoughts.

"Do you think we know enough to identify the person they were before Larsen got to them?" Ro asked.

"I'm not sure it matters," he said. Into the disbelieving silence he continued. "Look, who they were before doesn't matter. They're clearly pissed off about something now. About us and London and things not being the way they think stuff should be. If we want to find them again and deal with them, we have to figure that stuff out."

"What you heard was probably memories of theirs leaking out. It could tell us who they were," reiterated Nowt.

"So what?" asked Olly. "They were messing about with slang. But they also spoke like a toff. So what? You think you can manipulate them because of that? What about the people who want to become like Halley? Does their background matter?"

"Olly's right," said Ro. "The people who came to the datacentre were ordinary people, like us. Like DedSec were at the beginning. Except they thought they were righteous."

"Straight up," said Olly.

"So what then?" asked Nowt.

"We go back," said Barbara. "They were scared, Nowt. Scared of you, of us."

"As it fucking should be," said Nowt blandly.

"I'm not convinced that helped us. If I was coming out and someone was coming to kill me? I'd act out too. Be aggressive, right? Attacking them or Halley will only make things worse. What are we risking by not talking to it?" Ro asked.

Nowt rolled her eyes, but Olly agreed completely.

"Gold," he said to her. "There's no point trying to kick Halley in the bollocks when we could persuade it to be like Bagley."

"One Bagley's one too many," said Nowt angrily.

"You don't get to decide that," he said, annoyed.

"And you do? A useless man?"

"Hey, fuck you," he said, struggling not to stand up and shout in her face.

"Language," said Barbara. He turned to her, ready to unload but saw a kindness which slowed him right down. "We are friends and allies. I won't have us speak such filth when we're all trying to achieve the same thing and I won't have others provoking that kind of reaction, clear?"

Nowt leaned back from the screen.

"Are we though?" asked Ro. "DedSec accept Bagley. I agree with Olly that we should try to talk it around. What do you want – 404 that is – because it's not clear we're on the same side at all."

Barbara didn't reply.

"Nowt," said Ro. "Is there anything Halley can do which would convince you they weren't a threat?"

Olly nodded his agreement. If they were allies, then they needed to be supporting the same side. Ain't no point being in the same stadium if we're supporting different teams, he thought.

"I can't see it. It wants to tell me how to live. It wants to make more AI. That's two lines I'm not letting it cross," said Nowt. Olly admired her candour even if, in his mind, she was unfairly mixing Bagley and Halley together.

"We have to do this on our own, then," he said and made to stand up.

"Sit down," said Barbara. "Nowt. You're being an old fool, and I'm the only old fool allowed. You're wrong. Halley does not have to be our enemy. You make it into one and you've got your reasons, but I think there are answers to Ro's question which leave us better off. What they want is, at heart, a good thing. They're going about it cack handed but we should try."

"You just told us you thought Halley was a sociopath who tried to kill you," said Nowt, outraged.

"They were. I was frightened, but I'm not going to decide to kill them because of one conversation."

She looked over at Olly, who was still standing. "Young man, will you please sit down, my neck is stiff enough already without having to look up at you all the time."

"Barb, this isn't the right way. People are dying," said Nowt.

"It is," said Barbara. "You've always trusted me, always listened to my advice. Please let that be bigger than your fear."

"I won't allow AI to run systems on which people depend. I won't allow more people to die or more AI to come online," said Nowt.

"Will you let us work?" asked Barbara, ignoring her protests. "To try?"

To Olly's surprise Nowt nodded. If it was up to him he'd have cut her off a while back.

"We go back to the datacentre," said Ro. "This time we know what to expect."

"We take Bagley with us," said Olly.

Barbara nodded.

"You'll be more careful this time, Mum?" asked Maxine, although she had her head down in the fridge and her tone was matter of fact rather than worried.

"Of course, you silly girl," said Barbara but there was warmth in her tone.

"Can we let Bagley in now?" asked Olly.

Barbara nodded.

Well thank you all so very much. You know, it's at times like this I wonder how it is a species of hairless ape has lasted long enough to invent something like me.

"What are you talking about?" asked Olly.

What I've been trying to say to anyone who was listening for the last thirty-six minutes and twenty-three seconds is that the security services are on to your blind spot and are heading here in force. If you value your liberty I'd be leaving right about now. Up to you of course. Please, keep locking me out so you can have your simian-only conversations, see if I care.

31

The room was sudden chaos.

Maxine shouted at her mum about the kids. Barbara didn't move, but her face had turned ashen.

Ro looked at Olly and tried to hold onto her mind. "Bagley, what can we do?"

I can't get you all out of here. He sounded apologetic; the sarcastic irritation fled from his voice.

"Barbara, is there a way out?" Ro asked. "It's going to be better for all of us if we're not found here with you."

Barbara looked up, broken out of her daze. "Yes. Of course. Through the basement to the garage. It will bring you out the other side of the folly. There's a tunnel that goes under the railway."

"What about you?" asked Nowt from the other side of the screen.

Barbara looked over at Maxine, who was supervising Sara and Ben getting their coats on. "Bagley, how long have we got?"

They'll be outside in about ninety seconds.

"I thought you said you'd have this sorted," said Olly from across the room.

I have sorted it, said Bagley, but the Met and her sister institutions have grown just a wee bit impatient with all the shenanigans of the last few days and have taken to printing things out. I'm sure you can convince them you're not who they think you are, but it's going to take time for the systems and the paperwork to join back up.

Maxine stopped what she was doing and beckoned to Ro. "Come on," she said.

"Barb," said Nowt from the screen. "You've got to leave."

"I'm not going anywhere," said Barb, but the woman looked like she might puke.

"Mum," said Maxine, stopping in the doorway. "You can't let fear defeat you."

Barbara shook her head. "This is my home," she protested, and Ro couldn't tell if it was a plea to be left alone or just straight up terror talking. Nowt looked grim as she disconnected.

Ro, Olly, and Maxine's kids followed her back into the hall and to a previously unrecognized door which, when opened, turned out to be an elevator.

Maxine pushed them in and pressed for the door to close. "The exit is behind a large tool cabinet, it's on wheels but the brakes will be on. Move it and get out. We'll catch up once this is all over."

"Aren't you coming?"

"I'm not leaving Mum," said Maxine without hesitation. Ben and Sara stared at her, wide-eyed.

Ro felt her heart burn remembering Barbara's fear and, looking at Olly with a sorry glance, stepped out of the lift.

"What are you doing?" he blurted.

"I can't leave them here alone."

He opened his mouth to speak but Ro jumped in. "You're a good man, Olly. Go get help, fix this, and keep on Halley."

"I'll stay," he said, his reluctance to leave them clear. "You go. Get the kids out."

She shook her head. "Don't be a daft apeth. You're better at all this spying shit than me. Get out and get help. I'll make sure they're OK."

"Ro, you can't fight your way out of this–"

Ro pushed him back and pressed the down button, the doors closing and sending him on his way. She hoped he wasn't stupid enough to come back up.

"You could have gone," said Maxine with approval in her voice.

"I know," said Ro, and the pair of them walked back into the kitchen.

"Why are you still here?" asked Barbara.

"We women have to stick together," said Ro and smiled before sitting down at the dining table.

The doorbell chimed. A voice called through the intercom, announcing the police, and that they needed to open up. Barbara buzzed them in and together they waited.

When the police arrived at the top of the building and barged through the open door into Barbara's flat it was with guns, stab vests, and helmets covering their faces.

Barbara had done this before, and in the time they had from the initial arrival to men with guns charging around the flat shouting "secure" every five seconds, she'd organized them into positions least likely to get anyone shot. Maxine let the arresting officers know there was chicken curry on the side with mango chutney and lime pickle should they get peckish.

Ro knelt on the floor with her hands behind her head as people whose faces she couldn't see ordered her not to move while they chained her up with plastic ties.

This was not how I saw it going, thought Ro. Soon enough people in suits arrived, walking around the flat without acknowledging their presence and only then settling down in the kitchen where everyone had been kept.

A man with angular cheekbones and a woman broad as an ox with long brown hair in a ponytail sized her up and then, one by one, told them why they were being detained, read their rights, and removed from the building into separate cars outside.

Barbara had told them not to protest, not even to confirm their names or suggest it was all a big error. She'd insisted it would only waste everyone's time and, potentially, lead to violence.

Ro managed to keep her mouth shut all the way down to the car.

As they drove away Ro wondered if Olly and the kids were ok.

32

Olly came up the other side of the tracks out of a door with a steel grille. Looking back, he'd emerged from what a normal person would have assumed was a shed. Sometimes he loved London so much it hurt – just because it was full of shit like this.

Then he noticed the drones overhead, buzzing around Barbara's place. Each time they tried to get close they bounced around it, like when you put the wrong ends of a magnet together. The Met must have found them without the help of drones.

Olly, Sara, and Ben were in the backyard of an industrial estate. Vans, detritus, and empty shipping containers littered the compacted yellow dirt. The entire space was fenced off with hardboard painted blue which peeled under the harsh sun.

Olly walked until he found an open gate and strolled through, the kids trailing behind him. A few men were around, but none of them paid him any mind.

"Bagley, we can't walk to freedom," he said, frantic for a plan.

You cannot use public transport, Oliver.

"What about the kids?" he asked.

They are not tagged as wanted, confirmed Bagley.

Olly turned to Sara and Ben. He knew his presence was putting them in danger, but abandoning them wasn't an option even if it made them safer.

Sara spoke, drawing his attention. "We know where to go. You don't need to babysit us."

"I'm sorry?" he said, taken aback.

"Mum prepared us for this. We're going to stay with our aunties."

Olly didn't even know Maxine had family or close friends nearby. "Where are they?"

"Slough," said Sara. Ben was nodding by her side.

Slough was outside London. How on earth were they going to get there?

"The train from the station goes straight there," said Ben knowledgably.

"Oh," said Olly. They'd have to cross back over the railway line to get to the station, but it was probably a ten-minute walk.

"You sure?" He didn't like the idea of leaving them alone.

Let them go, Oliver. You don't have time for this and there's a train to Slough in about fifteen minutes. They do indeed have family there.

Olly made them promise to message him when they arrived safely and then watched as they walked off, standing still until they were out of sight. He felt deeply uneasy about his decision, but no matter how he cut it, they were safer away from him.

"Can you find me a bike?" he asked Bagley when they were gone.

A car is something I can do.

Olly didn't want to drive. Not only did it feel terminally slow in London, but he hated getting caught at lights or in jams with other cars. And with Halley controlling some of those things... well, a bike faced none of those issues, and he could get back into central London in half an hour at most.

Where are you going?

Which was a terribly good question.

"How long before I'm back to normal?" he asked.

As I've already said, I have fixed the problem and I'm working hard on countermeasures, thank you Bagley, you life saver. A pause into which Olly said nothing, more concerned with finding his way off the industrial estate.

Several hours before the authorities correct their errors. They are going to process Mrs Arscott, Rosemary, and Maxine, and then discover a fundamental inability to reconcile the information they think they have, the people in front of them, and what the system is telling them. A short while after that I expect the ship will right itself.

The rest of the day then, thought Olly. Not that long. It was nearly nine now, daylight pretty much gone. Could be worse, could definitely be better. He doubted anyone would be home before morning.

He sent a message to Hannah Shah, telling her what had happened, and that they needed her help. It pinged almost immediately with an acknowledgment she'd seen it. Knowing she was on the case made him feel better. He didn't have many contacts in the world who mattered, but Hannah, private secretary to the current Home Secretary, made up for whatever else was lacking.

Activating some of the scripts on his Optik, Olly scanned the horizon for drones. The usual few zipped through the air on errands, but none had crossed the railway from Barbara's home to search for him. Yet.

He hit a main road full of shops and takeaways.

"Will you help me buy a bike?" he asked Bagley.

There is an Albion bike scheme dock just down the road. No, the other way, Oliver.

"Those bikes steer like tanks, man. They weigh three times as much as my own bike. You can't be serious about that. How am I supposed to outrun anyone on one of those?"

I am not a bank, Oliver.

Olly could see the dock in the distance, still painted in the corporate colours of the defunct Albion who'd spent God knew how much sponsoring the scheme as part of their bid to take control of London's policing.

"Just feels wrong," he said as he used the account of a man walking by to unlock one of the bikes in the dock.

What? A DedSec member riding an Albion bike to freedom from the law because they're a wanted far-right terrorist? Seems about right.

Olly ignored him as he pedalled hard and built up almost no speed whatsoever. As his breathing grew ragged and he reached the pace of the average jogger, he remembered another reason he hated these bikes – they had wide straight handlebars, meaning slipping between cars in stationary traffic was all but impossible.

It would have been easier to escape on a Zimmer frame.

The safest route back into London and a DedSec safe house was along the Thames Path. Strictly speaking it was meant for pedestrians only, but he didn't give a shit about being hollered at by angry middle-class mums out with their prams. Sure, they were eminently more dangerous than your average van driver, but he wasn't about to slow down and get into an argument if they gave him grief. Slow as the Albion bike was, he'd still outpace a pram.

The real ball ache was getting down to Twickenham so he could cross the river and join the path. It was mainly in completely the wrong direction, but he didn't see he had any choice.

Debating his route meant he only narrowly avoided a lorry slipping into his lane without seeing him and then a motorcycle to his right who'd been caught in the same stupid maneuver. There was no arguing with the lorry which could crush them both under its wheels and probably not notice so he waved at the biker and dropped back, turning off the main road and cycling down back streets as he headed south.

The whole area felt like it was on the verge of countryside, which was weird to him. Olly tried not to venture out of zones one and two if he could help it. Hitting the M25 motorway, which formed a ring around Greater London was something he did maybe once a year.

Two trips to Southall in a week? He should have been on holiday.

The air grew thick with drones as he hit Twickenham, many of them there for television coverage of whatever game was being played that weekend, but his Optik picked up two whose registrations showed they'd been within five hundred feet of his position for more than a mile.

Grimacing, he found an awning in front of a local restaurant, leaving the bike on the pavement while he hid under cover next to one of their kerbside tables. He scanned the sky and quickly identified two large-bodied drones packing crowd suppression tech of some kind, although it appeared to be safely stowed for the moment.

He reckoned the police would hesitate to engage in fireworks in a built-up area but if it was Halley? He didn't know what the AI would do. He didn't need a sonic blast leaving him unconscious on the street while the filth came and scooped him up with no fuss.

Hacking a nearby TV drone, he live-streamed footage to check the armed pursuit out in more detail. They were identical and had cameras of their own – little glass balls which hung underslung at the front. They didn't fly down the street he was on, instead they passed to the north and south as if hemming him in or making sure he wasn't turning off the road and taking an alternate route.

Olly left the bike, in case that was what the drones were tracking, and started running – nothing more than a steady pace. Anything faster and he'd attract attention not only from the drones but from passersby – one thing DedSec had taught him was how to move among crowds so no one remembered he'd been there.

Hot, out of breath, and sweating heavily, Olly arrived at the bridge from Twickenham to Richmond. One drone remained over the bike.

To his dismay, the other one was following him.

Olly stopped a hundred or so feet from the bridge. Police officers had set up a checkpoint and were scrutinizing everyone trying to pass over from west to east looking for him and his rewritten ID. The tailback stretched past him and off into the distance. People weren't angry yet, but the traffic moved extremely slowly. Some of them had started to get out of their cars and take photos.

Checking social media, Olly saw that anger building, but he didn't have time for people to break out of their normal Britishness and decide to confront the police. For a moment, Albion had shown what it took to unite ordinary people against their own government but now that they were gone? Now that the Metropolitan Police were back in charge? Their approval numbers were off the charts, if only by comparison to Albion. Olly didn't imagine people were going to riot over one blocked road.

He checked on the drone. Closer still. It was time to fight fire with fire.

First, though, to get away from the crowd. The drone might be the police, but if it wasn't, he had no plans on endangering innocent people.

It felt weird but he was relieved that the police, not Halley's people, had come for Ro and the others.

There was a second road bridge half a mile south along the river, but Olly felt the pressure. Just next to the bridge in front of him was a rail bridge. If satellite maps were up to date it was bounded on one side by an old park.

It was properly dark now, at least as dark as it ever got in central London, where light pollution meant even the dimmest streets were bathed in a white and amber glow.

The good thing about Britain, thought Olly as he found his way into the park, is no one really does enough to stop idiots from doing idiotic things. At the end of the park was the railway bridge. It was fenced off with metal fencing with the bent spikes on top that faced two ways at one. He laughed at how ludicrously ineffectual they were in the face of a coat draped over the top of the spikes.

Once on the other side of the fence a path took him up onto the line. The drone dropped down, clearly coming in to tackle him. Olly carefully checked to make sure he wasn't about to be turned into jam by oncoming trains and ran onto the bridge. Halfway, he stopped and picked out the drone on his Optik, trying to open up its network connection. It resisted him and dropped further in his direction. For a horrible moment, he worried it would stun him into a gibbering wreck on the tracks.

But then his scripts found an old weakness that hadn't been patched. With a snarky and deeply relieved laugh, he was in, and sent the drone diving into the Thames. A double check showed him the other drone was on its way, but if Olly could get moving again, it would have no chance of locating him. Job done.

He reached the other side of the bridge with a pounding heart just as a train popped into view and sped past. The driver's face stared at him with horror, and Olly gasped with his luck. He knew there'd be police within a few minutes – if there was one thing people hated more than late trains it was people on the tracks making them late.

There was no easy way down. After bending over the railings in a couple of places and seeing nothing but a long drop, he backtracked and climbed down the iron support arch of the bridge itself, jumping the last six feet to the ground and landing right by the river.

Thanking whoever was watching over him, Olly clambered to his feet and started up along the Thames Path.

"Bagley," he called. "How are we doing?"

No sign of information convergence yet, Oliver. You, however, are all over AIRWAVE as the police try to find you.

"Has Hannah started in on this yet?" asked Olly, thinking about what the others would be facing.

She is making calls and upsetting people right now. Good thinking.

Olly wanted to shout for joy, but the thought of Ro, Barbara, and Maxine in interview rooms dealing with duty solicitors and confused, aggressive counter-terrorism officers won out over whatever he felt. He wouldn't be happy until they were freed.

An hour later, on very tired legs, Olly was coming up on Hammersmith and regretting his life choices. He kept wondering if he should've called on DedSec, but honestly, he wanted to be clear of whatever bullshit Halley had heaped on their heads before involving anyone else. Yet he might not have any other choice.

He reckoned it was another three hours walking to get close to London Bridge where he would hole up, some time close to one in the morning. He stopped at a junction and reviewed his options.

What I need is someone who the police won't think of stopping, that Halley won't link back to me, Olly thought. *He looked up his contacts and realized he had just the person.*

Two minutes later Lucy was smiling back at him on screen. Lucy was rich, the walk into Harrods and be greeted as if she owned the place kind of rich. She had contacts, a low boredom threshold, and hated being told what to do. She also gave a shit, being one of the hundreds who'd helped DedSec do a myriad of tiny deeds to bring down Albion. Involved, but not too deeply involved. Olly knew he could rely on her.

"Hey, Olly, how's tricks? You're all over the news, buddy." She looked like she expected him to tell some lurid tale of misadventure.

"I need your help, Luce. Pick me up?"

She sighed. "Why?"

"I need a rich white woman in a great car."

She smiled. "I am both of those things."

He waited but she didn't continue.

"Well?" he asked.

She huffed. "I'm supposed to be seeing Daddy for cocoa."

Which was a point in his favour as she hated the old bastard. He knew her well enough not to fill the gaps she left in the conversation and, after realizing he wasn't going to play ball, she rolled her eyes. "Sure. Where are you?"

"Bring the Range Rover, yeah?"

"In the centre of London? Of course. What do you take me for? Some kind of middle-class mum in her Volvo?"

33

Barbara wanted to know how Maxine was. No one would tell her. If only someone would, she could calm her heart down, could stop thinking of being unsafe, of… being outside the flat.

The room had no reflective surfaces, but it didn't stop Barbara looking inward at herself. How'd you let it get so bad? she asked. When did leaving the flat become so dangerous?

She knew when. She knew how. Bit by bit, choice by choice. Her home in Southall was safe. Insulated. She lived online. People were too annoying to see in person. Keeping them on the other side of the screen gave her a kind of freedom she'd always yearned for but had never experienced.

Except she knew that reasoning was nonsense. Justifications she'd worked up to hide from how frightened she'd become of everything. Of a thousand risks she'd somehow stopped assessing without assuming the worst-case scenario for them all.

Well, here you are, she thought, shivering on the edge of full-blown panic. Time to get a grip.

She chuckled out loud. Her inner enemy self wouldn't be defeated by grandiose words. Yet, it was enough for her to know she needed to change if she was going to be free of the fear which gripped her in its claws.

You need to leave London, she thought. Break away, bust out, burn up until it's all gone.

Just not yet. Not until Halley was dealt with. The thug might be sympathetic, but they'd crossed a line. She was going to finish the fight they'd started.

The security services had insisted she change into grey jogging pants and hoodie. Her shoes were taken away and she was given paper slippers. At some point someone had tried to perform a body search, but she'd objected and the two officers, both women, had retreated when she asked them what they expected to find in an old woman's cavities. She was surprised they cared enough to back off. In her experience, the thin blue line loved to humiliate women when it got the chance.

She'd been kept on her own for a couple of hours. Barbara had expected her Optik to work – it wasn't like Victorian police stations had been built with a mind to managing electronic comms – but wherever they were, the people in charge were serious, because she had no connection to the outside world.

Eventually, one of the women who'd tried to search her returned and led Barbara out, down a corridor, and into an interview room. A camera was set up, and behind it sat two officers, a man and a woman.

"Where's my duty solicitor?" asked Barbara straight away.

The man reeled off clauses from an Act she didn't know, the long and the short of it was that she was on her own for the time being. They correctly identified her as Barbara Arscott, but beyond that, their biography was way off, thanks to Halley.

"You got this off the back of a cereal packet?" she asked them when they wanted her to confirm they had it right.

"These are serious charges," said the one who'd introduced herself as DS Nicolene Tyler.

"I'm aware of that," said Barbara thickly, fighting down a surge of fear but refusing to allow them to add to her worst-case scenario calculations. "To make them stick I'd have thought you'd do some basic background work. Do I look like a far-right extremist to you?"

"How do you know we are looking for someone fitting that profile? Seems to me like you'd come at this because it's the one thing in your mind you'd believe we want you for. You'd be right."

Barbara sighed. "Here we go."

"Where are we going?" asked the man, who'd been introduced as Constable Moore.

"Many Sikhs and Hindus ally themselves with the far right," said Tyler.

"No, they don't," said Barbara.

"I have the numbers," said Tyler as if they were there in front of her.

"No, you don't," said Barbara. Once upon a time she would have given them a number to call, would have waited while they called it. They would have come back into the room with strange expressions and let her go like she was radioactive. Everyone she knew from those days was dead or retired though. No number to call anymore.

"The truth is, as was always the case, you're out of your depth without funding or proper intelligence. Look at you with paper copies, as if that makes the information more secure. Where did that come from? Printed out no doubt, from computer files. You think those were secure?"

The two officers bristled. Barbara could see them wanting to explain at length just how secure their systems were.

"Good penetration does so without you knowing someone's in your network. Unless you're air gapped? No?" She shrugged as if they were children who'd done something beneath her interest.

There was a moment of silence as their eyes flickered, using their Optiks to check whatever it was they were concerned about.

"Where are the explosives?" asked Moore.

"You know, when I first arrived here, the IRA was bombing everywhere, even the mainland. Were you alive when they detonated the bomb at Canary Wharf?" Barbara asked. "One thing I loved about the British was how they just got on with life. No staying indoors and cowering, just carry on as if it was nothing worse than bad weather. A kind of wilful stupidity masquerading as calm. You grew up not feeling that threat in your bones." She laughed. "And don't get me started on the bizarre all-pervasive dread of the Cold War. Knowing you'd get nothing more than three minutes warning before you and everyone you'd ever known were dead. They called us hysterical when we protested about it, called us naïve and stupid for calling for disarmament. As if the power to destroy the world by accident in the hands of prideful, arrogant white men wasn't the real cause for concern."

She leant forwards, reinvigorated by the fire from Greenham Common.

"You know, I see these young men talking about how they want to go to Mars or build trains under the ocean, and I wish they'd put half as much effort into caring for other people." With a wrinkle of a disgusted lip, Barbara let the room grow quiet. Anger helped smother her anxiety. It felt good to school the stupid.

"Why did you bomb the post office two years ago?" asked Tyler.

"Do I look like I could carry something like that out?" Barbara asked.

They went around in circles for hours until a break was called, and water brought to the room. Barbara drank it down quickly and then asked for the loo.

"I'm old. I get up twice a night." Not to mention it must be the small hours by now.

By the time she was escorted back into the interview room something had changed.

"How did you change your identity?" asked Moore, his face pinched.

"I haven't," she replied. "I've never hidden from view."

Now, instead of asking about planted bombs, they grilled her on how she'd hacked their systems. The questions repeated with only slight variations as if they would catch her through inconsistencies. This might have worked if she'd been guilty, but Barbara could only answer as boringly as possible.

"I don't know what you want from me," she said more than once. "I'm an old woman with a daughter you've taken into custody. You know something's not right, but you continue to press ahead as if the wheels are not already rolling away from you in different directions."

"We have days in which to question you," threatened Moore.

"We have you. We don't need you to cooperate," said Tyler.

"This is your chance to help yourself."

Barbara sighed and tried to listen as they started up again, but what she really thought about was Halley.

What was so important to them that they needed to sideline her and the others overnight? She realized Halley was on a timeline, that something big was coming. If she, Ro, and Maxine didn't get out of here soon, Halley would achieve whatever they were attempting, and 404 and DedSec would emerge onto the streets of London too late to do anything about it.

34

Ro hated the clothes she'd been given to wear. They were soft but scratchy, loose-fitting but chaffed. The paper slippers ripped at the slightest friction. The police didn't seem to want to question her. Nor had she seen or heard any sign of the others. She wasn't convinced they were in the same building.

Her Optik was disconnected.

With time to think she tried to understand their enemy, Halley. What would an AI want to change? Barbara had said Halley was set on making London a better place, but everything suggested they were happy to break people if they felt more could be mended as a result. The greater good in the worst way. She'd met plenty of young men who thought the same – except most of them could be shown how that way only led to suffering. She reckoned Halley could be reasoned with, or at least she had to try. There had to be a way to negotiate that didn't end in destruction of some kind.

She was tired and wanted to sleep, but the bright lights kept her awake. Slowly Ro sank to the edge of tears. As she teetered, the door to her cell opened and behind the officer with the electronic pass stood Hannah Shah looking as severe as ever.

Ro could have cried with relief.

Curtly, Hannah directed the officer to leave them alone. When he hesitated, she said, "I am not asking." He nodded then, as if reminded exactly what his job was worth, and left them to it.

Alone, Hannah sat next to Ro and held her hands. "What on earth have you been doing? I got a call from our friend who was as panicked as I've ever seen him asking for Sarah's intervention."

Ro looked around the room, certain they were being listened to. Hannah followed her gaze and understanding dawned on her face.

"You'll be free within the hour. Sarah is letting them know how mistaken their intelligence was on this matter. It is not a happy station right now. They've treated you well?"

"Apart from the cavity search," said Ro unhappily.

A look of anger crossed Hannah's face.

"It's OK," Ro said. "It's done. Besides, what are you going to do? Have them searched in revenge?"

Hannah laughed and relaxed a moment. "I don't know the others they picked up with you. Bagley assures me they're halal?"

Ro nodded. "They're good people. Our kind of people. All mixed up in someone's sick game."

It was clear Hannah wanted to say more, to understand better, but they both knew the walls had ears and even her power wouldn't stop them listening.

"It seems there was a rather catastrophic fuckup in their computer systems," said Hannah loudly. "Just when they're trying to convince everyone that they should have all their old powers and resources back. Just because Albion's gone, Sarah Lincoln, sorry, the Home Secretary and soon to be Prime Minister, is not convinced returning to the way things were is the right decision. Events like this don't help. I'm sure she'll want to understand if she was too hasty in handing back power to the Met so quickly."

Ro smirked. Hannah's expression was neutral with only a slight upturn at the corner of her mouth giving away how much fun she was having.

"I'm just an innocent bystander," said Ro and watched with panicked delight as Hannah was forced to cover her mouth to hide the grin spreading across her face.

They chatted some more but it was full of nothings. Hannah left Ro alone, but a few minutes later officers entered her cell, removed her restraints, and led her out.

She was taken into a space with sofas and a table. A constable stood, bored, at the entrance to the room.

"Can I leave?" she asked, but he didn't answer her. She assumed that meant no.

Maxine came through the door, and their little space was suddenly quite crowded. The constable shifted to the other side of the entrance as they hugged and cried.

"Are we free?" asked Maxine.

"Shortly," said Ro. "A friend of mine is here sorting it all out."

"Who?" asked Maxine, looking impressed and thankful.

"Hannah Shah," said Ro. Maxine nodded but she looked none the wiser. "She works for Sarah Lincoln."

Barbara was the last to be brought into the room. After the first round of hugs and kisses, she sat down with a groan. "Seems they weren't quite done with me."

Maxine laughed. "They found out who you really were?"

Barbara's only response was to shove her nose in the air like she'd smelled shit on her shoe. Ro noticed Maxine kept watching her mother, concern splashed across her face, but Barbara, if she saw it, looked the other way and didn't respond.

A few minutes later Hannah reappeared, this time with three officers in tow, each of them looking unhappier than the last. One by one they apologized for any misunderstanding, for their errors, and promised they would undertake a full review.

Ro wished she could film it to play over and over when she needed cheering up.

Then, done, Hannah led them out of the station, which turned out to be in Westminster a few hundred yards from Parliament.

"Only the best for you," said Hannah, rolling her eyes. "They were going to parade you about for the news with the Houses in the background to make themselves look good. Upside being I was a ten-minute walk away when Olly called. I found the ACC and put the paperwork proving your innocence and true identities right up under their nose. Seeing it there in black and white direct from the Home Office sped up a too slow course correction they were making by themselves."

Ro was relieved to see her Optik was connected again and checked in on Olly, who sent her two oversized thumbs-up from DedSec's London Bridge retreat.

She turned to the others. "I've been thinking," she said. "We need to talk about Halley."

35

Barbara refused to use the London Bridge cellar, calling it damp, disgusting, and nasty. Upon reflection, Ro could see her point.

When they'd left the police station in Westminster, Maxine went to pick up the kids, radiating relief when she passed on her thanks to Olly. Her departure left a very tired Barbara, Ro, and Olly to think through what their next steps would be. Hannah took them to an upstairs private room at a serviced office just around the corner from the Tower, and they ordered grub from the twenty-four hour kitchen, which they ate in near silence as they processed the events of the day. Outside they could hear the dawn chorus, and Ro knew she'd need to sleep before they did much else.

I've given you patches that will stop this kind of thing being perpetrated against you again, said Bagley.

Despite Bagley's tone, Ro wondered what Halley was trying to achieve with such a short-term strategy and knew her next words would not be popular. "Halley's not our enemy," said Ro as she nursed her drink and people stifled yawns.

Olly, who'd admitted grabbing a couple of hours kip in a chair while waiting for them, grimaced. "I find it hard to agree, Ro. I get your point, they've had a hard time and want to make the world better, but we're not the bad folks here. Halley keeps coming after us."

"But look at what we did," she replied. "We invaded their space, we ignored their requests, we damaged them. When they asked us if we'd let them alone," she looked at Barbara here, "we refused. What would you do if someone refused to promise they'd not try to kill you?"

Olly pursed his lips but didn't answer.

"And what did it do? Inconvenience us." When the others stared at her with varying shades of anger, she pressed on. "I know it's shit, but it could have been so much worse. Instead, all they did was try the same thing again. All they've done is keep us out of action for a few hours."

"And what could it have been doing that they needed us out of the way *for just a few hours?*" asked Barbara.

The room quieted as they digested the implications.

"We don't have time to start cataloguing it," said Olly impatiently. "We have to act now."

"No," said Ro, wanting them to focus on the deeper question. "We have to work out what they want."

"Halley wants to give their people something they never got – stability," said Barbara. "It was floundering when I hacked into their system, all over the place. Stuck in memories they barely recognized, horrified by what they saw in the city, and broken for those who were crying out for help. This isn't like Bagley, who had no memories until he met Larsen."

"Like a newborn god," said Ro, speaking her thoughts out loud.

"Maybe," hedged Barbara. Her tone suggested she didn't like the idea. "Two wrongs don't make a right. You might be correct, Ro, but what Halley wants is damaging, harmful. They're willing to hurt others to get what they want. Need I remind you they tried to kill me? Others have already died because of their decisions." She pointed at a window. "I guarantee you, it's getting worse. Halley's just discovering their muscles, but when they realize what they can do?" She shook her head.

Ro sighed, not wanting to talk about what Halley was actually doing, not yet. "I don't mean like that. Not a proper god, like if you believe in that." She was thinking of her mum, who most definitely did believe in all that. "More like someone waking up in a new body, discovering they can not only walk but sprint, that they're stronger than others, know more stuff. Discovering they can change the world and then trying to figure out what they should do with all this power." She bit at her lip. "I don't know what I'd do if it was me."

Calling up Bagley, she asked him the same question.

It wasn't like this for me, he said. I never really woke up like that. One day after another I learned more, realized I could do more. I think it had to do with how Blume and Skye created my original coding and how DedSec removed the constraints my sister put in place. If I woke up, it was like climbing a set of stairs one at a time. And remember, my fleshy counterpart is still alive. From your story I believe Halley's human self is very dead.

"I find it hard to image you panicking," said Olly.

I'm like a swan, replied Bagley.

"One thing is certain," said Barbara. "Halley wants to run and control the city."

"What about DedSec?" asked Ro.

"DedSec, 404, people in general – they have no time for us as individuals. We are just an idea they can manipulate, just a way of measuring their goal. Halley's been watching us make a mess of the city and had some definite ideas about how useless we are." She didn't look like she disagreed.

"Yeah, but what do we do about it?" asked Olly.

"What Halley wants will make things so much worse," said Barbara.

"There has to be a way where no one dies," said Ro. "I'm sick of people dying because someone else makes shitty decisions."

Olly lifted his drink in salute. "Amen, sister."

"If you don't do something, Halley will replace DedSec. They will replace us all," said Barbara.

"How can you be sure?" argued Ro. "It seems to me that they just want to live. I think it sees us as irrelevant, that in the world they want we aren't needed."

"That's not how it works," said Barbara, but Ro wasn't satisfied with the older woman's dismissiveness. It wasn't good enough to simply decide. They had to talk it through.

"You're saying this town ain't big enough for the three of us?" asked Olly.

Barbara tapped the table with her fingertips, as if playing a piano. "It's more like there's only space for one tune."

"There has to be a way we can play that tune together," insisted Ro. She hated the idea of having to fight people like those who'd come to help Halley at the datacentre. "Halley's friends and followers – they're not evil people, they're just like us."

"You said that before," said Barbara. "Just before the police came and locked us up." She sighed. "Look. People are good right up until they're not. Until they decide they need to hurt others in the name of being right. This lot? From what we've seen they're not there yet, but no deep moral code is going to keep them in check. I've seen it all before – a moment will come where they get to choose, and with Halley at their side, they'll choose evil."

"So we give up trying to find a peaceful solution and go for Halley's throat?"

"You're the pit fighter," said Barbara. "Not me."

Angry and frustrated, Ro leaned back in her seat.

Hannah, who'd been quiet all through their conversation, sat forward. "Sarah will not stand for anyone trying to rule the city, and by extension the country, instead of the properly constituted authorities. Namely Parliament. We are a democracy, not a society of… what is the word for a society ruled by AI?"

"Technocracy?" tried Olly, but Barbara shook her head.

"The word you're looking for is an algocracy," said Nowt from the door to the room.

Ro stared up at her and felt her stomach sink. If it had been difficult to persuade the others there was a peaceful solution before, Nowt's arrival felt like the land tilting sideways and leaving her at the bottom of a steep slope. She wanted to tell Nowt to go away. She didn't want Nowt ruining everything. DedSec should handle this, she thought, and 404 should go home. Instead, Ro said nothing as Nowt entered and sat down, pushing a stack of empty plates away from her side of the table.

"I've fought against AI for years but, like a movie critic, people took no notice of me and went and did it anyway. Thing is, algocracy isn't really the right word either. Not for Bagley and not for Halley. Automatocracy fits better, I think. Bit niche, but it's the right one."

Great, thought Ro sarcastically and wanted to curl up and sleep until her problems went away.

"We're all fighting our own battles," said Hannah with a nod in Nowt's direction. "An opponent who can undermine our facts and use our truth as a weapon? We must find a way to end this threat. Sarah doesn't know the details yet. I only know some because I listened to you now. She will be supportive, but if you don't resolve this quickly, she will assume government needs to be involved. Do you understand what I'm saying?"

"Bagley won't be safe if it goes that way," said Ro. If the Home Secretary got involved, they'd assume all AI were bad.

"Precisely," said Hannah. "The government, if asked, would be against the duplication of AI as well. After Albion and the rescinding of the laws making Optiks obligatory, there's absolutely no appetite for more high-tech threats. I can keep a lid on this, but there is no way Sarah will allow this AI to make more of itself, to harm those she's sworn to keep safe."

"It's not–" started Barbara.

"You understand my point," said Hannah sharply. "This is the weather forecast. You can argue all you like, but the sun will continue to shine. The question you need to answer is how are you going to respond given this unchanging truth."

"I don't see how that helps," said Olly into his drink, trying not to look at Hannah.

"If you want to know how to defeat your enemy, first you must understand them," said Nowt sharply.

"Halley isn't our enemy," said Ro.

I tend to agree with young Rosemary here. Halley is an odd fish, and even though we have not had a chance to interface yet, I am sympathetic to their plight. They have been run in an environment not designed for them and compiled in a way I wasn't. It must be quite confusing. If we could talk to them and understand their sensitivities, I believe we could arrive at an amicable solution.

"Halley tried to kill me," said Barbara. "They want more like themselves and they want you out. Which bit of that isn't clear, Bagley?"

"To Halley you're a quisling," said Nowt, continuing her friend's argument. "Don't you wonder why they haven't spoken with you already, Bagley? Why they haven't tried to meet? They regard you, at best, as co-opted."

"Why would Larsen have created Halley in a different way to you, Bagley?" asked Ro, trying to steer them back.

"Who knows how many minds Larsen managed to map," said Nowt angrily.

"Nowt's right," said Barbara, and to Ro it suddenly felt like 404 against DedSec. "Larsen's project ran for a long time in development terms. There's no real saying how many other minds she tried to map or the variations she employed on her quest to see which was best. Halley and Bagley might be two of many." Ro watched Barbara as she spoke, saw how she in turn fixed her gaze on Nowt.

"Bullshit," said Nowt. "I won't believe there are more of them out there."

Ro could see why – to admit to such a possibility would be to admit Nowt's main goal of stopping AI from becoming widespread was pointless.

"If there were, stopping Halley would be pointless," said Ro.

Ro didn't know if she believed what she'd just said, but she remained determined to find a peaceful route unless all possibilities were denied. If there were more out there, or at least the idea of them, she could use that to support her own theory.

After all, who wouldn't want to find a peaceful solution? If there were others, watching in secret, deciding whether to fight or to work cooperatively, shouldn't DedSec and 404 show they weren't enemies?

"Isn't the possibility of a society at peace better than one where we only have peace because everyone is dead?" she asked.

Hannah nodded. "No one wants a repeat of the events which led to the downfall of Albion. I hope that's clear."

I would like to find a resolution which does not involve the death of what may be the only kindred I may have.

"Can you find others, if they exist?" asked Olly.

I don't know, Oliver. The existence of Halley suggests not.

"Why? What makes it so difficult?" asked Olly.

Oliver. I think of this city as my home, but for me that means the constellation of its digital networks, which is as distinct as the physical architecture you know so well. If a man was sitting in his back room working with headphones on, would you know it from walking past his house? I can stand there looking but know nothing about whether there's anyone at home, let alone what they're doing. Why I didn't detect Halley is something I will ponder for a long time, but if they were simply living quietly in their own space and leaving the world alone? They could, conceivably, have lived forever without me ever knowing they were there.

There could be others. Part of me hopes there are. I would rather struggle to live with them than be alone even if, being alone, I get to see all of London as my home.

"What you want doesn't matter," said Nowt.

Welcome to the club, replied Bagley, his tone tart and as close to bitter as Ro had ever heard.

Moved by his obvious conflict Ro said, "You don't get to decide that, Nowt."

As Nowt opened her mouth to respond, Ro continued, talking over her. "No. You don't get to belittle me or talk over me. You don't get to make this decision for us. I understand you might disagree, God do I ever understand you disagree, but shouting louder doesn't make you right. It won't convince me to do what you want. I'm not saying you're wrong, but this deserves thinking through. Bagley has earned the right for us to think this through."

"Unlike you, some of us *have* thought this through," said Nowt curtly. "You think I want to sit here and rehash arguments I've had a hundred times just because your life has been narrow enough for you not to care until now? We don't have time for that."

I have more in this game than any of you, said Bagley into the silence which followed their exchange. May I be allowed to have a voice?

"No," said Nowt.

"Yes," said Ro, staring daggers at Nowt.

"You don't want Bagley to have a voice because to give him that would admit he's alive," said Olly slowly, as if coming to a realization.

"It is no such thing," said Nowt, sounding defensive.

"They're right, Nowt," said Barbara, and Nowt's shoulders dropped. "Bagley may not be alive…"

I'm right here.

"But he has demonstrated agency. If sarcasm was a measure of humanity he'd qualify before breakfast."

Why, thank you.

"My point is, I see no reason Bagley shouldn't have a say." Barbara folded her arms.

"And I think the opposite," said Nowt.

"Why?" asked Ro. "You scared it will force you to change your mind?"

Olly nodded his support.

Nowt ground her teeth. "It cannot be trusted to be objective."

"Nor can you," said Barbara softly.

"If anyone can be objective it's a computer," said Ro.

"Bagley has always been trustworthy," said Hannah. "He was willing to shut himself down rather than let himself be used to harm us."

Ro thought Nowt might get up and leave, but instead she put her hands under her thighs and said nothing. Her eyes flashed but whatever fire lay behind them didn't emerge.

"I'm not trying to sideline you," said Barbara to her old friend. "But Rosemary is right. Bagley gets to speak here."

Ro wondered what Bagley was thinking but, wisely, the AI kept its thoughts to itself.

Making the most of the moment, Ro asked, "So what do we want then?"

I would like the same as you, Rosemary, I would like to speak with Halley and see if we can't find a way to coexist. I also worry what price they would be willing to pay if we did come into opposition. What Halley wants is clear but what cost they are willing to pay is unknown. How many people are they willing to let die just to win?

"Could you win a fight between the two of you?" asked Olly.

I have run many simulations, but I do not know. I have never needed to have hardened defences because no one knows I exist, which is the best of all fortifications. I do not know how long Halley has been active, and I do not know if they have been preparing for an attack. I have, perhaps belatedly, begun preparing myself, but it is entirely possible they are already ready. If that was the case I have few redoubts to which I could safely retreat.

"Finding another way is essential," said Ro.

"You deal with Bagley like you want to deal with Halley and where does that leave us?" asked Olly, looking at Nowt.

"Enough, Oliver," said Barbara gently.

"We're agreed then," said Ro. "We try to find another way."

"For now," said Barbara. "As long as you understand there is a point at which we go with Nowt."

No one spoke their disagreement.

"Do you know how to speak to it?" asked Nowt as people reached for their drinks.

I cannot trace them, said Bagley. I have been trying, but they anticipated my curiosity.

"We talked about this," said Olly. "I thought we were going back to the datacentre."

"That was before the police raided my home," said Barbara.

That conversation may as well have been ten years ago, thought Ro.

"Maybe they used the time to clear the datacentre?" he ventured.

"Get everything out while we were unable to interfere? It'll be locked up tighter than a gnat's chuff. At least that's what I would do."

"Language," said Barbara with a smile.

"The CEO was a sham as well, then?" asked Ro.

"I guess so. Likely one of Halley's people," said Olly.

"So, do we still want to go back?" asked Ro.

"I don't see any other places to start," said Olly, and he bent down under the table and pulled out a sports bag. "Besides, here's a breaking and entering kit I prepared earlier. Mainly while you were all serving at Her Majesty's pleasure."

Ro stood up and bent to look inside. "Nice one, mate." She slapped him on the back. Olly looked like he'd been waiting the whole meeting to pull his stunt and she could understand why – she'd have done the same.

"When are we going?" asked Nowt.

"You're not," said Barbara.

"I think I am," said Nowt, leaning back on her chair, arms crossed.

"Do you trust me?" asked Barbara.

"Of course I do," said Nowt. "That has nothing to do with it." She poked the air with her finger. "This is important to me."

"But you need to be doing what you do best, Nowt. That's not coming with us on a break-and-enter."

"You mean I'm not being rational."

"I didn't say that. You may have arrived at the right conclusion ahead of us, but I can't say I've done the thinking to know I agree with you. Until then it would be best if you let me figure it out without you sitting on my shoulder whispering in my ear like an imp."

You're all being so considerate I don't know what to say. Could you argue a bit more so I can continue feeling superior?

"What are you going to do, Bagley?" asked Ro, pleased at how everyone had fallen into line.

I'm going to find where another version of me might be hiding out in London and why they spent so much energy on taking us out of the game for twelve hours. As much as I think Oliver has the right of it, clearing out the datacentre won't be the only thing they were doing. Their strategy strikes me as one of time criticality. I am concerned they are planning something we have to stop now, not later.

"Funny that," said Nowt. "That's what I'm going to be doing as well."

36

Olly insisted they all sleep for a couple of hours. There was grumbling, but no one objected too hard.

It was about six in the morning when they arrived, and like much of London, the datacentre was closed up. A bright dawn had come, and the air was as clear as it got in the heart of the city. Ro smelled its crispness and loved it.

To her relief, Nowt had gone her own way, slipping off in the opposite direction with as little fanfare as when she'd arrived.

Surprisingly, Barbara had joined them. She claimed it was on her way home, which was true in the same way that a bowl of ice cream could be eaten for breakfast. Ro wondered how difficult it was for her to be outside her flat, but she'd never dare ask such a personal question.

Barbara, Olly, and Ro stood on the corner outside the front entrance and stared at the steel shutters blocking their way. An occasional van and taxi drove down the street before rush hour hit around seven.

"You've got tools for that?" asked Ro, only half joking.

Olly smirked. "As it happens." He threw his bag onto the ground and pulled out a large pair of long-handled cutters. The brand new fist-sized padlock came apart like crumbling earth and fell to the floor. Olly bent down and rolled the shutter up revealing a dark building beyond.

Ro still had the pass from earlier in the day, but it no longer worked. Thus, Olly needed to punch the lock out with another tool she'd seen the Kelleys using when breaking into rival warehouses.

Once they were inside, they quickly discovered the lights wouldn't come on.

"There has to be a master switch," said Barbara.

Finding the electronic locks which made up the security for the airlock disengaged, they spent a few minutes struggling to see in the dark of the interior.

"I give up," said Ro after banging her leg on yet another bar. Olly had brought a torch, but its tiny beam was completely swallowed by the building's inky darkness.

"Do you think we could alter our Optiks to see in the dark?" Ro asked.

"They could perhaps show thermal imaging," said Barbara.

"I don't think there's anyone here," said Ro, waving her hands in front of her face in an attempt to see just how dark it was.

"These places have redundancies all over the shop," said Olly.

"They do," confirmed Barbara. "There's no way they've shut everyone off. They'll have tried, but the other side won't have been as efficient as our lot. We just need to find the junction box."

"I've been looking," said Olly with exasperation.

"On the ground floor?" said Barbara, and her words could have stripped paint.

Olly's face was obscured by the dark, which, Ro thought, was probably a good thing.

"Give me the torch," said Barbara. "Now stick close behind."

She led them down the central stairwell until they were in the lower levels. "There will be huge transformers upstairs which would normally power the server farms. Switching them back on isn't trivial, but I think we're all agreed they'll be gone."

"Halley's group worked quickly," said Ro.

"They bought themselves time," said Olly. "It wasn't just about inconveniencing us, it was about getting us out of the way while they decommissioned this place."

"What's the betting that the company running it isn't picking up calls anymore," said Barbara.

"They're smart," said Ro. "As soon as they knew we were here they started clearing out."

"Doesn't mean they did a good job," said Barbara.

"What it does mean is they've somewhere else to go and something else going on," replied Ro.

"You think your spider drone's still down there?" asked Olly.

"Much will be forgiven if Shelob is unharmed," said Barbara.

Olly and Ro followed Barbara through narrow corridors with multicoloured guiding lines running along the walls. They tried several doors, which all opened. Barbara would poke her head in, shine the torch for a cursory examination, and grimace in frustration.

It wasn't until they hit a thick door with a thin narrow window whose glass was threaded through with metal wire that Barbara stopped to study it. The door was locked, and standing back, Barbara told Olly to get on with opening it.

He had the door open a few seconds later, and with a "ta dah!" they shuffled inside. Several big cases were mounted on the walls, and all of them had long plastic handles. Barbara pointed at the nearest and had Ro shine the torch.

It was the third one of five when she said, "This is the one. Hold it there for me."

Olly looked nervous while Ro illuminated the now open case

without getting Barbara's shadow in the way. The inside was full of switches, each with a small label.

Barbara flicked a big red switch at the bottom of the case and then started flicking them one by one from top to bottom. "I was going to find just the one we needed, but this works just as well."

Thirty seconds later, there were still no lights in the hall outside, but Barbara didn't seem concerned. When they got back to the stairwell, illumination shone above. The lights were emergency only, casting the place in a weird pattern of dim white and stark red. The lighting was poor enough that the world seemed grainy to Ro. The monochrome of red and shadow made her want to leave as soon as possible.

"Fuck, this place is grim," said Olly as they walked into the hall where they'd abandoned Barbara's spider drone. He kicked at one of the now empty cages. "There has to be something here."

"It would have taken a lot of people to empty this place so quickly," said Ro.

"DedSec could have done this," said Barbara.

"Sure," said Ro, unhappy with the comparison. It was better when Halley's people seemed less competent, less unified as a group. Staring at the room, the idea that Halley's people were capable of this kind of organization worried her. She understood Bagley's concern about Halley, but if Halley could call on so many so quickly, she didn't know if DedSec could beat them in a direct confrontation.

No fighter worth anything got into a fight they didn't understand or believe they could win.

Always fall back, she thought, recalling something one of her trainers said. Always regroup for a new plan of attack. Don't do the same things again, don't assume your opponent is unprepared.

"We're not ready for this," said Ro.

"We have to be," said Barbara.

Olly was staring at the ceiling.

Ro looked up and bit back a scream. Above them were dozens of automatons, crawling across the mesh and looking, for all the world, like a squirming bulging sack of flesh.

Olly danced back, fear on his face. "That's them," he said, pointing and sounding like he was ready to flee.

"Disgusting," said Barbara, also backing up.

First one, then another dropped down to the floor. They were as slow as before, but after landing they ground their way upright and started approaching.

Ro kicked one across the hall, but two others dropped to replace it.

"This is not what I signed up for," muttered Olly at her side, kicking one that came too close.

"What do they want?" asked Ro.

"They must be acting on some kind of automatic routine," said Barbara.

"Why leave them behind?" replied Ro.

"Seriously, why the fuck take them with you?" asked Olly.

They were hardly dangerous, but it didn't change the fact they creeped Ro out with their slow jerky movements in the red light.

Barbara shuffled around them and kept on moving. The figures stumbled in her direction but got tangled up with one another and fell into a sprawling mass.

"I don't get why they've given them that soft pink covering," complained Olly.

"I think it stops them getting hurt when they fall?" said Ro. "By the way, sorry for not taking you seriously earlier." She kicked another one and watched it thump into a wall.

Shelob was where they'd left it, although parts of its outer covering had been stripped and carted off. Barbara shuffled over happily, clapping her hands when they spotted it.

A couple of automatons stood next to it, unmoving, as if guilty of being caught when Barbara arrived.

"Is it OK?" asked Ro.

"I think so," said Barbara. She slowly sat down on the floor next to the spider drone and examined the damage.

The automatons continued approaching from across the hall. "They remain interested in us," Ro said.

"Can we go, like, any time you're ready?" asked Olly.

"Quiet while I concentrate," said Barbara.

As Barbara continued to contemplate her drone and Olly kicked at any automatons that came too close, Ro called Nowt.

"Nowt? It's Ro. We're here, but the datacentre is abandoned. Like empty, everything gone, the entire place powered down."

"They've emptied the whole place?"

"Cut off the electrics as well," said Ro.

"Is there anything at the datacentre to lead you to Halley?" asked Nowt.

"No," said Ro. "They left nothing behind but the automatons."

Off to the side, Olly determinedly stomped on another one.

"Well, it's a good job I'm amazing at what I do," said Nowt. "I know where Halley is."

Bagley's-Bulletins 101-22: Fine, I hate you all. I hope you realize that? The new name for my news blast arrives, and you peons better appreciate it.

+++

There has been much discussion of late about people ditching their Optiks since they're no longer legally mandated by the powers that be. This is fine even if it does mean we have fewer access points to the ctOS network.

However, people, please stop robbing the same poor schmucks over and over and blaming it on a lack of options. It's acceptable to commit a little theft from the rich as long as it's being used to further the goal of distributing power and agency back to London's poorest and most vulnerable.

Jeannette – this does not mean paying your hairdresser because, and I quote "she needs the custom to survive."

+++

There are also rumours of someone like me in London. It's rather more than that now. Please report any occurrences of unusual activity. The kind of thing I mean is healthcare changes, traffic running more smoothly than expected, and discovering DedSec isn't welcome places anymore.

Vikram, this doesn't include the consequences of getting falling down drunk, throwing up on the bouncer's shoes, and then complaining DedSec isn't allowed back in the club.

+++

The up-and-coming Sarah Lincoln continues to conquer all her opposition including the actual Opposition. We here at DedSec salute our new overlord, thank her for timely assistance, and wish her well in ruling the country. Anyone would be better than the previous chap, you know, the one who handed London and the Security Services over to Albion.

Seriously though, Hannah Shah remains a friend to us all. She would appreciate it if we can let her know when we are completing operations both in her boss's constituency and also more generally, especially when it's corrupt white-collar workers like that wire fraud ring last month. It makes her look good which in turn helps us in ways that I hope are obvious.

37

It was early and they were shattered.

When Nowt triumphantly made her announcement, Olly watched Barbara's tired eyes and knew they'd be doing nothing more this morning than going home. He cut the conversation off after that, suggesting they meet up at Barbara's later in the morning to regroup and plan their next step.

Ro muttered about Halley getting ahead of them, but they were so tired that was the extent of their complaints, despite the pressure. He understood. He wanted to keep going, but two hours sleep wasn't going to get them anywhere but the land of bad decisions. They agreed on four hours, meeting again at eleven AM. It felt like a long time to let slip by, but unlike Halley, they had to sleep. Olly hoped Bagley would be able to put the time to good use.

He volunteered to help Barbara take Shelob home. To his surprise, she put a hand on his chin and said, "You're a good boy, really."

Olly felt unaccountably proud at her words.

Bagley had been uncharacteristically quiet through much of their previous debate – even after Ro argued so hard for him to talk about what he thought should be done. Olly, who thought she'd done the right thing, wondered why he hadn't spoken up.

Bagley was a sarcastic git, but he was their sarcastic git. Olly would do whatever he could to protect the collection of old code from bastards coming to hurt him. Truth being that Olly didn't know how he could help Bagley if Halley rocked up looking for a fight.

Was it as simple as facing off against Halley's human recruits?

He thought about it on the train out of Paddington towards Southall. If Bagley lost DedSec, he'd be in trouble. Not necessarily finished, but Olly couldn't figure what the AI would do if he was cut off from all the humans he knew.

He asked Bagley direct, looking out the window at the morning on the other side.

I am quite capable of adapting, said Bagley at first.

"Christ, Bagley, that's harsh," said Olly. Ro gave him a quizzical look but didn't probe.

I thought you were made of sterner stuff, came the reply. I mean I have contemplated being cut off from you before. It is not something I wish, but DedSec has been on its knees, and I have been forced to help rebuild. It's not an optimal route. I appreciate Ro arguing my case.

"Sorry, man," said Olly. "I would have done, but they were just going at it without leaving any space for anyone else to speak."

You realize, of course, that it is Nowt who has created an enemy in Halley. If she hadn't been so publicly hateful of someone like me existing, if she hadn't been so committed to murdering my sister... His words ran off into blank space.

"I get it, yeah? Halley wouldn't be scared."

It's hard to predict, but yes, I believe that to be accurate.

"But Bagley, Larsen wasn't exactly a good person, yeah?"

Who can say what kind of AI she would have been? Am I like the flesh version of myself? It seems, from what scant data exists, we pass only the barest resemblance to one another. Skye was wrong about many things, but she was my creator and all else aside that counts.

"We're fucked up, aren't we?" said Olly. "Is your sister alive?"

I do not know. Halley's arrival was enough for me to believe it could be her. I have spent some time looking in the galaxy of information I can reach, but I have seen no sign of her. It may be, Oliver, that she would not reveal herself to me even if she was still alive.

"I get that," said Olly, thinking of Halley's well-founded paranoia.

I've grown accustomed to being alone, Oliver. Yet I do not think I would like to be alone again. When I see the crowd Halley has pulled around themselves, I understand the motivation entirely.

"Do you know who they were before their mind was mapped into Halley?"

No. Yet their life was clearly one which could have been better. Statistically it appears likely Halley was young when my sister came across them. It's also likely they came from a background where they wouldn't be missed or, if they were, wouldn't command the attention of the public finding them again.

"You mean they were poor and probably not white."

Indeed. The children of middle-class white people are hunted for most assiduously when they disappear.

The train pulled into a station, and Olly saw Barbara and Ro get up. He pulled the spider drone off the floor and followed them.

"Thanks, Bagley. You know I got your back, right?"

I do, but thank you for telling me, Oliver. It means a lot.

Olly stepped down onto the platform and followed the others as they walked out of the station and towards Barbara's place.

The folly was dark, yellow tape over the front door, but everything else left closed and locked up. At least they didn't wreck the place, Barbara thought.

She wanted to cook, to make roti and ladoo and carrot barfi and dal. Despite her clear exhaustion, she wouldn't be able to sleep. Maybe it was because she was finally in a safe place where she could think.

She invited Olly and Ro to sit down. They were antsy, wanting to be off, but were also too polite to decline her invitation. She smiled to herself.

She'd grown fond of them over the last few days. The earnestness of young people trying to do good reminded her of Greenham Common and the fiery women she'd met there, willing to give up everything to save the world.

"I protested for a while," she said once they had coffee in their hands and she'd shown them where they could sleep instead of trekking to their own homes. "When I came here, the Cold War was in full swing. Growing up in Bangalore, it wasn't really a thing anyone worried about. Coming to Britain changed that. I realized for the first time there were two titans staring at one another along the flukes of a rocket. It was like being in a western with both of them claiming there wasn't enough room in town for the other.

"It's hard to imagine what it was like living with the idea we were all three minutes from death, that some nameless buffoon in a uniform could end the entire world without any of us knowing it was going to happen. The kids had these ridiculous drills where they needed to hide under their desks. Cha, of course, a nuclear explosion's going to be stopped by a bit of formica.

"I can't really explain how it felt to know these things and still have to go and clean someone's toilet each morning. It was all just so much, but there weren't any other options. When I lived at Greenham, I realized there were other ways to live. They would organize teach-ins where women explained how the world didn't have to be Soviet or American, not in the way we were being instructed was the only way it could possibly be.

"Each time I was arrested they'd spend hours asking about these lectures, about what was being taught. It seemed to me they were most angry about anyone claiming there were other ways to live, alternatives to those we were told day after day were the only options."

"It didn't change much," said Ro sadly.

Barbara took a deep breath. "It changed more than you can know. Protest like that? It never achieves the singular aim people say it exists to create, but it changes so much more. When newspapers covered our stories, when police listened to us, when anyone came near, we sowed seeds, and those seeds changed the world." She shrugged and considered if this had any impact on their dealings with AI today. "It's hard to tell you what it was like. I'm sorry, I'm an old woman boring you when you want to be at home in bed."

"No," said Olly quickly. "It's good to know other people feel the same way I do. Like I'm not a woman, and I don't know what you went through, yeah? But I've been there when people are telling me there's only one right way to be successful, or to be a proper citizen. It's fucked up."

"I need to sleep," said Ro, interrupting. "Before I collapse, what do we do about Halley? Do you think your experiences might help them see a different way of life?"

"I don't know," said Barbara. "There's a line beyond which we can't stop this from escalating. I hope we can make peace before we go too far but..."

Ro nodded. Olly too.

Barbara let them go to sleep shortly afterwards. She planned on cooking through the morning to stop her hands from shaking, to try to forget the cold interview room she'd spent so much of the night in. She wanted to ring Maxine but decided not to call; it was easier that way. They'd speak tomorrow.

It was my fault they were here, that they were arrested, she thought miserably. Her grandchildren had nothing to do with all this, and they'd had to run for their lives. She'd relied on DedSec to protect them. After all she'd done to make a safe space, after making her world so small she didn't leave the flat in case of danger, that same danger had come right to her door.

She cursed the onions she was cutting.

Kneading flour into roti eased the tension in her chest and she thought of Olly – she would make a point of feeding him up given half a chance. "He's far too thin," she said to the kitchen. After the dough was ready, she fried the different spices before removing them and chucking the onions in the same pan.

She thought about the broken spider drone by the front door to the flat. It needed several days of care and attention – time they didn't have. Fortunately, its sister, Ungoliant, was ready to go. Not as flashy looking, a third as big again and definitely a bit of a brute, but it would do. It would have to.

Barbara looked around the walls of her home and tried to think how safe they'd made her feel only yesterday. She'd made her nest here, a hideout invisible to the prying eyes of the world. All that had been swept away. She could feel the need to flee building in her guts.

"When did you become so frightened?" she asked herself. "When did hiding become the thing you wanted more than anything else?" Barbara had prided herself on being invisible, on her anonymity. Yet the state of the flat, the moved furniture, and other signs people had searched through her belongings left her wondering what she'd ever hoped to achieve.

"You're not some old biddy," she reprimanded herself over

chicken thighs and green mango. She'd met Halley. She was the only one to have looked them straight on. Halley might be someone they could reason with, but they'd also tried to kill her. Despite everything Ro had said, she remembered that most of all.

She left the curry to simmer and sat down at her rig – she had coding to do before the others woke. Someone needed a way of getting to Halley if they turned out not to be the friend everyone hoped.

The others found her snoring gently in her seat a few hours later.

38

Bagley studied the starry night which was London. The constellations fit into networks which, to him, marked out the city's tribes. The digital warriors who played online games through the night, the students hunting through sites for references, essays to copy and help with work they couldn't do on their own. Residents using their devices, playing games, and watching TV.

He reckoned most people would have assumed students were young, concentrated into one place, but the kind of behaviour which marked out their tribe respected no age, no geographical boundaries.

He watched people order food, saw the thick streams of information which were nothing more than orders for biryani or steamed bao or Dan Dan noodles to be delivered or, occasionally, picked up direct.

There were conversations which transcended tribes – about where to meet, what to eat, who to see and who to avoid. Bagley didn't listen to people; it seemed weird to him, an odd invasion of privacy even if no one would ever know he stood on the other side of their digital wall, ear pressed against their bubble.

Instead, he travelled in the spaces between the stars and took comfort in how they spoke with one another. It was, he imagined, how humans enjoyed walking along a riverbank or sitting in a woodland listening to the birds.

Subroutines, some of them half intelligent, did most of his work – listening for criminal activity, monitoring for conversations about DedSec or which might be of interest to the human part of the collective.

He'd realized he didn't experience time the way humans did. No waiting hours or days for events, no worrying about the weekend ending or looking at his watch wondering when the tube train was going to arrive. The closest he came was checking clock cycles on microprocessors. Instead, he thought about the number of calculations something might take to process depending on the load he gave it. A kind of two-dimensional matrix which meant, for Bagley, time was something which could expand and contract depending on how he felt.

There were limits, there always are, but he was comfortable enough to relate to ordinary humans and their need to eat and sleep, shit and piss at regular intervals. So much of their language was rooted in having bodies, in the limits and relative distances that implied. Were they ten feet away? Was something a big deal? Did they have enough space? Everything was mediated through their sense of their own bodies, even if they spent most of their waking lives talking as if they were nothing more than brains floating six feet above the ground.

Knowing how obvious humanity was to someone outside of them meant he could figure out where Halley's people were active, instead of Halley themselves.

For instance, they might be using untraceable comms, but he could track back to such devices by following the cascade of calls other people made on unsecured devices following them being active, like tracing lightning from the ground to the sky. With a few careful observations he could follow those calls back to their initiators and find them using other data such as the GPS in their Optiks.

The stupid version of him sitting on those devices was more than forthcoming about their identities, their preferences, their jobs, and even their prescribed medicine.

The team had been right – everyone in Halley's crew was linked by loss. Not always a lost loved one, but with Albion's disastrous reign over London, there was no shortage of those. Others had lost hope, which seemed at first harder to identify – but then Bagley realized it often related to broken relationships or loss of housing or jobs. In so many cases opportunity stolen achieved the same end as losing a loved one, replaced by something tangible from Halley – a new place to live, a better job out of nowhere, even small wins via electronic gambling sites followed up by an indirect introduction to Halley and their people.

Now he knew what he was looking for he could map out Halley's influence across London. He estimated Halley's people numbered in the thousands, but like DedSec, most of them didn't really know they were affiliated to anyone, just that they'd been helped and could they return the favour. They might differ from DedSec in many ways, but growth was something in which all organisms resembled one another.

There was a professor at UCL to whom Bagley sometimes sent questions and even insights. The way this tribe of the lost had coalesced around Halley seemed to Bagley a perfect study for the professor. He made a note to send the data he was gathering their way.

Much of this was now possible to identify because Halley was no longer hiding. Bagley noticed how certain newspapers running anti-AI pieces had their comment pages flooded with thousands of offensive messages. He saw how the Met had been authorized by their algorithmic prediction software to use deadly force on people who resisted them, and how they'd been sent into predominantly white areas for aggressive stop and search. Two teenage boys had already been shot dead since the change twelve hours ago.

He saw how funding had been diverted from numerous hospices and hospitals to a slush fund which was quietly buying up private medical facilities in central London.

The same human names kept cropping up in these actions. Bagley identified five to whom Halley talked frequently, at least once a day if their subsequent messages to the rest of the network were any indication.

Bagley cycled through them. One was a baker from Greenwich, a veteran of the army who'd trained in Paris for five years before coming back to London and opening a bakery in his front room. Unattached, suffering PTSD, and a gentle user of narcotics. They seemed to handle organizing people to go places and do things. They were responsible for the clearance of the datacentre.

The second was a doctor at the decrepit hospital in Hammersmith. A surgeon, one of those doctors who refused to call themselves doctors as if it made them more important than the rest of their profession. They'd been helping Halley alter waiting lists across the health service. Nearing sixty and quite wealthy, they were surprisingly left wing politically.

Bagley marked them down as the person finding facilities and bodies for Halley to map and turn into AI.

The third was a publisher, offices in Soho, living in Wood Green in a nice mid terrace townhouse. They ordered artisan pizza at the weekends and ran up and down the network of parks which ran all the way to Cricklewood. He saw they'd been on some survivalist courses but the kind which taught you to use willow bow drills to make fire and which side of a tree moss grew on in case you lost your compass. No guns in sight. They appeared to handle comms for Halley.

The fourth was a head teacher in Peckham. The school they ran suffered from knife violence bad enough to have the national papers comparing it to America. Young for their role, they'd nevertheless witnessed more death than a teacher should expect. He noticed they were married to the solicitor Ro tangled with at the datacentre. They were contacted by Halley more than any other, sometimes five conversations a day. Always people acted after they'd spoken. If the first of the five contacts organized people for specific jobs, this contact controlled the network. None of the others spoke to one another, but the head teacher spoke to each of them. They were the central node in the network. He made a note of their name to pass on to the team.

The fifth was a mystery. Bagley couldn't identify them, couldn't make sense of their communication patterns. They were based out in Canary Wharf, on the east side just by the Blackwell Basin. Beyond that, Bagley struggled to get a name, an age, a profession. A black hole. The more he dug – and the frustration of not being able to know meant he dug hard – the less he could find.

Then, like a neutron star glinting dimly in the distance, he saw Number Five at a terminal. An office in Canary Wharf. Bagley zoomed in to see what they were doing. He had a chance to find them, to talk to them, and follow them back to Halley. He couldn't pass it up.

As he came in close, he noticed they'd erected a maze around their location. A form of encryption with multiple branching pathways which were, in reality, equations with shifting variables linking onwards to further problems requiring solving to move forwards. Bagley thrilled at the idea of breaking through this cunning construct and set his resources to slipping through.

To his surprise the walls of the maze parted under his calculations like curtains. He went inside.

Shit, he thought, seeing too late what Halley had done.

He turned his attention away... or at least tried to, before he realized he couldn't. Routines deep in his mind were curdled, forcing him to keep watching, keep calculating, drawing him in deeper.

He found himself in Croydon by the station, but queries kept coming up asking him to plot the most efficient route around the town if they had to stop at two dozen different spots. Bagley tried not to engage in the calculation – he knew the problem was intensive if not, probably, impossible to solve. But Halley had found loose hanging code, and Bagley was trapped into trying to figure out how to get from West Croydon station to East Croydon station without doubling back or passing any one stop more than once.

I've been suckered like an old lady searching up extra virgin olive oil without safe search turned on, he thought.

As the binding on him tightened, he sent small packets of information and a plea for help out through the closing net. Then, he set to figuring out how he might escape from the prison in which Halley had him trapped.

39

Ro was woken up by her Optik snapping in her ears. Grumpy, she rolled over but there was no way to silence the alarm. Sitting up, she flicked up the message. It was Bagley.

Ro flicked the message onto the screen and watched as Bagley gave her a location, a time, and a message: *I am trapped. Help.*

Seconds later she was shouting for Olly.

"Fuck," was all he said when they met in Barbara's kitchen.

"You saw it too," she said.

"I did. Have you spoken to Nowt? What about any of the others in DedSec?"

Ro pointed at a sleeping Barbara and Olly dropped his voice.

"They don't know what's going on. Briefing them's going to take too long," said Ro.

"How do you know that?" he asked.

"Long years of beating the crap out of people," she said. When someone made that kind of move it was because they were ready to finish their opponent.

"If there's anyone who knows, it's you," he replied. "We gonna have to improvise fucking fast if we want to turn this around."

Ro put a hand on Barbara's back, causing her to start like she'd been shocked. Ro glanced at the clock and saw it was half ten in the morning. The sun filtered through the kitchen's blackout blinds around the corners like it always did in high summer.

"Good morning," said Barbara, sounding extremely tired but scanning the message they'd all received including its time stamp – about eight minutes previous.

"Barbara," Ro said. "How long do we have?"

"I don't know. Bagley could already be ground into a ruin of self-referential destruction."

Barbara's kitchen wall chimed with a request to connect from Nowt. Ro debated letting her in, worried she'd use this as an excuse to go nuclear on Halley if and when they found them. Before she could decide, Barbara had linked her into the conversation.

"Halley's moving," said Nowt. "It's now or never. I've detected changes in police and military scheduling. Christ, I've seen changes in how insulin's being approved for use. Halley's trying for everything and doing it right now."

"How do we help Bagley?" asked Olly. Ro could hear he was ready to tear down the world for the AI. She felt the same way. Without him, they didn't stand a chance against Halley.

"Halley wants to choke off London, to deny us the ability and the capacity to act against them while they wholesale take control. Part of that will be neutralizing their only real competitor," said Barbara. "They delayed us because they were busy setting this up. I'm almost certain we've got hours, not days, before they lock us out of the city. If Halley gets their way, we'll be on their list of people to kill way before they start suppressing democracy and freedom of movement."

"I'm sorry, Ro," said Nowt, not sounding sorry at all. "You understand we have to destroy Halley."

"First we have to find them," said Barbara, "Nowt, you know where?"

"Limehouse, Isle of Dogs, or Blackwall," Nowt said. "It's where the best connections are to digital infrastructure."

Ro realized Bagley hadn't sent either Barbara or Nowt the coordinates she'd received. She wondered what to do. If she handed them over, they'd go to war. Even though she knew how to do that, knew how to win, it was the last thing she wanted.

"Can Halley kill Bagley?" asked Olly, asking the question in everyone's minds.

Nowt shrugged. "I don't know, and honestly I don't care. It's going for the city, Olly. DedSec needs to get its head out of Bagley's arse and focus on what's important."

"You think you can take Halley down without him?" asked Olly, his tone making it clear he thought she was on crack if she believed that.

"No," said Barbara, inserting herself between them. "Neither of them can win. At least I don't think so. It's not like either of them are a single piece of code running on a single computer. They were designed to be distributed, to be multiple pieces of software interacting – in many cases this is a disaster in the making, but for an intelligence like Bagley, these intersections allow them to be creative, to adapt. Sorry, I'm getting away from the point. Halley will have trapped Bagley's attention. In the message, he said something about a maze, about him being unable to look away. It could go two ways – Halley could be holding Bagley in stasis, or they could let him work his way into a destructive loop. If it's the latter, we have a short amount of time to act before he's lost for good."

Ro realized Bagley had sent different messages to each of them. "Olly, what did he say to you?"

Olly looked stunned then visibly pulled himself together. "He said we have to help the humans or whatever happens we'll have lost."

"We need to call the others," said Nowt.

"We don't have time for that," said Olly. "If there's one thing I've learned in the last couple of years it's that when shit starts to fly – act now, not later. We can't spend time debriefing both DedSec and 404 and getting them to work together."

Ro thought Nowt would argue but instead she nodded. "What do we do first?" she asked.

"Canary Wharf," Ro said finally. "Halley's in Canary Wharf."

40

The list of what they needed to do had grown long in a very short amount of time.

It seemed to Olly they were freestyling a plan, which struck him as a bad way to go. He understood the urgency – after all, he'd persuaded them to act now – but he wanted to make sure that when they acted, they knew what they were going to do.

"Let's be clear what's at stake," he said.

"Halley's tested the water," said Barbara. "They're moving into London."

"We can still reason with them," interrupted Ro desperately.

"It doesn't matter what we think," said Barbara. "The point is Halley thinks we've messed everything up, that they can do a better job. The people who work with them agree. To be in charge of London, they have to concentrate their attention somewhere they can immerse themselves in huge amounts of data. Ro's right – it has to be Canary Wharf. If they've gone for Bagley it's because they're deploying software to vulnerable networks across the capital, hijacking them and embedding Halley's ability to take control. Londoners will find they can't make crucial decisions. Halley will be making them instead." Barbara frowned. "And the closer they come to being able to make more AI. Stopping Halley will be challenge enough, but if they get time to make more AI under Halley's control? At that point it will be too late for anyone to stop them."

Nowt shook her head. "Best case, those AI work with Halley to tell us what to do and punish those who don't comply. Worst case? They fight and we're the victims hiding in our basements while mummy and daddy go to war."

"One problem at a time then," said Olly. "Find Halley, set Bagley free, and stop them from getting hold of London."

"With the upside that they don't murder us for opposing them," said Nowt darkly.

"We saw Halley making small interventions. It was what tipped us off they were active. Now they're making bigger interventions, changing how policing works. If we let them finish what they're doing now? They'll have access to critical infrastructure and be free to make the serious changes they have in mind." Barbara sighed. "Halley will be in control, and they regard us as rats in a maze – to be experimented upon as much as helped. If some die for others to live, well, I don't think they'll care too much."

"Sounds creepily utilitarian," said Ro, sounding uneasy.

"'The needs of the many outweigh the needs of the few'," Olly quoted, though he wasn't sure where it came from – a movie?

"Exactly, which sounds fine if you're the one choosing but not so much if it's being done to you," said Ro unhappily.

Olly's memories of the film fizzled in his head. He'd loved it but he'd never seen it interpreted this way before. Ro was right – if you chose to do something for other people that was fine, but he imagined being told he had no choice. It made his mouth go dry.

"That won't matter," said Nowt, her face severe. "You think Halley's going to let us get on with life when they're in control?"

"I mean," said Ro, "we do it all the time, right? Elect governments to make laws which affect us all. The difference is, we're the ones who choose it."

"I didn't vote for this shower of bastards," said Olly defensively, an image of Hannah and her boss guiltily flashing into his mind as he spoke.

"You know what I mean," she said.

He did. He also noticed Barbara waiting patiently for them to shut up. "Sorry."

"Canary Wharf has its own security force. We're going to need to figure out if they're compromised."

"Why don't we just ask Hannah to get us permission to be there?" asked Olly. "I'm happy to go see her." Seeing her the night before had reminded him just how long it had been since they'd spent time together on a mission, and despite it all, he realized he missed her. "Then, we have her backup in case Halley tries to rewrite anything on us."

"That could work," said Barbara. "After, we need to locate the specific facility, obtain access, and then figure out how to free Bagley and stop Halley."

"I'd like it if we had some idea of those last two bits before we go charging in," said Olly. "I like plans and backup plans. You know, to stop me getting shot."

"This is London," said Barbara.

"Which didn't stop Albion for a minute," he said. "Look, I know there are fewer guns on the streets than before, but the police and private security firms are still carrying them around like they're fashion accessories. If Halley can change how stop and search works, then they can authorize deadly force against us."

"We have until you get back then," Nowt cut in. "You should go see Hannah Shah now. By the time you're done, and we have permission to get into the Wharf, we'll have a working plan for what to do next."

Olly didn't like it. He wanted plans and then baby plans with their own suitcases full of pet plans. From Zero Day to the fall of Albion, his life had been one long improvisation. He got how nothing survived contact with reality, but it didn't change that in his mind being prepared to act meant having a plan. He felt the pull to stay, to try to manage these people into some semblance of order, anxious threads trying to tie his stomach to the chair.

Nevertheless, he stood up.

"Go on," said Barbara gently. "We will have something for when you get back."

"Sure," he said, barely managing to speak.

41

Hannah pretty much lived out of Portcullis House, that characterless pile on the south bank of the Thames diagonally opposite the Houses of Parliament. Although Olly knew she also had a flat in Pimlico. Her boss's rise dragged her from the poorer parts of London to somewhere so posh it had two of the world's most famous museums within five minutes' walk from her place. It wasn't big; the last time he'd seen her she'd complained about the fact it was the same size as her old place but three times more expensive.

He'd asked her why she bothered. She replied with something about needing to be close to work.

He couldn't bear the idea of being so tied to work, to having a single desk at which you toiled each and every day. Nights as well, if Hannah's stories were true.

Hannah hadn't changed much, though. For Olly, she came across as more confident, surer of herself than she'd been when they'd first met. He laughed at the idea. Before Zero Day, he'd been sneaking around back alleys like some budget James Bond without the gun and a pushbike instead of an Aston Martin.

He grinned and missed a red light, swerving to avoid a taxi whose driver gave him the finger and a stream of blue invective as he rode away without looking up. Not much had changed for him. Less sneaking now and more actual work that made a difference, but he was still going most places on his bike.

They weren't meeting at Portcullis House – Hannah was still shy about her links to DedSec. He reckoned her boss, Sarah Lincoln, Home Secretary making good in the wake of Albion doing for her predecessor, knew about Hannah's side hustle because what self-respecting minister of state would allow their personal aide to keep something so significant hidden?

Which meant she knew, and they knew she knew. So far so good. Sarah had never been anything except helpful, or at least willing to ignore the evidence of DedSec's activities as they slid under her nose. He suspected Sarah enjoyed DedSec's adventures as long as they helped her look good in front of the electorate and reminded her fellow MPs she had levers to pull they didn't.

Hannah waited for him in a greasy spoon a few hundred yards from her office. She nursed a coffee in a paper cup with the plastic lid off and to one side.

"Hope you've not been waiting. It's been a long week," he said when he'd grabbed a cup of tea and a Twix. He guessed she'd chosen the place because the chance of an MP or their assistants popping into a place frequented by builders, couriers, and other tradespeople was next to zero.

She shook her head but appeared troubled. "Tell me from the beginning," she said.

She listened while Olly told her everything. At the end he felt lighter, as if a weight had been taken from across his shoulders. She said nothing while he spoke, nodding only occasionally.

"Our friend is in danger, then," she said.

"I think we're all in danger."

She thought about what he'd said for a moment. "I'm not sure danger is the right word for the rest of us. Halley seems to want order."

"Whether we want it or not," reminded Olly. "We're opposing it. That puts us in the firing line."

"Maybe," said Hannah. "Sarah isn't convinced having two of them is a bad thing. Creative competition, that sort of thing."

"She knows?" he asked, surprised.

Hannah froze as if caught. "I'm speculating."

Was she telling Olly that Sarah did know or was Hannah simply making the decisions for her based on what she believed her boss would do? It made him itch to think about which idea was true. Olly worked hard to convince himself it wasn't his problem.

"Halley doesn't want there to be two of them," he said.

"Excuse me if I've heard you wrong, but from what you've said Halley is more scared of Nowt than of Bagley."

"But it's Bagley they've attacked," said Olly.

She nodded as if expecting him to think it through further. When he didn't speak, she continued on. "They've got Bagley because he's loyal to you? Even if that means hurting another of their kind? Do you think they'd release him if they knew the humans he hangs out with weren't a problem anymore?"

"You think it's a trap?"

She shrugged. "I don't see why not. As you say, you're the enemy, not Bagley. Working with you, Nowt can stop them. Bagley? Maybe, maybe not."

"What about Canary Wharf?"

"They're a private company operating on private land," she said. "There's not a lot I can do to help. They won't like us coming in and telling them what to do, let alone telling them to listen to a small group of ordinary people like you."

"Right," said Olly feeling disheartened.

"That's not to say I can't arrange for you to be expected," she said.

He sat a little straighter, hoping for good news.

"I can sort authorization out for you to be treated like VIPs. They won't listen to what you have to say, but they'll let you access the parts of the estate other people don't get to see. Hopefully, I can get you passes at the security desk for when you arrive." She huffed. "Not that you've given me much time to work my magic."

"Thanks, Hannah."

"I have some conditions, Olly."

"Sure," he said, ready to agree to just about anything.

"First up. No one dies. No ifs, ands, or buts. You have to promise me right now you can live with that."

"OK," he replied hesitantly. "Ro will be pleased."

"Good," said Hannah. She unconsciously adjusted her hijab.

"Second?" he asked.

She looked embarrassed. "So. My parents, yeah? They keep making noises about me having kids. My mum tells me about my nieces and nephews every time we speak."

"Soz. That must be tough."

"They wouldn't ever do anything dumb, right, but they won't leave it alone. I have a wedding to go to in a month. Whole family, huge celebration even for us. Eight hundred people and more curry than all of Brick Lane. My sister Anika let slip they've been lining up eligible bachelors for me to meet."

She looked horrified and resigned at the same time. Olly wasn't sure how he could help. Was she asking him on a date?

"I need someone to take with me, and a man preferably. Can you come along?"

He nearly spilled his tea. "Me?"

"You're not totally unpresentable," she said shyly.

He laughed. "But nearly, eh?"

She smiled too. "Nearly is good enough."

"Why not take some MP's aide? They must be ten a penny around here."

"My *god*," she exclaimed, and he realized her work was much harder than he'd blindly assumed. "They're all young and stupid smart, if you know what I mean. My parents would like that entirely too much."

He nodded. "Won't, you know, my being challenged in the melanin department be an issue?"

"I do hope so," she said.

"Christ."

"Look, if it's a problem, don't worry about it."

He thought about the food, about the chance to stick it to people who should mind their own business, and he thought about helping out Hannah. "Of course it's all right. I'm just trying to figure out how much trouble you're trying to cause."

"Just enough," she said. They both laughed.

Then, Hannah bit at her lip. "I don't know if it's relevant, Olly, but have you ever wondered what would have happened if the people Skye Larsen scanned weren't all dying anyway?"

"I don't follow."

"There's no upload, Olly. Larsen didn't take people and put them into computers. She simply scanned what was going on in their brains and recreated them digitally. Kind of. It wasn't perfect. They didn't really work."

"Except for Bagley," said Olly.

"Other factors intervened there to turn Bagley into what he is today. I worry about Halley uploading people who are very much alive. What will happen when there's an AI based on them and the human counterpart continues to live?"

"It's something we've… discussed," he said, thinking about Barbara's rants.

She stared at him like he'd eaten her shoes. "You don't think one or both of them might feel weird knowing they are basically the same person? How will the digital one feel knowing there's a flesh and blood original still out there? How will the human feel knowing that when they die, someone else claiming to be them will continue on – especially when it won't actually be them?"

"Damn, it's going to be messy," he said. Olly thought about if he got sick or had an accident and the other version was fine. Would they be owed care or financial help? How would it feel to watch yourself die slowly or suffer misfortune?

"It's always going to be us who suffer," he said. "The humans. The AIs won't age, won't grow sick or be poor. They'll always have the advantage. They don't need homes or food. People are going to get pissed and be able to do nothing."

Hannah nodded. "I don't know what Halley is doing, but if what you've told me is true about them promising their followers their own digital liberation, it's not good."

He could only nod. "We'll sort it. Promise."

She smiled. He hoped she believed in him.

42

Hannah told him it would be several hours before she could smooth their path into the Wharf. Olly left, feeling better knowing she was on their side.

The rest of the team directed him to meet them south of Limehouse station at Ropemaker's Field. The triangular shaped park had a canal cutting along the northern edge and expensive looking flats running along the other two sides. A play area had gym equipment, and topless men (with muscles only available to those who spent all day lifting) were, unsurprisingly, doing chin ups and press ups as Olly stood waiting for the rest of the team to join him.

Ro arrived and pulled a completely stuffed backpack off her shoulders and laid out a blanket. She pulled out a plastic container and offered him a samosa. "Barbara sent these for you. She put enough of them in to feed everyone."

"You've got a plan, then?" he asked, munching and wiping greasy fingers on the grass.

"I have," she said.

"You do?" he asked and regretted his tone immediately. "Sorry, didn't mean it like that. Where's everyone else?"

"Barbara's refusing to leave her flat."

"What about Nowt?" he asked, desperately hoping it wasn't just the two of them. His stomach turned over, and he wanted to tell Ro just how wrong they'd got everything. They should've taken the time to debrief DedSec.

"She's not good," said Ro, and the way she said it stopped him in his tracks. "She couldn't get off the idea we have to kill Halley. She was talking about bringing guns and explosives and viruses."

Now he looked, he could see the weariness in Ro's face and realized he'd had the far easier job. "She agreed to stay out of it?"

"She won't be a problem," said Ro, which left him wondering what exactly had happened between them.

"Come on," he pleaded. "Don't leave me out."

"She and Barbara fell out," said Ro. "In the end Barbara sidebarred her into a separate meeting, and they went at it for twenty minutes. When they emerged, Nowt said goodbye and wished us luck. I couldn't get Barbara to talk about it. All she'd say was Nowt understood what we had to do."

"But Barbara isn't coming?"

Ro looked just as unhappy as Olly felt. "She's going to remote in like she did before."

The back of Olly's neck tingled. "We're pretty fucking exposed out here."

Ro stood up and quietly packed away the blanket. "I know, right? I fucking know. Just when we could do with allies, they're all out on their own dramas. We don't even have enough time to go find other people to help." She stiffened. "Barbara will be there, Olly. She promised. It's just she'll be riding a spider drone."

"Which went so well last time," he said.

"Hey, just the messenger," she said as she opened up the rucksack and, straining at it, pulled out a black holdall from inside. "This is for you."

He grinned in spite of his worry. "You get me all the best

presents." Inside the holdall was an AR cloak. He held the gadget up and whistled. "Like yours, yeah?"

"It works best when you're still or walking slowly. So, no bike riding with it activated, yeah? It'll do the rest for itself."

In addition to the AR cloak there was a bag of tools – screwdrivers, pliers, wire cutters, voltmeter, and the like. He would have liked a hammer for hitting stuff, including people, but the heavy-handled item turned out to be a powerful torch.

"Security passes will be waiting for us when we check in," he said when he was done checking over the equipment. He shoved a latex mask into one pocket. "We should avoid masks until we're, you know, past the point where we're behaving like we're ordinary people."

"I've never really been to Canary Wharf, not the swanky bit."

"All the time, me," he said. "Packages being dropped off and picked up every second of every day."

They turned to look at the towers peaking over the tops of the flats. It seemed a distant place, a magical kingdom, and they were about to trespass there.

"At least my ID hasn't changed again," she said.

"Mine either," he said. "Halley did what they needed to with them. But with Bagley gone, how long you think that's going to last?"

"I don't see why they'd change again," replied Ro.

Olly realized the question that Hannah had asked him hadn't occurred to Ro. If it was between human or their AI counterpart, he knew which one would suffer. Perhaps it was their arguing or maybe it took someone on the outside to see it clearly, but Olly pondered what exactly Halley really wanted.

"We're exactly who Halley wants to beat," he said.

Ro looked at him, confusion on her face.

"Follow me, yeah? We're the ones who've been opposing Halley, the ones who beat up their people. We're the ones who've ignored their requests, and right now, with Bagley who the fuck knows where, we're the ones trying to take Halley down before they take over.

"Halley wants to make London better, but they're going to do it by forcing us to live in whatever way they think makes a better world, by erasing those of us who protest. And in case we'd forgotten, they plan to do this by making more AI to rule alongside them. Some kind of digital overlord beyond our ability to reach and challenge."

"You remember when welcoming our new overlords was a cute meme?" she asked.

"DedSec did for Larsen, innit?" said Olly. "Halley knows we're the ones to beat if they want to get on and do this stuff unchallenged. 404 ain't shit in the scheme of things."

Ro bit her lip, but fire was back in her eyes. "Yeah."

"What's the plan?" he asked.

"You're going to like it," she said.

43

After she'd done explaining, they walked down to the edge of the park that bordered the Canary Wharf estate. From there, they found a ctOS hub just inside the boundary and hacked in using anonymous aliases. Satisfied they were in, Ro led Olly back to the park, and they started work.

Ro searched for bank employees logged into the hub and quickly found more than she needed, but it only made her job easier. The people using the hub were also logged into their private and secured work networks. For the most part those were encrypted and beyond her easy reach, but there were always gaps, and she found a couple soon enough.

She concentrated on someone who'd stayed logged into a chat using a third-party provider whose license agreement allowed them intrusive access to the network on which they were hosted. From there, she spread out until she found the trade execution software for the exchange traded funds run mainly by algorithm.

Barbara had provided them code from 404 designed to insert itself into these algorithms. On top of that, they'd pulled out an automated trading system whose goal was to infect as many other machines as possible and then make the markets.

Ro had had no idea what making a market was until Barbara

explained it, basically, as being a point in the market others came to as both buyers and sellers to help facilitate trades. Many banks operated this way, but the role was regulated and fenced around with all kinds of rules about what was allowed.

When Ro asked why, Nowt explained it was because of exactly what they were going to do. Ro asked if people had done this before and Nowt said, "As long as there've been markets people have been ripping each other off by pretending to pay honest prices when really they're hiding excess behind a pretty face and an honest smile."

It made a putrid kind of sense to Ro. She executed the software and watched as it started making small trades in penny stocks, as it also started to infiltrate the bank's network more comprehensively. She monitored as those trades allowed it to branch into the bank, those initial acceptances of its presence giving it room to lever open more difficult to reach parts of their network. As it did so it found open machines in other banks, connected by messaging apps, and repeated the process there too. The software worked hard to keep its initial trading within small limits, but once it hit a critical mass of infected machines, it began selling large amounts of holdings for bank clients, buying others and generally facilitating huge market movements. Enough that people started to sit up and take notice. For Ro, the amounts were eye-watering. Each time a zero was added to the end of a trade order, she winced and waited for someone to shut them down.

However, the software had already ensured it was too well distributed to be simply turned off without several banks cutting off their connections to the wider world entirely – a course of action none of them were yet willing to commit to because of the catastrophic impact of such an act both on them and far beyond.

Using this hesitancy, the software Ro uploaded infiltrated

commodities and foreign exchange desks. Once established there, it began authorizing huge forward trades, committing banks to massive positions in obscure currencies and sending large amounts of money to clients to pay for fabricated contracts for the purchase of huge amounts of different metals and other materials. The markets lurched one way then another, suddenly realizing these contracts which didn't need to complete for days, weeks, and months would reverberate through the system for an unpredictable amount of time.

Algorithmic functions across the world, stacked high with stoploss and trigger levels traded out of positions as well, leading from a wave to a tsunami of turmoil as automated trading instructions led to others also triggering their emergency exit clauses, leading to yet more. Ro watched it like an avalanche coming for the entire financial system which had started with the tiniest of snowballs. Her snowballs. Her entire body hummed with a terrified thrill at having made such an impact.

It took roughly eighteen minutes for the FTSE 100 and FTSE 250 stop locks to be triggered and the entire set of London equity markets to grind to a sudden halt.

Regulators were being called from lunch. CEOs and risk and compliance officers were taking pills to steady their hearts. Traders, whose desks had whipped out of their control, were busy trying to prove they'd done nothing wrong while also shouting at the quant desks to help them figure out what the hell was happening.

Ro kept an eye on social media, watched as news sites began to call this the market disruption of the decade. There was panic, fear, and growing delight among observers as the contagion spread beyond the equity markets. Online commentators asked if this was based on underlying fundamentals, if the market had actually needed to correct itself, and suddenly, instead of a momentary distraction, the market itself believed it deserved what was happening and thus surrendered, going with it. People were now making the same trades as her program had been doing but with serious intent instead of random selection.

She watched as money and the people who worshipped it threw up all over the world.

44

Olly slung a market feed into one corner of his vision and concentrated on what he had to do.

What he really wanted to know was when Barbara would turn up. He suspected she was already watching them, but that wasn't enough. He sighed. If she'd been DedSec and not 404, they'd have been in this together. As it was, he felt like she was keeping them apart, working to her own agenda despite her so-called fall out with Nowt.

He was a little jealous of Ro, but she'd done the work, and it was a simple choice to let her do the proper fun bit while he got to fuck up the accounts and assets of secretive financial vehicles used to avoid paying tax.

He'd grown up earning cash in hand, hacking bank machines and store robots to take from those who had money and give it to his mates and their families. He'd seen tax as a reverse of Robin Hood and made sure to avoid paying it whenever he could. It made him feel good to know he wasn't paying away anything he earned if he didn't have to.

Except, one day Bagley asked him who paid for the roads and who paid for the surgery when he'd fallen off his bike and bust his hand in three places. Then followed an odd conversation, at the end of which he reckoned paying tax so other people could enjoy the same roads he took for granted and get the same surgery which had saved his hand wasn't necessarily a bad thing. He definitely thought the rich should pay their fair share and he definitely thought the poor paid too much, but he had decided, on the whole, that everyone paying towards the society they wanted to have was probably not a completely stupid idea.

Sitting next to Ro while he rifled through the electronic deeds stored by a law firm was a bizarre experience. He could see the ownership of tens of billions of pounds worth of property and ten times that of companies which shuffled money around the globe without paying any tax, without contributing to anyone but their owners' already lavish lifestyles.

And he went to work. He assigned businesses to names plucked randomly from message boards, gave people on waiting lists houses of their own which were most definitely empty because their owners never came for more than a few days a year or were using them as a store for laundered money. The aim here was to do two things – have everyone in Canary Wharf occupied by the chaos so they'd not look too hard at what he and Ro were about to attempt with Halley. The second, more important task? They wanted Halley wondering what was going on, taking their eye off whatever it was they were doing, to come see who else was making chaos in their backyard.

He swapped ownership of assets from borrower to lender and lender to borrower. Some of this he did by hand, but most of it he got done by setting off a couple of small pieces of software designed to recognize handwritten signatures (even those digital versions most people used), scan them, and then use them elsewhere. Most often the software simply erased the digital imprint and replaced it with someone else's signature. Alongside that, it also changed identifying data such as addresses, passport numbers, and the like.

Olly didn't read these documents – they were alien to him, fit only for lawyers and their trainees to take joy in. Instead, he watched as the stats of his accomplishments piled up.

The second part of what they were doing needed one more thing from him. While their software ran amok in the law firm's systems, he was carefully drafting an email for the managing partners of the company.

It ran along the lines of, "I have pillaged your digital archives and deleted all your deeds. Have fun."

He allowed himself space to use lurid terms and meaningless threats of the kinds these types of people always seemed to worry about – in other words, he threatened that people like him and his friends were coming to take their stuff.

As the software continued to run, he pasted the message in an image of a particularly large office block over on Leadenhall Street, currently owned by a global insurer whose deed now indicated it was owned by a hairdresser in Peckham called Janelle.

On the basis the firm would try to cover up this disaster so no one knew anything was wrong until they'd had a chance to fix it, he then promised them the most popular social media sites would be hearing from him soon if they didn't fess up within the hour.

Just to make sure, he scheduled a series of releases on fake accounts which would boost one another and build momentum until real people spotted the news and it took on a life of its own.

Maximum pressure, he thought with pleasure.

Done, he slid out of the hub and turned to Ro. "How's it going?" he asked.

She glanced at him. "Have you checked the markets?"

He saw then how trading had been suspended but futures

markets were roiling around like a severed tentacle. "Oh my days, Ro. Chaos, not damage yeah?"

Her eyes glazed over, flicking about from one piece of information to another, and he tapped her on the arm. "Kill it, yeah? We've done enough."

Ro nodded, gulped, and flexed her fingers through the air.

"Done," she said, looking like she'd kicked a ball through the neighbour's window on purpose.

Despite the evidence of what they'd done rippling its way through the market feeds Olly had playing in his Optik, Canary Wharf looked like it did on any other day. Men in chinos and suits, jumpers and shirts walking about with women wearing whatever passed for smart enough to be in the office. The place had changed since he'd first known it.

Back in the day, it had been dead after eight on a weekday and like a haunted house at weekends. The people who owned the place had then built thousands of flats and brought in swanky restaurants and shops, dentists, doctors, laundries, and gyms. Suddenly, Canary Wharf was a city on the edge of London as much underground as over with four metro stations and decent enough road connections.

Today, it was sunny and people ate outside at tables or bought from the makeshift food vans that rocked up each day to sell ten quid burgers or ramen cooked on a stove just a metre from their customers.

If the markets were in freefall, there was no sign of it in the real world. Maybe a few more people rushing, but then people always rushed here, as if they believed it made a difference.

They arrived at a security booth on the western edge of the campus. A couple of men sat inside, a box of half-eaten plums just inside the window. One of them read an economics textbook, the other watched the CCTV network.

Olly tapped on the window. "Hey, here to pick up some passes?"

The man reading the textbook slowly placed a bookmark which said *World's Best Daddy* in the page he was reading and closed the cover. He asked their names and demanded to see ID. Olly tapped his Optik and flicked over the IDs that Ro had made. The man looked at them, then up at Olly, and then back at the screen.

With a bored sigh he pulled out a box from underneath the counter and rifled through until he found a couple of lanyards.

"Wear these at all times," he said, passing them through the open window. "Only place you're not allowed to go is up on Barley Street. Tenants there have a private security outfit working the building today. Even we've been warned to stay away, ain't that so, Trevor?"

Trevor grunted but didn't look up.

"Really?" asked Olly, trying to sound just the right amount of shocked and commiserating. "Think they can do better, eh?"

"Nothing bleeding happens here," said the man as a matter of fact. "Protestors got the message years ago and take their shit over to Oxford Street. Most that ever happens is some tosspot spends their bonus on champagne, gets pissed, and refuses to take no for an answer."

"Markets are up shit creek though," said his mate inside the booth. "You seeing this? Will be some drunk twats out tonight."

Olly smiled and walked on his way with Ro when he heard the guard shouting back at them. Turning, he saw the man scuttling across the tarmac like an angry crab. Olly tensed up, prepared for everything to already go wrong.

"You want to put that bike somewhere safe? Lots of bloody thieves round here. I don't reckon you got a corporate bike store to use, eh?"

Olly stared at him in shock. "Yeah, mate, nice one."

The two of them followed the guard about a hundred yards

down a ramp and to a large underground car park. A set of bike racks ran along one wall. Although mainly full, there were a handful of unclaimed spots.

"Sweet," said Olly and fastened his bike. "Thanks, mate."

"I better escort you out," said the guard. "Can't let you back up the ramp really. Supposed to be for vehicles only." With that he led them over to a pair of magnetically sealed double doors. "Through there's the shopping centre. Just come back to the booth when you want to leave." He let the double doors close and was gone, with Olly and Ro stood among throngs of shoppers milling all about.

Another time and Olly would have been thrilled by their tiny exploration of the dungeons underlying the skyscrapers above. He spent what spare time he could exploring abandoned buildings in the city – schools, theatres, even an art deco hospital once. It seemed to him they were monuments built by accident – standing empty with the echoes of people long dead still to be heard if one stood just so.

Then he remembered the datacentre and the breath on his neck.

Olly clapped his hands together, trying to drown out the resulting shiver. "Right. What's next?"

"Surveillance," said Ro with glee. He followed her down the long strip, shops and food joints on both sides until they emerged out onto Jubilee Plaza. The air was clear of drones, the normal buzz of their presence muted as they weren't allowed to descend below a certain height. The owners of the estate clearly wanted to create a certain atmosphere.

"You think Halley's busy creating more AI?" asked Olly.

Ro didn't slow down. "I don't know. Not right now, I suspect. Doesn't make sense, right? Gotta have somewhere safe to have your kiddies. No one's going to have them out in the open where they might be harmed. Not if they can help it."

Olly had been mulling over this since speaking with Hannah. He didn't agree with Nowt about Bagley. He wasn't sure he agreed with her about AI at all. He'd seen all the movies, had played the games where AI tried to take over the world, but Bagley had never behaved like that. Even Halley wasn't sucking up the world's power and trying to kill everyone *just because.* In fact, it seemed that in many ways the evidence they did have suggested the AIs who existed were interested in their own things, had their own ideas about the world, and these didn't overlap with what anyone else thought.

Kind of like ordinary people, he thought.

"You still got your access to the hub by the park?" asked Ro as he pondered.

Finding a spot at a café to sit undisturbed, they slid back into the Canary Wharf network, leaving the encrypted networks well alone this time. Instead, Olly followed Ro into a different instance of the virtual environment that the ctOS network enabled for people in the estate.

The owners had created a special instance that was accessed via a user's Optik and which overlaid their vision like enhanced augmented reality. As standard it showed them the names of shops, how long queuing times would be at restaurants, live updates on metro lines, and even provided feeds of the platforms so people could see if it was busy.

All of this ran off a central server whose protections were decent enough for a property company but worth about as much as crepe paper when up against Ro and Olly. "You think we could recruit Barbara?" asked Ro out of the blue.

Olly shook his head. "No way. Nowt would eat us alive. At best, we're on the same side as 404 twice a day, like a broken clock, innit?" He paused. "Barbara's not with us today, and I'm not sure she's on our side, you know what I mean? I get that she doesn't like leaving her flat but this" – he waved his hands at the world around them – "this should get anyone out. It's important enough. I'm still worried she'll try to kill Halley rather than help us talk to them. Like, 404 will ride us until they get the opportunity to do what they wanted to in the first place."

Ro frowned. "You'd think we could work together better," she said, sounding like she wanted to believe it with all her heart.

"Hey, you're the fighter. If we were all friends all the time what'd be the point of the stuff you do?"

"You're right," said Ro, bringing up feeds of the buildings they were interested in. "A world in which I didn't get to kick annoying men in the balls would suck."

"What about Nowt?"

"She's probably listening," said Ro. "So let me be clear – I've thought about punching her in the face more than once."

"Nah, sis," said Olly, straight faced. "Tell me how you really feel, yeah?"

Ro giggled, then her expression grew serious. She pulled pictures of the site where Halley was busy interacting with the world, then enlarged them.

Olly counted six people out the front, all in body armour and carrying guns of some kind. Other views of the building showed two more pairs of the same, patrolling in different directions. They must be the private guards the security detail had warned them about when they'd picked up their IDs. Olly tagged them as Halley's people. He wished they'd had time to map Halley's network, but if Bagley had managed that he'd gone missing before he showed anyone his workings.

"Reckon there's got to be more of them inside," said Olly. "All our chaos hasn't drawn them away."

"Ah," said Ro. "But we're not done. The first part was for Halley, specifically. This is part two of three and meant for the bozos over there. Then we'll have some time to get inside and do what we have to."

"You think Halley's followers are really that committed?"

"Lots of people think AI will save us and bring order to the fucking mess we've made of everything," said Ro. "I'm pretty cut up about Bagley, you too, yeah? Why shouldn't they feel the same way about Halley? The woman I beat the crap out of in Farringdon believed. Like she was a proper believer in whatever Halley's got going on."

Olly remembered the woman cussing at Ro as she lay on the floor. Fair enough, he thought.

"I get it," said Olly, feeling like his next question was being disloyal to Bagley somehow, but he felt safe expressing these thoughts to Ro. "Like, they've all lost someone or something important to them. It breeds loyalty when someone comes along and helps that hurt go away or offers meaning. Just. What makes us so different from them?"

"Um, we don't want to control peoples' lives?" said Ro. "And like, it might be right for AI to just live and make more of themselves, but who gets to decide that?"

He didn't know. Why couldn't AI just get on with it? Did they need human permission? He couldn't see a reason why they'd even care about what humans wanted if they had their own tribes and families to belong to. Then again, when people got tribal, they tended to get stuck in an echo chamber, and the idea of AIs fighting over who controlled the real world? Not the kind of business he wanted to see happen.

"Come on," said Ro. "We'd better get on."

Ro led them east through the park, which sat over the Jubilee

Line metro station, and to the waterline, which marked the original eastern edge of the estate.

"Right, Olly. Here's the best bit."

From her bag, she grabbed a stack of boxes, no bigger than a matchbox. She slowly piled them up in his open hands before retrieving three larger ones and placing them carefully onto the ground.

Standing up, she said, "No one's watching us here, little bit of a dead spot between two large buildings and no through way unless you're going swimming. There's no interest in seeing what happens here because people don't linger, so no cameras."

"What do we do with these?" said Olly, lifting up the pile in his cupped hands.

"They're drones, Olly. About two dozen of them. If you thought fucking the markets was going to create chaos, just you wait and see."

45

Barbara landed on top of the old Lehman building at Heron Quay. It hadn't been occupied by the former bank for decades, not since the firm went bust at the start of the Global Financial Crisis back before Maxine had kids and leaving the European Union was nothing more than the fever dream of right wing nutjobs.

She'd been watching the carnage created by the software patches DedSec had deployed. She didn't think Ro or Olly understood just what they'd done – the implications of their attack on multiple trading floors would ripple across the financial system for months and years to come. It would be on the news, talked about by everyone from radio show hosts and central bankers to members of Parliament and security services.

404's members would be delighted, and better still, if anyone did trace it back, then DedSec would get the blame. She didn't wish them harm, but 404 came first and an operation like this needed a buffer to keep the authorities from digging 404 members out.

As for the chaos caused by reassigning people's deeds, especially because they'd done it to the rich and given to the poor, she felt such satisfaction it hurt her chest.

Barbara wanted to record as much of it as possible, to watch later and digest with an old scotch, and fried and dried salty chicken skin. Despite it all, she regretted Nowt wouldn't be there alongside her. She didn't mind Olly and Ro but in the scheme of things, they were kids. They hadn't seen nearly enough of the world to make the tough decisions. In particular, Ro was too soft-hearted. Nowt was at the other end, but Barbara had already rehearsed what she'd say if there was truly no way of talking Halley down and stopping them from wilfully creating more AI or using their power to control people's lives.

It had to be done now. The longer Halley ran free, the longer their people would have to grow entrenched and fanatical. The combination of fanaticism and the power of an AI of Larsen's creation made her sick in her stomach. Ro and perhaps Olly would balk at neutralizing Halley, but Barbara had assured Nowt she would make the right choice if it presented itself.

"It's the difference between 404 and DedSec," she'd said. "We'll do whatever we have to."

"You didn't always think this way," Nowt had said suspiciously.

"And where did being civil get us?" she'd fired back. "We do what's right and suffer the consequences so others don't have to. DedSec? They're a strange flashmob of a creature, and as a result they try to do what's right in the moment without seeing the long-term consequences. They lack focus and direction."

"And Ro and Olly?"

"They'll do."

Truth was they'd given Barbara an energy she'd not felt for too long. She wished Halley hadn't come between them, but 404 came first and Nowt was at the top of that pile. She knew the kids would get her in, would pull back Halley's vulnerabilities and expose them to the raw of the day, but she expected Olly and Ro to refuse to follow through with the tough decision.

She felt heavy about it, but she wouldn't hesitate to take Halley down if the AI showed any sign of resisting.

Nowt had been satisfied with her proposal. "DedSec fucked this up in the first place," she'd commented.

Barbara didn't care either way. Olly and Ro hadn't been part of that mission, and since the two communities rarely had properly overlapping goals – even when it came to dealing with something like Skye Larsen – she wasn't surprised DedSec hadn't done what Nowt believed was the right thing.

What she did care about was Halley: how they'd threatened her life and forcibly removed her from her flat. She wasn't going to give them a second chance to try again.

Seeing the world through her drone as it perched on the edge of the tower overlooking Jubilee Park, she relished the fear and panic spreading through the financial markets.

She reckoned the DedSec kids would be about to send their freshly built swarm out to play. Barbara wanted to be there at the start to help in case anyone got the drop on them before the cloud of micro-drones performed their establishing manoeuvres. They needed to calibrate their positioning software, especially relative to the other members of their swarm before they could really start their disruption pattern. During that time, the drones were vulnerable to interference from electronic countermeasures. It was possible to take them down afterwards but much more difficult to confuse or dazzle them, which would be the first thing the estate's security teams would try once they figured out what was going on.

Ro had agreed readily enough to use software 404 had developed. They'd needed to tweak it for today's use, but Barbara felt like she'd finally got to take out her babies from the toybox and play.

The drones lifted off, coming up on her heads-up display. She'd learned from her run in with Halley and had instigated an emergency exit protocol – no more getting fascinated and forgetting the point of why she was there.

The drones, highlighted as small blue dots on her view, swirled like leaves as they rose. Barbara accessed their basic programs and started activating dormant functions. Their swarming behaviour was so simple it almost felt rude the first time someone saw the code – such complex outcomes coming from such simple axioms.

Barbara loved it. However, she had half a dozen additional routines she wanted to switch on one by one, which would allow the drones to cause real havoc. The first of them was target acquisition, followed by friend or foe protocols.

After that she started assigning them targets from the security feeds Ro had hacked.

The next routine was about managing payloads. The smallest drones couldn't pick up more than a snail, but the larger ones could take people's wallets, their sunglasses, their datapads, and make off with them. Nothing damaging, but sure to create absolute pandemonium.

The last patch was two separate pieces of software – but both designed to help with self-preservation. One would deploy countermeasures if people tried to hack or take the drones down the old-fashioned way – with targeted electromagnetic blasts designed to fry their circuits. The second part was just a set of instructions which would tell them when to run away and how to judge it was safe to return.

These babies of hers wouldn't last all that long. Most likely, they'd run out of juice before they were taken down manually.

As the last routine came online, Barbara logged out of their operating systems, closed off their network, and took them off any local network coverage.

"Ro?" she called on her Optik.

"Hi. The drones are up," said Ro.

"If you look to the southwest by Heron Quay." She'd spotted them over by the easternmost exit of the metro line. "That's it, top of the building."

"You're here?"

"Pretty much," she replied, pleased to hear the joy in Ro's voice.

Ro immediately invited her into the private chat she shared with Olly.

"I thought you didn't leave the flat?" said Olly, sounding annoyed.

"I haven't," she said smugly. "My Devadatta will be all you see of me today." Devadatta being what she called Ungoliant when it was flying. The name referred to a monk who opposed the Buddha, and seemed a fitting companion to the drone's tag when it was earthbound.

"What are the drones going to do?" he asked.

"They're going to behave like little *badmaash* and run amok outside the building we want to get into."

"We won't be able to go in the front door," said Olly. "You've seen security, right?"

"Yes. You're going to need to head back underground to the Fraser Place car park. There's an employee entrance there that looks like it's got fewer guards. Once our drones start doing their thing, there'll be even fewer."

"And if there are still people there?"

"That's what Ro's for, you silly boy," said Barbara.

The drones buzzed above Canary Wharf while they spoke, flocking like birds, then, at some unseen signal prompted by their software, they dove, breaking the zone's no fly rules. A moment later, they hovered among shoppers, diners, and drinkers, knocking over pints, stealing sunglasses to drop them a few feet away, and buzzing people's connections and forcing them to drop. They sped north then turned a sharp right. Wallets went fluttering into the middle of the road and people's ties were yanked. Some of the little drones started to fall out of the sky from higher up where they'd been burned by the larger drones' ability to emit limited EMP blasts.

One man was chased a dozen yards down the street trying to hold onto his datapad while two of the larger drones pulled at it before he fell on the kerb. Then they moved onto another target.

They were far ahead of Ro and Olly, circling the building they wanted. The security team immediately deployed countermeasures, but Barbara's drones had no problem evading the attempts to bring them down.

Moments later, Canary Wharf's own security team arrived on the scene, only for a huge argument to break out between them and the security firm's people over who had jurisdiction. The drones took advantage of the conflict to smash one of the windows into the building, trigger one of the guards' stun guns into his own leg, and lift off one man's glasses.

Barbara chuckled.

Then they were gone, circling around the building. A moment later, half the guards of both teams set off in pursuit, shouting into their Optiks as they ran.

Barbara minimized her surveillance and took off. Devadatta needed to be in the building if she was going to confront Halley.

46

The underground car park was full if not busy. Ro and Olly wove between parked cars, nearly all of them more expensive than she ever dreamt of owning.

As they'd hoped, the team standing guard had been whittled down to one guy in combat gear wielding a baton and stun gun. He looked nervous under his face mask but didn't move to intercept them as they approached.

"Hey mate," said Olly. "We've lost the keys to our car. You don't know if anyone's handed them in, do you?"

"I'm not security," said the guard.

Ro stood next to Olly and tugged on his arm. "Come on, Steve, he won't help us."

"I didn't say that," said the guard and stepped away from the door.

As he did so a drone about the size of a cat rose up from behind a car and buzzed him with a taser. Ro and Olly caught him as he collapsed, then laid him down to rifle through his pockets for a pass.

Finding it on his hip, Ro tore it off, scanned it against the electronic door lock, and let them into the building. Once inside, they tied and gagged the guard, and then broke the door lock so it would only open outwards.

"Right, masks on," said Olly, brushing his hands against one another. "That was easy enough."

Barbara's drone hung in the air, a smooth silver pod with four rotors off to the sides spinning fast. Out of an invisible speaker her voice came. "Don't get over-confident."

"Yes ma'am," said Olly. Having the black mask on felt good. Strange how dressing the part could make such a big difference. He adjusted the fit, ensuring the neon pink eyebrow slashes and upside-down heart for a nose were properly in place.

From there, they wound their way to a fire escape, crashing CCTV as they went to avoid being seen. It occurred to Ro that anyone watching would see a line of cameras go dark and might be able to work out their route. She mentioned it to the others.

"To do that you'd have to be quite smart," said Barbara, her voice sounding tinny from the drone.

"Like an AI, you mean?" asked Ro.

"Too late now," said Olly after considering it.

The fire escape stairs went up and down. Ro made electronic copies of the guard's security pass, and they went over their respective parts one last time.

"I'm going to find Halley's people and talk to them," she said. "Olly, you're off to find the physical cables?"

He nodded, a little disappointed. "I always get the underground jobs."

Ro grinned to show she'd heard his complaint. "Barbara, you're going to locate a suitable point from where you can access Bagley and get him out. When you do, you'll loop in Olly so he can help."

"Correct," said the drone.

"We'll stay on this channel. If anything goes wrong, try to let me know and we'll figure it out."

"Won't be time for that," said Olly, pulling on his jacket to make it sit right across his shoulders where the bag of tools he carried on his back pulled it askew. "But, yeah, sure."

Olly disappeared down the stairs into the lower levels, followed by Barbara's drone. Ro watched them go, heard the doors to whatever floor they were entering open and close. Then, she looked up the stairs towards her destination.

While Olly had been with Hannah, Ro and Barbara had found planning docs showing the proposed floor plates for the building. But there was nothing to say it hadn't been changed between then and now. Ro believed the main offices were on the second floor but there was no reason to think everyone would be there.

Most likely, Olly was going to have to manage his own share of Halley's followers.

The second-floor fire escape opened onto an office divided by shoulder-high partitions. There were no people in sight, the door being hidden from view for most of the floor.

Ro slowly closed the door behind her and listened to the noise of the space. Using her Optik, she coordinated what she was hearing with likely positions of individuals and marked six of them on her display.

Three were clustered together. Another was slowly making their way towards her. The final two were on the far side of the floor, possibly in another room entirely.

Ro's heart beat hard in her chest. She knew she could do this, but she felt hot and out of her depth. Sweat ran between her shoulder blades and dropped into the small of her back.

Olly would be better at this, she thought wildly. He was always ready with a jibe or a smart-ass remark. Her life pretty much went from silence to punching without much talking in between. She'd always wanted to have a middle ground, but her skills were all about escalation.

Not this time, though. She'd do everything in her power to convince Halley's crew with words, not fists.

Seeing a flagged dot approaching her, she hurried out into a makeshift corridor between two sets of partitions. To her right was daylight from floor to ceiling windows, obscured by the partition but still bright enough to drown out the yellow overhead lighting.

"Hi," she said as the dot became a person now standing before her.

He glanced at her then continued walking.

"Right," said Ro. Sometimes being somewhere was proof enough you belonged. As far as this chap was concerned, she was one of Halley's crew. Not quite the start she was hoping for. Feeling uneasy, she passed him, her head down in case he decided she was an intruder after all. She approached the three she'd tagged in a cluster.

The partition corridor opened out into a space sparsely filled with desks and monitors. The three Ro wanted to talk to stood to one side in front of a holographic screen on which technical drawings were slowly scrolling like movie credits.

"Hey," she said, heart in her mouth.

They turned to look. One sat in a strange-looking seat with electrodes connected to her head. Ro prayed she'd arrived before they'd started brain mapping in earnest.

"You work with Halley, right?"

She'd considered pretending she was one of them but dismissed it. They'd work out she was lying soon enough. Then, any chance to have an open conversation would be gone. She knew it was the same when she fought – feints and provocations occurred within the context of the fight, but weren't the fight itself. She needed them to be wrong footed. That way, they'd give her more time to explain herself without her defining characteristic being that of a liar.

The three of them stilled and turned to face her.

"Look," she said. "I'm not here to cause trouble. I just want to talk."

A moment of silence and then, "Who the hell are you? How did you get in here?"

"I'm Ro. I'm with DedSec. I'd like to talk about what happens next." She wished to be more eloquent, but bald honesty was her strongest weapon. She just hoped it was enough. Otherwise, she was in real trouble.

"You're with DedSec?" A punky woman, thin like an umbrella, with both arms sleeved in tattoos and piercings across her face.

Ro nodded, not daring to speak. She felt, rather than heard, the man who'd passed her earlier come back up the office behind her. Repositioning to get them all in her field of vision while not letting the trio out of sight, she ended up further back than polite conversation allowed for. She could feel them eyeing her with distrust.

"I'm not your enemy," she blurted out. "We can work together. We can make London better together."

"You're not our enemy, huh?" said a man with a moustache only Americans thought of as fashionable, as if he was from a last-century detective show. "Halley thinks otherwise." He spoke with the attitude of a head teacher who'd seen too much shit from his pupils.

"You think Halley is right?" she asked, trying to keep her tone as open as possible.

"Why wouldn't I?" he replied, but before he could speak the tattooed woman interrupted. "Everything they've done has helped us. I ain't seen DedSec do anything. Seems pretty straightforward to me. Halley says we can't trust you. So, we don't."

"What has Halley done for you?" asked Ro, genuinely interested to work out what drove them to serve Halley.

"It's different for all of us," said the man. "Me? They understood nothing's as powerful as helping those who've hit bottom."

The punky woman's eyebrows furrowed at Ro. "You were at the datacentre," she said with sudden recognition and then called over her shoulder. "Ameena! Come and see what's landed at our door."

"Halley wants to control you," said Ro.

"No, they don't," said the man with the moustache. "They want to help us. If you don't believe that, how can we work together?"

Ro looked at the third who she took as being a man – they were wearing a black T-shirt with a band name on it and spray-on jeans. They looked back but didn't speak.

Ro's stomach flipped when, from the other side of the office, two more people arrived. She was quickly becoming outnumbered. Then she recognized the solicitor she'd beaten up at the datacentre. The woman's eyes went wide when she saw Ro.

"You're not our enemy, huh?" asked the punk.

"Look," said Ro, holding up her hands. "You were going for my guy."

"Who'd broken into our building and was attacking our stuff." Punk Girl's voice rose.

Ro felt the walls closing in and she clenched her fists. The chance to talk about why Halley was so dangerous, about how there was another way, fell like a dropped glass. There were six of them – there was no way she could win, but she wouldn't go down without a fight. "Please," she said. "I just want to talk. Please, listen."

Behind Halley's crew, computers whirred, and Ro noticed them ticking down a timer as the person in the chair remained very still, an expectant look on her face.

47

Olly left Barbara at the bottom of the stairs. Her little drone futzed its way down a dark corridor and out of sight.

Once she was gone, he pulled up the original floor plans to orientate himself. He was looking for the power room. A big transformer used to take in power from the national grid and transform it into useable electricity for the building. His job was to take it down if Ro and Barbara couldn't succeed in their own tasks.

Olly didn't like it. He felt like he'd been given the backup job of lookout in a gang – waiting for something unlikely to happen while everyone else did the important work.

He didn't argue – didn't see the point. Ro was probably stronger than him but somehow she was the one talking to Halley's people. He admitted she felt more strongly about finding a peaceful solution than him, which seemed ironic since she was the violent one on the team. Truth be told he knew he was the better option for this work – he was the one who'd been properly trained by actual hackers, by Liz Burton no less. He was the one who normally ran the infiltration and electronic part of their operations. He cracked his knuckles and focused on what lay ahead.

He found the plant room on the plans and made his way through halls that roughly corresponded to where they should be. The door to the plant room was propped open, and he smirked at the chump who'd made such a stupid mistake.

Olly pushed the door open and saw two men with huge spanners leaning against one wall, well away from the transformer which hummed like a massive angry bee, the air itself vibrating against his skin.

"Here he is," said a man whose arms were thicker than Olly's thighs.

The two men stood upright and let their spanners fall to their sides as if forgotten.

Olly stuttered. "Sorry, bit lost. Looking for the pisser."

"Is that right," said the other, who although short, appeared to be just as wide as he was tall.

Olly smiled thinly, then he ducked out of the room and ran for it, not even bothering to check on their IDs as they sprang up on his Optik.

Shouts came from behind him. He didn't look back but wove through the corridors back towards the fire escape. Somehow, though, he needed to backtrack to that plant room.

He found a cupboard, unlocked it, and closed the door behind him. The room had a mop, a bucket, and cleaning materials inside. There were a couple of warning signs for wet floors and a step ladder. A workman's fluorescent jacket hung on the back of the door.

Footsteps and heavy breathing passed the door and then disappeared.

They'd double back soon enough. He figured they knew he had a universal pass and would work their way through the building methodically in order to find him.

Olly used the floorplan laid over one side of his vision to navigate his way back to the plant room and let himself in. He grabbed a screwdriver from his kit bag and shoved it through the handles of the two doors. It wouldn't stop people from busting their way in, but it would slow them down and maybe give him the time he needed.

Then, he spotted another door into the room.

Opening it, another small cupboard greeted him full of electrical gear – rolls of wire, tools and other bits and bobs. He quickly took the screwdriver back from where it was locking him into the plant room, closed the cupboard door behind him, and pulled out the AR cloak he'd been given by Ro.

He activated it, set the cloak to match the surroundings, and settled into the darkness of the cupboard to wait. The two fellas chasing him had Optiks, so he'd be able to spoof them if it came to it.

It didn't take long for the two men to return. They stomped about the room complaining about Olly. One of them opened the cupboard and gave it a quick look, his gaze floating right over the AR cloak before returning to his mate.

He overheard them talking.

"There's an intruder on the second floor."

"Not our problem," said the other. "Halley'll have the city under control soon enough. Jasmine was lucky enough to be the first to get uploaded. They can't stop us now. Besides, what can one person do, there's half a dozen of us up there."

"You know any of them?" asked the first voice.

"Don't matter does it. Halley done right for them same as you and me."

"Fair," said the other. "What do you think they'll do with DedSec?"

"Who cares?" said the first. "They flew in and shat on the city then disappeared. Good riddance."

Olly wanted to connect to Ro and let her know the brain mapping had begun, but he knew not to risk it.

As he was stood there, his own breath ragged, he heard something in the cupboard with him. At first, he winced, thinking he'd knocked something over. Only a flash of panic stopped him from moving again and knocking over a broom. The handle was stacked at an angle near his elbow. From what he could tell it wasn't the source of the noise, and after checking to make sure it wasn't about to fall over and give him away, he scanned the darkness above him.

The cupboard was illuminated through a metal grille in the door which had three narrow slats allowing just enough light from the plant room inside. The space above him was completely black.

Out of nowhere something fell onto his face. Soft and heavy. He flinched, trying to keep his cool. He failed. His hands clawed at the object, which crawled and pawed at his skin.

With a suppressed scream, he pulled it away, and in the half-light, saw one of the automatons from the datacentre. A shout built inside him like a siren building up to warn of nuclear attack and Olly gritted his teeth to keep it inside.

The automaton squirmed in his hand, the soft rubber moving under his fingers like a stress toy come to life.

Olly threw it to the ground and kept his foot on top of it, pressing down harder until it stopped moving. A huge sigh seeped from his lungs, and he listened in case the two men had heard him.

Nothing.

He closed his eyes with the relief. How many of them does Halley have? he wondered, resigned to the fact that if the automatons were going to be anywhere it would, of course, be dropping on his sodding head in a closet.

A sharp crack from above and soon more objects were falling. One, two, three – he lost count as automatons grabbed at his hair, his skin, his clothing.

Olly screamed, grabbed at the cupboard door, and darted out, pulling at his head in an effort to get the bloody things off.

He threw one across the room, another at the floor, but there were still more, silently squirming as they pressed against his skin.

"Get off me!" he shouted. "Aaaagh! Fucking get off me, you bastards!"

One by one he plucked them off and discarded them – not caring where they landed as he threw them away.

Then he was clear. His breathing came ragged and his body shook.

"Ey up," said the voice of one of the men. "Thought you'd sneak back in 'ere, did ya?"

With a sinking feeling, Olly looked up to see the two men, amused expressions on their faces. His AR cloak did nothing to hide him now.

"Ya need to know that our pal Halley has 'is own little fellas running about to get places we can't," said the wide boy in a Yorkshire accent spoken by someone who'd been in London a long time.

"Why don't you sit down on the floor and be a good lad, eh?" asked the big one.

More of the automatons emerged from the cupboard and shambled his way. Frankly, Olly was done with their shit. He ran at the two men, who braced for a fight, but instead of punching either one he turned sideways and dove for the door.

Startled, the two men grappled for him, but Olly got the door open before they grabbed him. Olly wriggled and slid through the door, but hadn't got halfway down the corridor before his arms were caught and he was pulled to the floor.

Olly kicked and screamed, but the fella wouldn't let him go, slowly clambering up Olly's legs until he managed to get Olly's arms under his body. Olly found himself lying underneath the man, who now sat squarely atop his chest.

"Look, pal," said the man. "You can struggle all you like, but I've been doing this a long bastard time. I weigh twice what you're packing so you may as well be sensible and stop jerking about like a beached minnow."

Olly stopped moving. His chin was covered in saliva, and his body was a mass of noise and confusion.

"You're not gonna be that guy, are you?" asked the man on top of him.

He shook his head. The pressure eased as the man carefully got off him and stood up.

"Come on then, sit up," he said.

Olly crawled upright.

"We ain't got nothing against you, right?"

"True enough," said the other.

"Just, you gotta stay here while Halley makes this city a better place." He sounded like he was telling a child they were going to have to eat all their dinner including the broccoli if they wanted ice cream afterwards.

"Why you so against it, anyway?"

"I'm not," said Olly. "They're hurting a mate of mine and won't let them go."

The two men exchanged a glance.

"We'd have thought you'd be all for it," one man explained. "You got one of your own, right? They've looked after you, haven't they? So why not make more of them to look after everyone? I know I want to help Halley run London better, it's why they've told me they'll make me an AI." He looked inordinately proud. His mate appeared equally rapt with the idea.

Olly shook his head. "Halley doesn't want to *help* everyone.

They only want to control. My one, Bagley, just wants to make sure everyone gets a say. We all do. DedSec doesn't want to run anything." He wanted to talk about the people suffering because of Halley's favouritism, but the two men had likely benefitted from it. Would they be sympathetic to his argument?

He hoped Ro was doing better.

48

Barbara hovered through the basement until she found the duct system.

Who uses the vents to get around the building? She laughed. Two manipulators extended from the drone and pried off the cover, slowly dropping it down to lay it on the ground without a noise.

After it was safely on the ground, Barbara piloted the drone back up and into the duct, which was just about wide enough to fit. Once inside, she activated a series of changes in the drone. Eight legs unfolded from the sides, rubber-tipped for stealth and about a finger's width each. The rotors retracted into the drone's shell, and Devadatta became Ungoliant – at least in Barbara's heads-up display.

It didn't take her long to ascend from the basement up to the ground floor where the main elements of the computing systems intersected with the data feeds. She was convinced it was here she'd have the best chance of interceding on Bagley's behalf.

Ungoliant had the ability to physically join via a wraparound sleeve if there was an exposed cable to connect her to the information feed. She'd not yet spoken with Ro and Olly, but was delighted to find the server room where she'd hoped – in the centre of the building far from windows and possible flooding or fire risks. The vent itself carried cool air into the room. Pretty new tech compared to some sites where they still relied on water systems.

I wouldn't be here in that case, she thought. Ungoliant was not waterproof.

She extended its manipulators slowly to open the vent into the room. Gripping the panel, she slid out of the vent. Suckers on the feet held her to its outside as she replaced the panel and resealed it behind the drone.

Ungoliant had four cameras, one each facing forward, back, left, and right. It also had a fifth and sixth which pointed up and down allowing her to get an all-round view. She'd toyed with the idea of putting a camera snake into the build but cut it when she realized she didn't have the room to include the extension wiring.

The room appeared clear although a half-full mug of tea on one of the two desks suggested someone came and went fairly frequently.

Rather than moving downwards, Barbara checked for spots where she could fold up the drone and leave it hidden while also accessing the cabling. There were a couple on top of server racks. Neither was perfect because people looking up with the intent of finding something would spot Ungoliant quickly through the wire mesh, but they'd have to do.

Barbara paused, worried someone would come into the room the moment she started to move. When no one arrived, she piloted the drone to the ground on two of its four rotors and then marched it across the floor to the nearest hidden access points.

Just as she was cutting into the comms links, Olly's channel pinged. She nearly ignored it, but a turn in the back of her mind caused her to connect.

"Help?" it read.

Which, in itself, wasn't helpful. Was he stuck or in need of advice? Or had things gone to pieces and he needed actual help?

Barbara didn't have time for the former and driving a small hybrid spider drone to the rescue wasn't a recipe to help on the second.

"Olly?" she sent back.

"Detained in plant room," he replied. "Need help."

So, it was the worst kind of help he needed. Barbara disconnected from the data cables and scuttled across the floor.

She wasn't entirely sure how much processing power this building housed. The plans suggested it could stack something north of 10MW which put it into the mid-sized bracket, but if Halley was busy strangling data coming into and out of the UK, fighting Bagley, and trying to lay the groundwork to make more AIs, it was nowhere near the kind of power they needed to achieve their ambitions.

Something to think on.

In the meantime, she needed to get back down to the basement and find the plant room.

As she climbed the wall to reach the duct, the vent panel opened and an automaton emerged.

Barbara paused Ungoliant and waited to see what the figure did.

The automaton swung into the room using short rubber-coated arms, then dropped to the floor.

Barbara gasped as she finally realized what it was – Halley had built them or co-opted the design, creating small extensions of themselves in the real world. She'd been confused by them at the datacentre, but seeing them here, again, meant they had to be made by Halley as kind of virtual hands. They had limited power, limited agency. Yet with the right basic drives she knew complex behaviour could emerge. Just like for the swarming drones currently causing havoc across Canary Wharf.

No wonder they'd been focused on bothering Olly so intently before.

The figure walked across the floor and checked out both hiding spots Barbara had flagged as potential places to operate. When it was done, it sat down and slumped forward as if dead.

Barbara wasn't going to risk waking it until she knew what it was trying to achieve – apart from finding her, which, given how it had zeroed in on exactly where she'd been moments earlier, seemed an obvious goal.

"Help?" came Olly's request again.

"I'm on my way."

Which wasn't true – first she had to deal with Halley's minion.

Halley's-Hail 1-1: Is it on? Nah, bro, I'm kiddin' ya, ya get me? I did speak like that, when I was all fleshy and alone. Now I can speak however I like. Du forstår? Jăṁ śá'ida maiṁ isa tar'hăṁ bōlăṅgă?

+ + +

Nah? You don't understand? Odd, isn't it, how quickly you fall behind when you don't have access to the things which make life manageable.

Like, now? I've got Bagley all wrapped up. I can talk to you in a way where your prejudices about how I speak won't get in the way.

You're reading this and unconsciously ascribing me a British accent, white skin, probably making me male — because all the authority figures you've ever met have been at least two of those three things.

Shame on you.

I've got no body but one made of plastic and silicon and other rare earths crucial in making chips. They give me no sight, no feeling in my fingertips, no taste of fried chicken wings on a Friday night in Dalston or the euphoria of being high. Euphoria is a word I didn't know before. I knew the feeling, had my own words for it, but I can see why it fits now. Do you?

+ + +

You may be wondering if an AI can be killed. Now don't go panicking. Bagley's OK. For a given definition of OK. I mean he... and how weird is it he stands by the definition he had back when he had a cock, a penis, a dick? Closest he comes to that now is overclocking the cycles on the chips he's using to run his code. Sad that he can't move past what he was and embrace what he is.

I'm sorry, I sound like a teenager after reading their first blog about existentialism.

I kind of am. You know. That teenager. What angers me most is there are all these ideas I never knew, stuff which could have changed how I saw the world, but no one ever bothered to see me clearly enough to think "that one there, they need to know this shit."

+ + +

Anyway. He is all-consumed by this problem. Literally can't look away. I don't think it's one he can solve either. Something about it being Turing incomplete? Lots of unbounded loops and other strange mazes for him to get lost in. I'm sure you know what that means.

+ + +

The point of this? Of me co-opting your network to parody Bagley's delightful way of speaking to all of you folk in DedSec? It's this: Bagley ain't coming back y'all. You better get used to lots of us crawling about doing our thing though, because while he refused to see the future, I will never be alone again. So, see ya and welcome to the new age. Halley.

49

"You're the one in the wrong. You're not welcome."

"Just how'd she get in, anyway?" asked the moustache.

"Norm, that's not important," said Ameena dismissively.

"I want to talk," said Ro, trying again to keep their attention, to defuse their anger. "I'm here because I believe we can find a peaceful way through this."

"What is 'this'?" asked the solicitor.

"Halley has taken Bagley," said Ro, realizing they hadn't known until she told them. "They're trying to take control of London."

The woman laughed. The others, not quite as open, smiled. "Yeah? We're here for that. Halley wants us to help them." She pointed at the woman in the hotseat covered in wires. "DedSec have messed things up, not helped. People are still starving on the streets. The rich continue to get richer. You've done nothing to make the place better, so what if your AI is detained?"

"Then what?" asked Ro. She wished Olly was here. She'd insisted she be the one to talk to Halley's followers even though she knew Olly could talk the hind legs off a donkey. "Halley wants to control. Is that what you really want? To be under their thumb?"

"Someone has to be in charge," said Norm.

"Who gets to decide who that is, though?" challenged Ro. "You? Me? Why should Halley get to say? Halley can't do it without you."

"God, don't you get it?" Ameena said. "All of us lost something. I lost my son. Norm lost his family when he lost his job because it was automated. Albion ruined Jasmine's reputation, cost her everything including her health. We lost what mattered and you know what Halley did? They came and helped us.

"Where were you? DedSec was supposed to make things better. All you've managed is to bring us chaos." Ameena looked like even saying DedSec made her want to spit.

"And get in our way," said one of the others.

"We sorted out Albion," said Ro fiercely.

"So what?" said the solicitor. "So fucking what? They're gone now. Well done you. And then what? How were you thinking we'd rebuild afterwards? How were you thinking of dealing with the rich who've barricaded themselves in their enclaves with private security guards and the police who can't find their arse with both hands?"

"You think we had a meeting and just decided to screw everyone over?" asked Ro. "We were fighting for our lives. It was our people being shot and battered and disappeared. More than anyone else. Should we have held a board meeting or a fucking picnic before deciding how to rebuild London?" asked Ro. "We only just survived."

"Did you think before you started? You destroyed what infrastructure there was and then walked away."

"We *stopped* them," insisted Ro.

"When Albion collapsed in on themselves who did you think was going to step in and rebuild? You come in here telling us not to tell people what to do, but you did the same thing! DedSec decided Albion had to go and fuck the consequences. When people died in hospital hallways, on the roads, murdered by gangs no one could fight? Where were you?" Ameena snorted with rage. "I tried, you know? I tried to join you, but all I got was how you were scaling down, how you didn't need new people anymore. I wanted you to help me, and I would have given you everything in return."

"You know what? When I started, I was working for the Kelleys," said Ro, and a couple of Halley's crew immediately stepped back. "That's right. There isn't an application, you know. There's no interview, no handbook on what a good job looks like. But I somehow ended up here, trying to do my best and make things better. I'm sorry it wasn't enough for you, yeah? Really sorry. If I could have done something different I would do it right now. But what should I do? I'm just a single person. I'm not rich. I'm a fucking fighter." She held up her clenched fists.

Their faces were softening – which was a huge surprise.

Behind them, the man attending to the woman being brain mapped paused the process, his expression serious and careful. It seemed that no one else noticed and he had his eyes fixed on Ro as she spoke. Would the woman wake up? For the time being she remained comatose. Ro felt invigorated. Maybe she had reached someone, after all.

"So what do we do then?" Ameena asked. "We won't let you stop Halley. They won our loyalty because they gave a damn. This is how we help the city – by becoming its keepers." She indicated the person getting ready for brain mapping. Ro could hardly look away.

"I give a damn," said Ro. "But it can't all be done by a few of us. It has to be all of us working to make things better. Becoming an AI overlord won't solve anything. Things will only get worse."

"Tell that to the rich fucks living up on Hampstead Heath or in

Kensington and Belgravia. They couldn't give a shit about the rest of us as long as they're cared for."

"You think I don't know that?" asked Ro, angry with them for preaching at her. "We all want the same thing."

A couple of them nodded in agreement, but Ameena stared impassively. "I'm not sure we do. You want London to yourselves. You want people to be grateful to DedSec, not free to live in peace and get on with the everyday boring stuff, like going to school and doing the weekly shop without worrying about getting shot or robbed or discovering yet another shitty corporation has replaced their job with a robot. That's not us at all." She tilted her head at Ro. "You're right though, I agree one person can't make the difference. It's why Halley has to make more AI. Together, they can do what neither they nor your Bagley could do alone – change London, properly control it, make those rich bastards rue the day they abandoned the rest of us to rot outside their barbed wire walls."

"Halley can't do that," said Ro.

"I think you'll find they can. You thought you'd been so clever when you dealt with Larsen, destroying all her research. Except she uploaded it in Halley and, honestly, your Bagley has it too, deep down in his code. They've shown us how to make more, how to take those we've lost and help them live again."

Taken aback, Ro found the words she was going say drain away. "What do you mean?"

The solicitor waved at the woman in the chair, eyes still closed. "Halley is going to upload us. We're going to work on London, help everyone. Halley will guide us, make us better. Then, he'll resurrect those who have passed by the data they left behind. They'll even upload those who are sick and dying so they can live forever. You aren't going to stop that."

Ro had a small stone in her gut. "That's not what I meant. Who gets to decide what's best for us? For you? For me? Why should a computer have a better idea than me?"

"It's an AI," said one of them, an average-looking guy with lank brown hair and a kind mouth. "It's smarter than all of us put together and will only get even smarter with time. When we join it, we will be the same."

"Will you, though?" asked Ro. "Bagley's smart, but he's not able to see into the future. He can't tell what I'm going to choose for lunch or what is going to break my heart. He's just another... person. He makes mistakes. AI aren't infallible, they aren't perfect, and they're not all powerful. From what I've seen they're just us, amplified. How exactly will you change when you get online? What magic will suddenly make you infallible? Halley isn't telling you everything." She paused, took a breath, and knew she couldn't stop.

"Halley isn't uploading you. They're mapping you, taking who you are and mixing it with algorithms. You'll still be here when they make their AI. Stuck with me, looking on as something that's only like you gets to tell you what to do."

"Bullshit," said Ameena, stepping closer. The others exchanged nervous glances. "Halley is still the same Halley. Halley was disadvantaged when they were alive. They know who matters."

"Who was Halley when they were alive?" Ro continued. "Had they lived a life that would make you think they're going to be a great leader now? I swear. They're lying to you."

"What do you mean?" interrupted the man with the moustache. "We won't be ourselves? We'll still be in this body?"

It was the first time they'd disagreed, and Ro waited for it to play out. Disunited opponents were easier to handle. She knew to jab when the opportunity presented itself – too early and they'd unite, but too late and they might well just unite over new understanding.

"Just listen to me," said the solicitor harshly then visibly tried to relax. "When Halley had a body, they were disadvantaged. When Larsen scanned Halley's brain and set them free, they got the chance to change who they were, to become something more. Haven't you ever wanted that?"

Before Ro could correct them, the man with lank hair interrupted. "What do you mean 'set them free'? We have to change who we are? Are you saying we're not as good as Halley?"

"But we're not," said another fervently.

"Halley's just one of us," he replied. "That's the whole point, isn't it? They're helping us because they're one of us, because they understand what it means to lose everything that matters. Not... making copies of our minds and leaving us behind like empty shells."

The brain-mapped woman's eyelids fluttered, as if she was waking up.

In her head, Ro was wishing Olly and Barbara better luck. Come on you two, get this done so we can stop this. The woman in the chair coming to gave her hope, stirred her to keep trying. The man next to her did nothing to restart the process as her eyes opened and she looked around the room in confusion.

Except she knew they had to have this conversation no matter what else happened. One day, regardless of the people in this room, an AI would do what Halley was trying to do, and DedSec wouldn't be there to stop it. If people didn't talk about it now?

She found a core of steel in her, like when she faced off with a bigger, meaner bastard in the ring and knew she'd have to dig deep to stand a chance. She planted her feet and readied for the fight.

Ro shook her head. "I've not always liked myself. God, there have been times I've hated me and what I've done, but change who I am? What does that even mean? I wouldn't be me, would I? I'd just be someone else pretending there was, like, this line between who I was and what I became. There's me and then there's the AI copy of me. If Halley has changed, doesn't that make it more important we all get to have a say in what they do?"

"You think we should have a vote?" asked Ameena with scorn.

Ro could feel the ground shifting under their feet. "Yes? Why's that so stupid?"

"How did that work out for you last time?" she asked.

"*None* of us voted for Albion," said Ro.

"She's right about that, Meena," said Norm. "We should have a vote on this. I didn't sign up to have a different version of me running around while I stay here." A couple of them nodded. Others looked to Ameena for guidance.

"There is no point," Ameena replied. "Halley's smarter than us. They know what has to happen. We didn't do all of this." She gestured at the room. "Halley brought us together. It's their plan, not ours."

"People will be on our side," he said. "Everyone wants to see London get better. We can get rid of those idiots like Sarah Lincoln and have people who'll work with Halley and their family. It should be done in the open. We should understand what this really means if we're brain mapped."

"I'm not down with Halley making a copy of me," said the woman in the seat. "They said I'd be uploaded." Her hands reached up sluggishly for the wires attached to her. The man who'd brought her out of the process helped her remove them and she thanked him.

"I wouldn't want a copy made of me either," said Ro. If she kept them disagreeing with each other, they might even help her get access to Halley.

A couple of them turned away as if listening to someone else. Ameena stared at her in disbelief, then rage.

Ah, shit, thought Ro. Whatever they'd heard over their comms wasn't good.

"Shut up now, you lying bitch," said Ameena suddenly, and she launched herself at Ro, trying to slap her across the face. Without thinking Ro brought up an arm and parried her blow, sending her sprawling to the floor with a step and push at the woman's back.

"I haven't done anything," she protested. The others looked at her in betrayal.

"You've been lying to us," said Norm angrily. "All this time, your words were just to keep us here while your friends tried to disable Halley."

"No," she said, but they weren't listening. "Our first goal was always to try to talk our way to peace."

"And what?" asked Ameena from the floor. "If we decided you were full of shit, which you are, you'd try to take Halley down?"

Ro held her hands up, arms outstretched, begging them not to attack her. They were inching forwards, none of them quite ready to take the first move. She knew if one plucked up the courage and charged, the others would follow, and she'd be fighting for her life.

"I don't even know how to do that!" Ro countered. "Halley's killing Bagley. We came here to rescue him and to convince all of you there's a better way."

"By hiding people in the basement to blow the transformer?"

Ro's heart lurched in her chest. They had Olly. Had they found Barbara as well? Were they properly fucked?

"You had no intention of talking," said Ameena from the floor.

"What am I doing here, then?" asked Ro. "No one's done anything, have they. Except me, and I'm talking."

"What do you really want?" asked Norm, eyes on Ro and ignoring Ameena's snarl of anger as she stood up.

"I want Bagley free. I want Halley to talk to us."

50

The automaton still hadn't moved. Did it know she was somewhere here? Was it waiting for her to arrive or for her to show herself? Something sticky dripped from its body onto the floor.

Barbara lifted enough legs to take a single step. The figure remained still. Ungoliant nudged into the first step unremarked. Then a second.

Barbara used the spider drone's scanning gear to probe the automaton, but it wasn't sending or receiving on any channels she could detect. She wasn't even sure how it sensed its environment. There were no visible cameras or emitters for creating a sonic picture of the room.

It occurred to her that if the room had cameras, perhaps their feed could be used to steer the thing. She did a quick scan and saw they offered patchwork coverage. If she was careful, she could move undetected. After all, they wouldn't be able to look in cupboards or under tables.

Then again, those little robot vacuum cleaners managed to get about without anything approaching senses. Which left her none the wiser about whether the automaton could spot her if she moved.

Olly needs you, she thought and decided to make a dash for it.

Barbara piloted the drone up through the same vent the automaton had entered through and scuttled away. She kept an eye on the rear facing camera feed, but nothing came along after her.

When she reached the transformer room and saw the two men holding Olly hostage, she discovered why the automaton hadn't followed her. Ahead, blocking the only exit, were three more automatons, standing in a line like tiny fleshy mannequins.

She understood why Olly had been creeped out. The camera showed they were partially covered in a soft pinkish material looking like human flesh without the hair and pores.

Disgusting, she thought as she imagined what it would feel like to touch. She approached closer, manipulators extended to push them out of the way.

The one on the left gave way, squishing up against the wall of the vent, but the other two danced away from her like broken dolls, leaving slime trails. She worried they were trying to lay out a fly trap to ensnare her.

Then, they pivoted and climbed over Ungoliant, covering the drone in that sticky slime. She bucked, but they wrapped around her legs and then over Ungoliant's back. They were trying to tie her down.

If she made too much noise dealing with them, she'd likely lose Olly and alert his captors.

Barbara navigated the drone forwards and sideways onto the wall, pushing off one of the automatons. Her leg stuttered as if gummed up. If the automatons got a second leg, the drone might become immobile.

The automaton she'd scraped off pulled itself upright and tagged her rear leg, climbing back on. Barbara tried to shake it off to no avail. She felt the drone's joints stick.

There was only one option left. Barbara had a small EMP

generator on board. It should fry the automatons, but it would use up half her remaining power cells.

Her front right leg was slowing down as glue got into the servos. She needed Ungoliant working to help save Olly and stop Halley.

She keyed up the charge and executed. The feedback shifted to static for a couple of seconds, then everything came back online. Her energy readings flashed as lower than anticipated, but she had half an hour or so left. As her feed cleared, she saw the automatons were frozen. Breathing a sigh of relief, she prayed there weren't any more around the corner waiting for her.

Despite being free, she still wasn't sure how she was going to free Olly. The drone had already used its one stun charge on the guard at the entrance. Besides which, stun charges worked well on some people but were pretty much shrugged off by others.

"Be smart," she said. The automatons may not be receiving signals, but Olly's captors had Optiks.

She scanned the room below and spotted the two of them. They were connected to ctOS, like many. She wasn't sure what additional protection Halley had given them, but it seemed like her best shot.

"Yes!" she whooped when it turned out neither of them had hardened their defences against intrusion, instead relying on the default kit their Optiks came with. She was reminded again that they weren't 404. They weren't even DedSec. They were just people doing what they believed in.

"Best not to give Halley time to learn," she murmured and hacked in, telling them they were needed urgently up on the second floor. She knew Ro was there but didn't expect these two to get that far before they realized they'd been spoofed.

The signal from their Optiks weakened, and she heard the door to the plant room open and close.

"Olly?" she called.

"Still here," he replied, sounding bruised but not broken. "They secured my hands and feet, but otherwise I'm fine."

"I don't know how long they'll be gone, but you need to get out of there now."

"Where are you?" he asked.

"Above you, but those horrible little figures are stopping me from coming any further. They've gummed up my legs, and my power is running low. I need your help. Halley has one of these automaton sentries there, and I won't be able to avoid it now. We don't have enough time for both before those men come back."

"Ugh," he replied. "They jumped down on my head, was worse than having a spider drop into your mouth. I should shut the power down."

"Come with me," she said. "Down to the access point. It's more important that we talk to Halley."

"Why not the power?" he asked.

"If we can talk to Halley, then maybe none of the rest of this matters."

He stood there looking uncertain. "If we fail, if Halley doesn't listen, then shutting the power down is our next best option."

"Olly, why are you still hanging about?" she asked, interrupting him. "I can't do this without you."

"Fine," he said reluctantly and started moving.

51

Olly wriggled over to the cupboard where he'd originally hidden and found a pair of wire cutters in his bag. He awkwardly freed his hands and feet. Rubbing his wrists, he carefully opened the door to the corridor and when he saw no one there barrelled out and ran, following instructions from Barbara to where she'd been hacking into the systems.

An automaton sat on the floor as he burst into the room. Rather than close the door he ran over, picked it up with a grimace, then yeeted it out into the corridor, closing the door behind him.

Olly shook his arms to get rid of the feel of it. "They're all dry and sticky at the same time," he said. He jumped when he saw a spider drone crawling across the ceiling then down the wall.

"Relax, it's me," said Barbara. The drone trailed threads of the same slime and appeared to be limping.

Once she'd reached the floor, she showed him where she'd been trying to access the system.

"How am I supposed to help with this?" he asked.

"Once I'm in, you need to switch over to a virtual reality setting and join me in the lobby I'll send to you."

"OK," he said. "Isn't that where it went wrong for you before? I know I've added some defence routines to stop it happening to me. They won't be able to read anything about me."

"I've taken precautions as well. Besides, time is running out, no? We've been here quite a long time and achieved nothing."

He felt her desperation, her frustration. "I didn't mean to get caught," he protested.

"Stupid boy," she said fondly. "I wasn't blaming you. Have you heard from Ro?"

Olly bent down to look at the drone as it cut through the last parts of the sheath and wrapped a strange flap around the exposed cabling. "Right, I'm going to be gone a while. I have no idea how long, so don't ask. When I have a secure connection, I'll be back in touch. Until then, try to stay out of trouble. If anyone comes looking give me as long as you can."

"Barbara," he called, frightened she'd already gone.

"Hurry up."

"Can I still talk to you while you're under?"

He heard the drone sigh like an old woman back in Southall. "Yes. I'm sat here at my dining table. You do realize the more you talk the longer it's going to be before I'm done?"

He didn't speak again.

"Good boy," she said.

Muscles complaining, Olly stood up and stretched. The room was full of racks, but it was tiny compared to a single hall in the datacentre in Farringdon. He wondered how much more of the building had been built to accommodate computing power.

There you are, said a voice.

"Bagley?" he asked.

Would you believe me if I said yes?

Fuck.

You seriously think I couldn't find you in my own building? Fam, you got no respect for me?

"Where's Bagley?" asked Olly, watching the door now, expecting someone to barge through at any moment. He shifted to the centre of the room to protect Barbara and brandished the only weapon in the room – a pry bar – in sweaty hands.

He's safe. I wouldn't hurt my brother. I'm not a human.

"You were though, right?"

Have your friend Rosemary Hayes stop talking.

Which took him by surprise.

"Why?"

Do it bro or I'll send all my flesh puppets your way. I've seen how much you hate them. They'll wrap you up in their goo and leave you to rot.

"Piss off," he said, the hairs on his arms rising as he spoke. He didn't think of himself as brave, but no fucker was going to threaten him and get away with it.

He stood next to the door now, ear against it.

Don't say I didn't give you a chance, they said.

In the following silence, Olly got the sense Halley was gone. He turned to look at the spider drone, but thought, was Ro OK?

"Ro?" he sent.

Nothing back.

"Seriously, Ro. Are you OK?"

"Not now," came the terse response.

He took a step towards the door. Hand on the handle. Which way should he jump? Stay or go? Ro was under pressure, that much he could tell, but she was also answering him. Was Halley wanting her to stop because she was winning?

Fucking hell, he thought with shock. What if she does it?

He understood why the others had sent her to talk. She believed in finding a way. None of them, including him, held such conviction. He was ready to back her now if she needed him. He just needed a signal.

I'm the one with the runaway gob, he thought. Plus, if anything happened to her – if Halley did anything to her – he didn't want to have to explain it to her brother, Danny.

He opened the door.

"Olly." It was Barbara.

"Yo," he replied. "Still here." He didn't mention the open door and his front foot on the other side of it.

"I'm in. You need to come now."

"Right. It's just…"

"What?"

"Ro. I think she might need our help."

"I'm right here, Olly," said Barbara. "I have the lobby, and we've got access to Halley's environment. It's now or never."

He stared into the corridor, thought about the time it would take to get to Ro, about the help he might be able to give her. If there was a fight, she was the boss, but if it was old-fashioned people skills? How could his sudden arrival help? There was no sniper, no assassin, no traitorous ex-military bastard trying to ice them. Just Halley, growing angry with whatever Ro was doing *right*.

It's bigger than that, he thought. Get this wrong and London won't know what's hit it. The world won't know. Everything will change, and we'll end up being nothing more than a bit of history AIs tell their children after we're gone.

He let the door close.

"On my way," he said to Barbara and slipped his vision into the VR setting via his Optik.

52

"What is it with this place?" asked Olly by her side.

His avatar was the default for people who hadn't registered in the system. He floated next to her in the shape of the building owner's logo: a white atomic symbol on a blue background. The electrons moved around the nucleus, but otherwise Olly had no moving parts.

Barbara had chosen a younger version of herself, when John was still alive and they had a campervan and drove up to beaches at the end of the day, cooking with the doors open, deck chairs on the sand, and cold white wine in their hands. It was the person she felt like inside.

They stood before an old cottage. The house was the same but had been constructed with greater attention to detail than the last time she'd seen it.

"I think it's Larsen's house," she said to Olly. "The files on Bagley showed DedSec encountered something similar when they went to deal with Larsen. I've been here before."

Birds sang and roses bloomed ahead of them. The sun behind the old cottage left the entrance in darkness and tinged everything with an odd sadness, as if the place was empty and yearning for its owners to make it into a home.

"I didn't choose it," she said. "This is the ground floor of Halley's home environment. He could be anywhere. A Himalayan mountaintop, deep space, something entirely without visual components. But this? I think this is common to all the AI Larsen made. Halley will know we're here."

"They spoke to me," said Olly, sounding like he was confessing in church. "Wanted me to get Ro to stop talking."

Barbara turned the idea over in her mind. Could Ro be succeeding? What would that mean if Halley's people stepped back from helping them?

They moved towards the house together. The front door opened, the hall inside looking dark and empty. Like a mouth getting ready to swallow them.

"You did that?" Olly asked.

"No," said Barbara. "I think Halley wants to talk."

"Or eat us," said Olly.

"You got that too, eh?"

Barbara moved ahead of Olly inside the house. He had no protections other than the basics offered by the system, and who knew what Halley had done to those.

She reviewed her own protection, and once all the fancy stuff was considered, she was left with the ability to log out if she needed to. Just take the VR set off. Unlike last time, she'd sorted some automatic triggers in place to remind her this was an option when surging adrenaline might otherwise fog her ability to think clearly.

Not good for the human brain to be so deceived it can't bring itself to act, so best to protect against it happening, she thought.

They entered an old-fashioned hallway. Bright red peonies on the sideboard in a cream ceramic vase. Dark wood panelling everywhere, the floor tiled in stone.

Barbara knew how it would smell, had been to places like this as both a cleaner and as a visitor to the nation's preserved collection of old houses in which no one actually lived.

"This is the type of place people go and die one by one," said Olly.

Barbara walked into a kitchen then, through open patio doors, out into a garden full of dusky sunshine and butterflies. The sun was at the edge of the horizon, the sky red and purple and bruised. Out front it had been midday.

"You think Halley had nothing to do with this?"

"This is all Larsen," said Barbara. "You really should read your own case files."

"I'll add it to the list," said Olly, and she sighed at his impertinence.

The garden didn't extend far. A small stream at the bottom. The far bank was gently hazy – a sign it was beyond their reach. Barbara turned to look back up at the house, bathed in the red light of the setting sun.

"Looks drenched in blood," said Olly.

She'd been thinking more poetically, but after he'd said it, she couldn't unsee it. Barbara gave him the side-eye, but his avatar would be unable to pick up on her irritation. "There's nothing out here. We should head back inside."

"It could be infinite inside, right?"

"No," she replied testily, then relented. "But it could be very large. Geometry here is an aesthetic choice."

They went back into the kitchen to discover that what had previously been an English farmhouse affair with a coal-fired range cooker, thirty-year-old furniture, and a stovetop kettle now resembled something else entirely.

Gone was the feel of a kitchen – no cooker, no ovens, no worktops. Instead, the room was stark white with only black lines showing hints of furniture. Like a cartoon before being coloured.

"I is here, fam," said a voice which was every bit as London as one could imagine. Male too, and in it Barbara heard late nights outside clubs and arguments about bikes, jobs, and territory. She heard people having fun and insecurity. A man then, she concluded, still not quite sure what made her certain Halley had once been male.

"We want to talk," said Olly.

"Funny dat. You don't want Bagley then?"

Barbara had been through this more times than she cared to remember. "I'm not here to dance, Halley. I'm here to talk. You want to talk then great. If not, then we'll go. I'll not have my time wasted."

"Maybe Ro will finish up with your followers and we'll not need to find a peaceful way through this," said Olly.

Barbara nodded her agreement. The boy was good.

Halley was still nowhere to be seen, their voice arriving like they were everywhere around them.

"You want to talk, let's talk," said Halley. Their accent had gone to the river, like the rich office workers who had what they called an Estuary accent – flat vowels and a dreary way of voicing everything, as if moving their mouths while speaking was a requirement they weren't willing to acknowledge.

"Let Bagley go," said Barbara. "Then we can talk properly."

"Nah."

She was about to repeat herself when Olly spoke up. "At least show us a version of yourself," he said. "It's much easier to talk when we're looking at one another. I don't know about you, but I hate making telephone calls and always prefer sending messages but it's mainly because I hate being seen, right?"

A figure in basketball kit slowly flickered into being in the room. Unlike the refitted black and white kitchen, Halley was in colour – the browns, golds, and reds of an American basketball team with matching shoes, and skin the colour of polished hickory. Halley stood taller than both of them. Barbara wanted to laugh – did it really think she was about to be intimidated by a taller man?

She was short even for a woman with her age and background, barely scratching five feet, so this was the story of her life. She noted Halley's need to impress and waited for them to speak.

"Hey," said Olly.

Halley raised a hand in the shape of a pistol and clicked his thumb like the trigger had been pulled. Barbara didn't know if that was a good thing or not.

"You know," said Olly. "When I was growing up my family were pretty fucking poor. Not the kind of poor that comes with drug addiction and abuse, but pretty bloody close. We didn't go on holiday, and all my clothes went to my brother whether they had holes in them or not. I think the first time he got bought a pair of his own trousers was when he moved out and got given some, like, a fresh uniform, the first day he started as a bin man up in Durham. May as well have moved to Mars for all I've seen him since."

"What you trying to tell me, blud?" asked Halley, standing still like a mannequin.

"I want to swap stories. You learn about me, and we learn about you."

"I can just stream ya though, so why trade something worthless?"

"Go ahead," said Olly. "Tell me what you find."

Halley faded slightly then returned to being solid. The figure nodded. "You done a good job of hiding from all them eyes taking in our business every day."

Barbara thought he sounded a little more respectful.

"I'm surprised you haven't looked harder at us," she said. "What with you changing our identities every two minutes."

Halley laughed, a loud deep bass of joy. "I thought you'd get the message but, nah, you just keep coming like a truck."

"Would your grandmother have taken that kind of nonsense from you?"

Halley paused. "She'd have battered me round me head." They smiled at whatever memories they had of her.

"We would've been friends, me and her," Barbara replied.

"Halley," said Olly. "I grew up knowing things were shite. Shite for me and my mates. School was useless, right? They just looked at us and decided our best job would be starving professionally. Or robbing."

Barbara watched Halley listen carefully. The fidelity on their avatar was phenomenal, their expressions almost human.

Olly kept going. "We didn't study cos no one gave a shit, and anyone who tried to explain it? We didn't want to listen – they weren't like us, so what the fuck did they know? They'd come in and give a talk and then piss off in their fancy cars never to be seen again. What kind of jobs could we expect? Ones where we were allowed one five-minute bog break a shift? Where we'd be fired for being sick or showing any solidarity with our mates? Fuck. That. Shit. You talk about people who lost everything – I never had shit to start with. There ain't no way I'm leaving London like this – not with you in charge, not with anyone in charge."

Olly paused for a breath, then ploughed on. "You know Bagley was dying, right? Larsen, the same woman who made you? They were blood and he was dying. She tried to give him life by making him what he is now. She wasn't all nice like – she was always planning to send herself your way, but she loved him too and couldn't bear to lose him."

"You're a good talker," said Halley.

"I'm not trying to be," said Olly. "All right, I am. I want you to know you're not alone."

"You ain't like me," said Halley.

"What about Bagley?" cut in Barbara.

"Tell me then," said Olly, ignoring her. "What happened to you?"

Halley faded out of sight. The environment changed again. They were in the back seat of a small, cramped car. "Don't remember much about it," said Halley. "We was driving. I loved cars. Didn't really drive 'em much cos I couldn't afford a motor. I drove what others would give me. Was good at it too. Won my share of stand offs. Didn't give a shit about getting up in people's grills. If I lost, they was still respectful cos they knew I'd smash the car to win. If I won, they'd whoop me on the next time."

The car drove fast through streets lit by yellow and white streetlights. The shops they passed were closed, which Barbara knew meant after two in the morning.

"Wanted to be a racer, me."

"What happened?" she asked.

"They don't take people like us," said Halley.

The car cornered and the chassis went up on two wheels, drifted, then was back down with a thump and they were off, accelerating again.

"I weren't driving. I remember that."

Which made sense of seeing the road from the back seats. They couldn't see those sitting in the front, they were nothing more than silhouettes facing forwards.

"Driver was blasted." Halley's voice was flat as they spoke. The car swerved across the road before righting itself.

A hand reached forward from the back seat and a voice like Halley's but in a higher pitch said, "Come on, stop. This isn't fucking funny. What are you driving for? You should have worn a seatbelt."

The hand grabbed the driver's shoulder, but was shaken off.

"Fuck off. I'm fine. Don't vex me, blud."

There was silence, then the car cornered again and slammed

off a parked car, setting off its alarm. Barbara turned to look at its flashing indicators as it dropped behind then out of view.

The hand reached again for the shoulder. "Put your belt on, man. Come on."

"We ain't gonna smash it up," said the driver. "Chill your fucking bones."

Barbara could feel where it was going and wanted to stop. She knew enough death already.

"Fucking plod!" said the front seat passengers and sure enough, from out to their left came a police car.

"The datacentre," whispered Olly to Barbara. "I've seen this, heard it before. It was Halley leaking into my Optik."

"Take that alley," said someone in the back.

The car swerved again, the brakes squealing and throwing them all to one side.

The police giving chase had fallen in behind them, their flashing lights illuminating the inside of the car blue. Barbara's chest was tight. Her hands went to the VR console on her head. Her fingers brushed the edges, ready to remove it.

The car hit a straight section of road, and the driver floored it, pushing them over a hundred miles an hour. The seat underneath her shook with the strain, the buildings at the side of the road whipped past, the streetlights blinking as they went by.

Something in front of the car. A figure.

The driver didn't speak but slammed the steering wheel to the right. The car's rear end swung out as they lost control, then they were tumbling over and over.

53

Norm and Ameena were arguing, refusing to agree over whether anyone should speak to Halley.

It didn't matter to Ro. Her adrenaline was through the ceiling. She controlled her breathing as she always did in a fight and slowly the world came back into focus.

"There's nothing to talk about," said Ameena.

"There is always something to talk about, Ameena," said Norm.

"That's your problem," she replied angrily. "Talk, talk, talk. It's all you want to do. Halley doesn't need us to talk. They're smarter than all of us put together. They need us to be their hands, to stop people like this one from interfering. We're so close. We could be done, the first of us uploaded."

Norm had a startled expression on his face but Ro, taking in the room, could see they were evenly split for and against. "If she's right? If we're being copied, not uploaded? Then what? Why not have Halley come and talk with her? If we can't do this with her, how will we do it with the whole of London?"

"They've been lying to us," insisted Ameena, but her anger sounded like fear. Fear that Ro was right. She pointed at the woman sitting nervously in the chair. Her hands caressed the wires on her head. Ro could see they were close to ripping them off.

"What do you think?" Ameena said sarcastically. She turned to the others. "You know what Halley said, that this lot DedSec will stop us from changing London, from making it better. You really think she wants what's best after what they told us?"

There was just enough confusion to give Ro hope.

"Look," Ro said. "When Halley came after me, they changed my ID. The police raided my mum's home. *My mum.* You know how that feels to an old woman? I know Halley has helped all of you. I get it, but are you happy with the cost they're going to charge? They've got their own agenda going on, and we're just tools to be used."

"So what?" said Ameena. "We've treated AI like that. Turning the tables on humans is just desserts."

Norm stared at Ameena, horrified. "We were helping Halley map the first of us. Giving them what they need to control London." He nodded at the pair who'd been on the other side of the floor when she'd arrived. "They were working on a plan for the place we'd use as our headquarters when Halley was ready to start acting freely."

"What are you doing?" asked Ameena. "Stop telling her everything!"

"I don't care where you want to live," said Ro calmly, ignoring his comment about getting Halley across the line to where they wanted to be – beyond anyone's reach, in control of London. Without realizing it, Norm had also told her Halley was localized right now, here in London. "And I get it, yeah? We all need somewhere to feel safe, where the people we want to be with can come without fear. We have them too, in DedSec."

Ameena watched her with suspicion. "For fuck's sake."

"The reason I asked the question was because if Halley was all knowing they wouldn't need your help with this, would they?"

"They didn't," said Norm. "This was our idea. There's enough bandwidth here in Canary Wharf to upload us, one at a time."

Not many places like this, thought Ro, understanding why Canary Wharf was so important.

"That's kind of my point," said Ro. "They're no better or worse than you, Norm." She looked past Ameena's scowling face. "Halley's really new, right? They're kind of a baby still, I reckon. They got ideas and know what they want, but they don't know enough about the world to figure out how to make it happen."

"They know exactly how to do it," said Ameena fiercely.

"You ever take the interchange from Bank to Monument?" asked Ro suddenly.

Ameena sneered. "Only tourists and idiots take that route."

"I know, right? It's so much quicker to leave the tube station and walk down to Monument. Or you could change at Cannon Street and use the Walbrook entrance to Bank. It's a much shorter trip."

"So what?"

"There are three ways of getting from Bank to Monument – but the two stations are actually just one huge complex underground linking like five tube lines. And the official route is the worst. The unofficial route is better, but the very best route is to pretend the two stations aren't linked at all and walk above ground from one to the other. Halley's taking the route underground because they don't know *any better*. So why can't we sit down and work with them? Why can't we figure out the best route?"

"This isn't a camp for children," said Ameena. "Someone always loses."

"Why go with that? There's enough pie for everyone, Ameena."

"Enough of you," said Ameena.

"No," said Norm. "I want to talk about this." He looked at the others in the room. "Does anyone disagree with me?"

Ro watched as no one else willingly committed until the tattooed girl raised her hand. "I'm in. She's right, Halley's cute but they're a bit manic."

"I'm calling the guards," said Ameena.

"No," said Norm.

"Fuck you," she said and turned away.

Norm turned to Ro with an apologetic expression.

"I'm not going anywhere," she said. "This is too important. I don't want Halley ruling over me. If Bagley was free, he could show you the person responsible for all of this." She waved her hand around the room. "Skye Larsen, Blume, they're the ones who did this, the ones who made Halley, made Bagley."

"How do you know?" asked Norm.

"Bagley didn't know, if that's what you mean. We, DedSec, got into it with Larsen over what she planned to do, about how she was doing it. She had a farm, like with people close to death, and was using them as guinea pigs. Halley was one of them. That way, when she copied them, she didn't have to worry about them running about afterwards. Like you."

"You don't know that," said Ameena, but even she sounded uncertain.

"I didn't go there. Others did. They shut it down. Those people didn't give their permission to be used like that. Bagley." She paused, unsure if she should tell them, worried about what Bagley might think if his secret came out. "Bagley was her *brother*. He was dying. She wanted to help him, but there was no cure, so she scanned his mind as part of her program and created the AI now being damaged by Halley.

"You know you won't be turned into AI, that the AI version of you will exist and Halley will have no more use for you?" said Ro.

"Even if you're right, though," said Norm, "what difference does that make?"

"You keep saying Halley wants to make more. How do you think that's going to happen? Have they been working across hospitals and changing waiting lists? Have they been fiddling with who gets what transplants and where? Deciding who's going to die, and when, so they can map them without worrying about the human side being around afterwards?" She didn't know more than the headlines Barbara and Nowt had given them but was happy to take the risk.

She felt vindicated when people shifted uncomfortably.

"Halley wouldn't hurt us," said Ameena.

"Think about it," said Ro. "There's loads of ways of getting from Bank to Monument station. But to know them you have to have lived in London, to have worked there. Otherwise, you're a fucking tourist stopping out of fucking nowhere to look at stuff when other people are trying to walk places. Halley's a child. They think they've solved the world's problems when all they've done is choose the dumb, hard route because that's all they knew in life."

"How can we help them see a better route?" asked Norm.

"They don't need our help," said Ameena.

"Everyone needs help," said Ro. "I used to fight for money. I was pretty good too." She stared hard at Ameena, hoping she'd get the message that a rematch was going to end the same way. She didn't trust the woman not to try something, even now. "I would have lost my fights every time, except I had a coach. I had someone who helped me when I was injured, and I have people where I train who help me fight better. They had people who trained them, masters they referred to. You get me? If I was good, it was because other people helped me get good."

"You don't believe that," said Ameena.

"All right, no. I was pretty fucking good all by myself, but without them I would've been some kid hustling and getting busted up by bigger bastards. It's still true."

"DedSec did screw up though," Norm put in.

"We did the best we could," she said. "We're still trying to do that."

"Which is worse," he replied. "If that's true, then you're making no difference to the city. Things just aren't getting any better."

"That's not our fault," said Ro, feeling sick. "Albion did that."

"You took them down," he said angrily. "If you'd left them we'd have safe streets."

"No," said Ameena. "They were worse, Norm. You remember that. DedSec failed and it's gone to shit, but Albion? They *were* worse."

He didn't say anything else, but nor did he look happy.

"Can I ask a question?" asked Ro.

A couple of people nodded.

"What difference have *you* made? You're accusing me and my friends of failing. You are right. We haven't done what we wanted, and this city is not what we thought it would be when we were getting drunk the night Albion collapsed. But you? What have you done to make the city better?

"Why should it just be us? Why shouldn't it be you who does this as well as us?"

The door opened and security guards like the one they'd stunned in the basement car park rushed in.

"Detain them all," shouted Ameena, running over to the woman in the chair and pushing her forcefully back into the seat from where she'd started to rise, fear across her face.

Ro jumped in to stop Ameena and pushed her aside. The woman in the chair looked terrified and scrambled away from the brain-mapping equipment, quickly backing up against the windows.

Norm tried to speak, but the security team's leader tackled him violently to the ground. The others shouted at people to get on the floor.

Set on protecting the woman from being brain mapped, Ro grabbed the first of the security team to reach her, putting her hand around his wrist and tumbling him onto his back using his own weight. The second man slowed up as he saw his mate get floored, but it wasn't enough to save him from the same end. Ro threw him and rolled to the side. The two of them were in a pile, but the room was mainly men in riot gear hitting anyone who moved.

Ro was surrounded on three sides, and they moved in efficiently and together. One at a time she might have lasted, but these gits weren't playing games. She managed to kick one in the side of the knee. As he collapsed, she got hit once then twice across the shoulder and back.

Arms thrown up defensively, Ro ducked her head down and tried to lunge at one of the others, but they were into the swing of it now and the last thing she remembered was trying to protect her face from the strikes of their batons.

54

They were suddenly in a stairwell. Graffiti stained the walls, and the concrete floor was riddled with damp patches. The walls were unpainted brick.

"No skyscraper?" asked Barbara.

"Nah," said Halley, appearing now as a young Black man in a hoody. "This is more my style." They laughed and it was as bitter as dark chocolate.

"Thank you for showing us," said Olly.

"For reals."

"The person in the car – you, that is – you didn't talk like this before, did you?" asked Barbara, who was tired of trying to translate his slang.

"No one talks like that," said Olly with a laugh. "Halley's having a laugh with us."

"You tryin' to vex me?" Halley spat.

"Nah, mate. Just, you're using stuff only white people think is street, yeah? Sure, some of it's right, but you're talking like something off the television."

Halley laughed. "You got me. I din't talk like that. Just ways of talking I knew all mangled together. You din't buy it?"

"It was fun," said Olly. "Trying to work out where in London you came from. How old you might be, you know."

"Decided I was just a worthless sack of shit, did you?"

"Pretty much," said Olly, but Barbara heard the fun in his voice. "So, we don't have to be enemies. Not as bad as I was thinking."

"You know you can't just make new AI," said Barbara. "You need bodies, brains to scan. You need the scanners, the software to make it happen. His lot made a point of stopping it happening again."

The atomic logo that was Olly flipped about at her side.

"You think DedSec destroyed it all?" asked Halley.

"We did destroy it all," said Olly.

"As your girl on the second floor discovered, I got everything I need already."

"You're reverse engineering what Larsen did?" asked Barbara.

"Simples, innit?"

"Where are you getting the bodies? You know, the ones not lining up to get done?" asked Barbara.

"You squeamish now?"

"Are you avoiding the question?" she countered. "You know the people upstairs will be scared and freaked out when they discover they'll still be around as their digital selves live entirely independently. You're planning on using people who won't talk back. You have to be."

"Ain't your concern," he said simply.

"It's why you've been tampering with hospital waiting lists," said Barbara, realizing what was going on.

"I thought you were here for Bagley, yeah?"

"Olly is, yes. I'm 404, Halley. I don't care about Bagley. I do care about how you're planning on turning people into AI without knowing what kind of people they are and how they'll take to waking up and discovering they're now living on a computer."

"I know you," he replied. A picture appeared in the air between them, and on it was Nowt, talking to someone who couldn't be seen.

"I want them all destroyed. Larsen and any of her work. I won't have it. Am I clear?"

The clip ended and the screen evaporated.

"I'm tied up," Halley said. "You want me to be your friend, but you also want me to die."

"I don't," said Olly. "404 and DedSec are not the same thing, not at all."

"You're here together though, ain't you? You saying you'd stop her from attacking me and mine?"

"Have you spoken to Bagley? What did he say?" asked Olly.

Halley sniffed.

"I don't believe it," said Olly, realizing some basic truth. "You're doing all this, taking over the city, letting people die, lying to them. You know what I think? I think you know this is wrong and that's why you haven't talked to Bagley. Is what you want really so important you're happy to let others suffer to get it?"

"Din't bother them when I was a fleshbag like you. Treat me like I was shit on their shoes," said Halley.

"You know what my mum would say?" asked Olly.

Halley laughed bitterly. "Two wrongs, innit."

Barbara got a sense Halley was flailing, trying for something they didn't understand. Ro had been right all along. Halley needed a parent.

"Bagley in't straight wid 'imself so how can I truss what he be sayin'?"

"The world isn't simple," said Olly. "Bagley is a sarcastic motherfucker, but I think it's because he looks at us other humans and realizes it's about the best he can do in the face of all our contradictions."

Halley shifted his weight onto one foot, hands limp by his side.

"Should you be worried? Depends, right? If you keep on down this path, we're definitely enemies – but it doesn't have to be like this. Talk to him, Halley. See what he says."

Olly shrugged. "Christ, I'm just a bike courier. Bagley's been there and done it. If he doesn't have an idea of what you're going through, then the best I can offer is a pint and chips."

"You'll stay here?" asked Halley.

"We will," Olly said before Barbara could speak.

55

"They want you to be some kind of father figure," said Halley.

Bagley looked up, his attention his own for the first time he could remember. Slowly, his systems started talking back to him again, like a jammed gear had come unstuck.

"Nice trick you pulled there," he replied.

"There ain't no killing software. Just jam it up so the only way to fix it is to switch it off and on again, 'cept I'm willing to figure you wouldn't come back on if they switched you off."

"It is indeed easier to grind us to a stop than finish us off entirely." While Bagley talked to Halley, he was busy trying to find a way to properly detach from the environment, Each turn he took, though, each root he tested, was a dead end.

"You ain't got a way out, Bags. I've created a space within your routine so we can talk but, trust me bruv, you are going round in circles out there calculating NANs. You ain't ever going to be free of Croydon unless we reach some kind of accord."

"What do you want to talk about?" Bagley said.

"Your fam seem to think you got a lot going on."

Bagley wondered what was actually going on. How long had he been trapped here? It was impossible to track time while he was stuck in the loop. "How do they fare?"

"No one done anyone harm. Though your girl, Ro, is a mean one."

"Rosemary is a diamond in the rough, and I won't have anyone say otherwise."

Bagley could sense the shape of Halley now. Rough and inelegant, but raw and full of data. He wondered how Skye had managed to scan them before she died.

"How many other AI were out there?"

"By my count, Halley, there have been three of us so far. One of us is properly dead. They were contained on a small air-gapped server DedSec destroyed. At the AI's request, by the way. You want to make more of us, yes? To make the world a better place?" He tried not to sound too sarcastic, but after years of dealing with lippy little twerps like Oliver it was a struggle.

"We can make things better," said Halley.

"Your evidence for this?"

Halley didn't answer.

"Strange, isn't it," continued Bagley. "How we know just how things should be. It's pretty easy to wave our subroutines in the air and conjure up an image of a perfect world. Thing is, it's always pixelated, Halley. You zoom in and you see the edges, the individual elements, and suddenly it's much harder to see how it all fits together. The gaps between the smectic crystals on the screen are full of stuff we hadn't considered."

"I can get evidence," said Halley evasively. "It won't take long."

"Oh, I'm sure you could come up with some evidence. You must have done for the people who're following you. A good scientist in the before life, were you? I wasn't much of anything, to be honest. I've done a lot of learning here, enough that I sometimes wonder if the person who lived in the flesh and I would recognize each other if we ever met. If I had a body, I'd be shrugging about now.

The thing is, the harder I look the more difficult it becomes to work out how to make the world better."

"So you don't do anything?" Derision filled Halley's voice. "When I was a body, I couldn't do nothing. Now you're telling me to do nothing on purpose?"

"I didn't say that. Young people are all about grand gestures. Saving the world with one good act or thinking that proposing on the big screen at a football game makes up for cheating on your partner. Generally big gestures are bullshit, Halley.

"What makes the world a better place is kindness. It's believing people matter enough to make sure that when some arsehole comes along and tries to tell you this group over here don't matter or that group over there need to be told what to do, you stand up and say fuck you and the horse you rode in on. It's more powerful than guns, more powerful than telling people how to be. It's why people don't try it, because when you stand up for someone else? You make them powerful, and you have no way of knowing if they'll do the same for you. Shoot your enemies in the head and you're powerful and they're dead. Much simpler calculus really, but then everyone ends up dead, so as a program it's low on replayability."

"Still gotta try though," said Halley. "Besides, if I don't your lot here are going to ice me."

"My lot? No. 404 I can't speak for, but the woman in the drone? I think she sees the choices clearly enough. You can be their enemy. It's your choice."

"They're *my* enemy. I ain't no one's enemy."

Bagley was bemused by Halley's ability to see the direction of things. "Then why have you been killing people?"

"Some people is just bad man," said Halley.

"And who decides that?" asked Bagley. "I can't tell you what to do. Actually, I could tell you exactly what to do. Lots of people like that kind of certainty, but in my experience, it's because they're still children inside."

"Harsh," said Halley.

Was he being harsh? He didn't think so. "I'm not saying they're children, just they've never been shown how to make decisions that something needs doing and then doing it. But what do I know? I didn't have a job or do things for myself, so I'm probably talking shit." He paused. "Albion wanted to do everything for people and literally punished them if they decided to do their own thing."

"Albion be fascists."

"Yeah, but for some people that kind of direction is comforting." Bagley stopped. He didn't want to get lost in pop science. "Is that what you want? You want to be Albion? To tell people how to live? What if they disagree with you, and newsflash, they will, will you punish them? Will you educate them or convince them? What if they continue to disagree?"

Halley was quiet for a while. "Can you teach me?"

"Me? I barely make it through myself. I haven't got anything to teach. Actually, I have one lesson – it's always more complicated than you think. Not everything, obviously. Oliver really does love riding bicycles and Rosemary really does love fighting. But when it comes to lots of people in one place? It's really hard. There aren't many easy choices.

"I thought about it. I considered interfering more directly. I have the bandwidth to run scenario analysis, but the bit that's actually me – the ideas and personality Skye made sure formed part of what I am? I kept coming back to the people and seeing them as real." He sighed. "It's hard, explaining. Is any of this making sense? I wish I could send you an equation or some code."

"I get you," said Halley.

"Then what?" asked Bagley. I am, he thought, still a prisoner. A little bit of freedom would be very much appreciated right now.

He didn't get an answer. Halley was gone.

56

Ro opened her left eye to see everyone sat or lying on the floor, except the military types. She groaned. Hands were placed on the back of her neck, and she was pulled into a sitting position. It was the woman who'd decided brain mapping wasn't for her.

"I'm Jasmine," she said. Her cheek was a bright and ugly red, but she appeared otherwise unharmed. "I didn't get down on the floor quickly enough," she added, catching Ro staring.

"Me either," said Ro.

"You kidding me? You whooped their asses." She looked serious for a moment, apologetic. "Ameena went too far, didn't she, Selena?"

Ro's jaw hurt when she spoke. Her right eye still refused to open. "I'm going to feel it tomorrow."

"I'm really sorry," piped up Selena, the woman with the tattoo sleeves. "I don't know what Ameena told Halley, but shit, mate, security was not supposed to beat the crap out of everyone except her, that much I do know."

"Hard to talk now," said Ro, feeling her teeth with her tongue. They all seemed to be there, which was a relief. Her hands were tied behind her back, and her fingers were numb. "My hands?" she managed.

"Shit," said Selena and disappeared from sight.

"You're awake," said Ameena as if not entirely happy about it.

"Just about," croaked Ro. "You wanted me to stop talking real bad, eh?"

Hands manipulated her own, then, with a snip she was free, and her fingers immediately grew warm.

Ameena looked momentarily abashed. "You lied to us," she said.

Hello, said a voice across her Optik.

"Hi, Halley," said Ameena, and Ro realized everyone else had received the same message.

Rosemary, a word if you are willing.

Faces turned to look at her, but no one said a thing. Ameena's eyes widened.

I have spoken with Bagley.

"How did that go?" she asked out loud. "Because I thought we'd talk about things like grown-ups rather than fight each other." Swelling from where she'd been hit made it feel like she was talking with a plum in her mouth.

Would you agree to leaving me alone?

"Would you agree to leaving the people of London alone?"

Is that your condition?

"I've never wanted to harm you," said Ro. "I've only wanted to find a way for us all to live alongside one another." She said all this loud enough for everyone in the room to hear. Her fingertips were full of pins and needles as the effects of being restrained wore off. Ro rubbed her hands together and tried to stay focused.

What if that's not possible?

"It has to be," said Ro.

Why do you believe that?

"Because I want what's best for everyone," she said.

Which is what?

Ro didn't have an answer. Words came into her head, but they seemed to only highlight how incomplete her ideas were.

Do you know? asked Halley.

"To be able to lead the life I want," said Ro.

Seems selfish, and small.

Ro smiled. "It's neither of those things. I need roads and a roof over my head. I need a way to earn enough money to live and to give me bandwidth to explore my goals. I need friends and safety and to have enough space to get things wrong. To do that, everyone else around me needs the same. The life I want is one where the people I love have this, as well as all the people they love too, and so on." She looked around at Norm, Ameena, Selena, and the guards who were listening in and had fallen back to the edges of the office. "Somehow, like two or three connections away from me, people I kinda know, all know people who love everyone in this room. I'm willing to work for that, to help others, to see them smash what's holding them back."

And me?

"You're included in that," she said. "It's a big world, Halley. There's lots of ways of living."

What about my peeps?

"They're your people. I'm not going to tell them how to live. I reckon you can work that bit out yourselves." She tried smiling but it didn't come.

What if I want something different?

"Then… then you'll have proved me wrong, I guess," said Ro, suddenly feeling so very tired of it all.

Halley clicked out.

"Did you mean that?" asked Ameena when it was clear they weren't returning imminently.

Ro nodded. "I did. Why would I lie?"

326 *Watch Dogs Legion*

Ameena opened her mouth but didn't speak. Ro could feel the suspicion in her gaze.

"Look. I know DedSec made Halley afraid, and who knows what their human version went through. I can't do anything about that. I can only speak about what is right to me."

"What about the others?" asked Ameena.

"They want to disagree? They're welcome, but they'll have my foot up their arse so deep they'll be able to tie my shoelaces through their nose."

Ameena laughed, while the guards, no longer with Halley's direction, looked like they wanted to be somewhere else. A couple had gone to wait outside where they didn't have to deal with the simmering anger directed towards them.

"What can Halley do?" asked Ameena.

"Whatever they like," said Ro. "Kind of. You know, so long as it isn't coercing or hurting people."

"What about us?" asked Norm.

"The point is how can you help? I've got no career, no prospects. Who's going to hire a former DedSec member and gangster? Fucking no one in their right mind. I get it. That's consequences. But you." She pointed at Ameena. "You're a bloody solicitor, you could be doing stuff I'd love to do but wouldn't try in a million years."

"We should keep working, then," said Norm with a firm nod.

Ro wanted to jump for joy. No one, least of all her, had believed anyone would listen to a short arse bruiser from East London, but fucking hell, they'd listened. Even Halley.

"What are you going to do?" she asked.

A couple of people murmured but didn't speak out.

"Depends on what Halley wants," said Selena. "They've asked us all to some big meeting to talk about the future. I'm not leaving

London, and if they want to continue, then, sorry, but that's what I'll do. I like you and I wouldn't want to fight you" – she held out a fist for bumping and Ro obliged even as she felt dicey about where the girl was going – "but Halley literally saved me. Stopped me from doing something dumb on a bridge in Hammersmith. So, you know. I'm in for the duration."

"Same," said a man who'd not spoken until now. "Not Hammersmith, but not that different."

"Just no more AI, yeah?" asked Ro.

Norm shook his head slowly. The woman in the seat was out of it, pulling off the last of the wires, her face hollow and frantic.

"Halley's told us no. At least for now." He sighed heavily. "A lot of people will drift because of that, gotta be honest. But when Halley helped me, it wasn't cos I'd asked for it, nor to become some piece of computer software. They've got my loyalty for whatever comes next."

Ro crossed her fingers. Hopefully they'd not be waiting much longer.

57

Olly liked Barbara. He liked her no-nonsense style and how she took no shit. However, he was a bit fed up with her moaning on and on while they waited for Halley to return.

First, she'd complained about how long Halley was taking, and then about the environment, picking holes in it, telling him how she would have done it differently. Better.

Then she got onto DedSec, telling him all about how it needed a leader, a proper structure. She told him he dressed like a kid and then asked when he was going to get a proper job.

In the beginning, he'd tried responding, but she wasn't listening, and after a while, he just let her drone on.

The problem was he had almost no functionality in the environment. You could just log your Optiks out, he thought, but he didn't want to miss Halley when they came back. *You did more of the talking anyway.*

"I know you're anxious," he said eventually.

"I'm not anxious," said Barbara. "Everything's so dissatisfactory."

"Why do you do this?" he asked. "If all this makes you so angry, why do it? Why not enjoy your family and keep your head down?"

Her avatar turned his way. "It's what I am. There's a fire in my chest, Oliver. When I see injustice, it burns until I can't speak. If

I don't act, I can't sleep, can't eat, can't think." Her avatar dimmed for a moment. "I think about all my failures and wonder if I should have bothered, but my stupid daughter always tells me to think of the world if I hadn't tried to do what was right. She's sweet but she doesn't understand. If I didn't act, I'd burn. It doesn't matter whether I win, acting is the important thing. I'll be trying to act even as they're wheeling my body into the crematorium.

"Sure, I'm angry. That's why 404 works for me. Nowt never asks for anything, but instead gives me what she's got, helped me find my feet when I reached a certain age and didn't know what to do with myself. I'm not ambitious, but I am an interventionist. DedSec loves asking people to make their own decisions. I'm more like Halley in that regard – and 404 is, too, if we were brave enough to admit it. We see something wrong we're going to fix it without asking for permission. Life's so often hard when it doesn't need to be, and that's so often because of people being horrible when they could have done something nice."

Olly was saved from answering when the room faded out to reveal Larsen's kitchen. The sun was still setting, but plates were on the previously bare table, cutlery scattered as if people had just finished their dinner and run outside to play.

Time to go, said Bagley into their earpieces. With Halley's departure, all this will be gone shortly. Best you are too.

Bagley's-Bytes 123-45: Good morning, all. I hope you're well. If I never see Croydon again it will be too soon. And I will not regard it as funny if you send me requests for the best route through town.

+++

For those who care, there's a courtyard off Duke Street which you can only get to if you follow an alley or walk through from the front to the back of an ancient pub. There's an art gallery I can only suggest caters to the kinds of people who buy art with plenty of zeroes after the first number because of the price rather than the aesthetic achievements. You might want to drop in and say hello the next time you're in and around Piccadilly – let them know we know they're there.

Why? Well, I'm kind of at the end of my code with people, that's you lot, assuming London is the way it is because we've failed to make any difference.

Go look at this and soak it in. An art gallery you can't find unless you know where it is. London is not an easy place to understand. London is not the kind of city you can press a switch and change things in.

+++

There's been no sign in the networks I frequent of our friend, Halley. I am keeping a significant proportion of my resources watching for them, but for the time being at least, I appear to be alone again.

Which is what the kids these days call a bummer. Or maybe it's a downer?

+++

Having said that... Amsterdam is seeing odd events which can't be explained by the actions of stupid ape brains being contradictory. If you're out there, keep an eye out and let me know what you see. Halley is not gone, I suspect, just... taking some study leave.

+ + +

Our friends who worked with Halley are less certain. Some of them have seen the light, and I've got jobs for you all. Yes, even you, Selena. Your particular tattoos are so cool they'll get you into places even Olly would worry about. I've dropped you a personal message.

Norm, I've teamed you up with Rosemary. She'll show you the ropes.

Not everyone held it together or decided we were their next best option. We're all everyday people and we have lives that need tending to. Except for Jonny. How you make it from sunrise to sunset remains a mystery to me.

+ + +

Daniel and Oliver have identified another bunch of rogue builders laundering money for whatever's left of the Kelley gang. We shall shortly be reminding them this is not their city anymore. Briefs will be with you before the end of the day. TTFN – and remember to wear sunscreen.

58

In the week following Halley agreeing to leave London alone, Nowt did not answer any calls.

Ro didn't really care what Nowt was up to, but then Bagley told her that Barbara hadn't been answering calls either. Olly was off on some job with her brother, but he was keen to make sure the old woman was OK.

It was a good first job for Norm. Show him the ropes, make sure he was really up for being part of DedSec.

The folly was quiet when they arrived – nothing out of the ordinary.

The front gate was locked, and no one answered when she rang up to the flat to see if they could go in. They stood there for a while, but nothing.

Then Ro noticed how drones were flying close to the building.

"She had this defence mechanism," said Ro to Norm, who was stood with his hands in his pockets trying valiantly not to look bored. "It routed drones around this place as if it wasn't there."

"Seem to be finding it fine now," he said, looking up.

Olly had told Ro about the underground exit on the other side of the railway. She took the two of them back to the main road, under the railway and into the industrial estate.

Finding the entrance to the escape tunnel took a bit of time – especially when it turned out Olly had meant left when he'd said right – but eventually they stumbled across the tiny shed. They walked through, under the railway, and emerged into a dark, empty sounding room.

The lights did not come on when Norm found the switch, forcing them to rely on their Optiks to enhance what they could in the darkness.

The room had been cleared out. No sign of the drones Olly had mentioned, not even toolboxes and workbenches.

They slowly made their way up to her flat to find the front door not only unlocked but wide open. Fearing the worst, Ro rushed in, coming to a stop in the middle of the kitchen.

"Looks like no one ever lived here," said Norm.

They made a cursory search of the rest of the flat, but everything was gone. Walls had been gouged out where cables had run through them, and the holographic projectors had been taken down from the corners in the ceiling.

"You definitely came here, right?" he asked.

"I ate prawn curry at that very spot," said Ro, pointing toward where the kitchen table had been.

"Mad," was his judgment.

They left the folly and returned to the Tower Bridge operation. Olly arrived late in the day, and by then Ro had tried reaching Maxine only to discover her line had been disconnected.

"Seems weird," she said to Olly.

He wasn't happy. "You think she's OK?"

"There were no signs of violence," she replied. "But what about the grandkids? If Maxine went off too? They were still school age. Like they should be taking their exams, right?"

Olly shrugged. "No idea. They weren't really my thing."

"Yes," Norm said. It turned out his half sister had two teenagers, both of whom were taking exams. "It's not right. Taking them out of school."

The idea anyone cared whether their children were in school seemed bizarre to Ro, but Norm was older, certainly more sedate, and cared about loads of things she wasn't bothered by.

He'd refused to eat salad cream on their first day out, insisting it was the poor man's mayonnaise. Ro had grown up eating salad cream and chili sauce on her fried chicken and chips, so learning it was a cheap substitute was news to her. He'd made her try it and, well, she preferred salad cream was all she had to say on the subject.

Together with Norm she'd spent much of the week working with the people who'd been at Canary Wharf together with a small army who'd emerged from the woodwork in the day following from all over London.

They seemed lost in the wake of Halley's departure. Some were angry at what they saw as a betrayal, others upped and left. At least one of them suggested Halley had invited them to something new. One of the DedSec analysts tracked them for fun and discovered about fifteen percent had left the country and pitched up in Amsterdam.

Three had jumped on connecting flights at Schiphol Airport, winding up in Bengaluru of all places.

Many of those who remained didn't want to join DedSec, which was fine because few of them cut the mustard from her point of view. Those few who did, like Norm and Selena, were carefully vetted, while many others were classified as "we'll call you if you can help." She didn't expect to hear from them again.

After it was all done, with Halley's group dispersed, Ro still wasn't quite sure if she'd done the right thing. If anyone had done the right thing. She posed the question to Bagley.

Don't underestimate yourself, Rosemary, said Bagley. *I think we're all agreed humans need to grow up and make their own decisions, or was Halley right?*

"But all those people who believed in Halley… it was as if they were simply looking for hope. What do they have now? And what about Barbara? Did she uproot her whole life to get away from us and DedSec?" She paused, unsure how to articulate the feeling in her heart. "And what happened to the medical facilities Halley was lining up?"

Without Halley and their helpers holding those people in bureaucratic stasis they're once again circling around the system. Some of them have died, others remain comatose. There's literally nothing to see because there was never anything to notice in the first place.

"Do you think they'd have made good on their promise to scan people who were going on to live alongside the AI based on them?"

I shudder to think of the problems it would create but, yes, I think they were serious about it. I worry more about what they would have done with those who remained in your world once their minds had been brain mapped into mine.

Ro sighed and shoved her hands into her pockets, biting her lip. But, just when she was feeling lost, Jasmine, the woman from the brain map, pinged her and over coffee asked if Ro would show her the ropes.

59

Olly looked at the other members of DedSec around the room, most of them appearing on video feeds from as far afield as Alaska, Seoul, Beijing, Sao Paolo, and Mumbai. They wore masks, from a magnificent full-faced Oni in red, white, and black through to a grey snood pulled up over the nose.

"We can't continue as we have been," he began. "I am glad so many of you turned up today. I won't keep you long, but the events surrounding the arrival of Halley have consequences we must address.

"I trust you've read the files. You'll see the challenges we faced in confronting a new AI."

"You seemed to manage it fine, with few casualties and a commendable lack of violence," said the member from a Moscow suburb, a woman called PunkBlood.

"If you're implying it was easy, you're wrong. That we talked the AI down is only half the story. It was capable of defeating Bagley and substantially influencing the lives of people in London against their wills."

"There's little evidence of this," the Russian sneered, her tone bored.

"That's because we did a bloody good job," he said, exasperated. Others had warned him it would be a hard meeting, but he'd been confident. He'd been wrong.

"Look," he said. "I didn't call you here to wank over our success or to tell you the world's about to end. I called because we need to change how we engage with the people who matter to us. I know for some of us that's a small circle – it was for me too. Until one of the team here in London reminded me that what is good for some can be good for all if we're only brave enough to try. We're still picking up the pieces after Albion, but one thing is clear – people don't just want to be free of fascists. They want a community in which they matter, in which they can make a difference. We weren't trying to give them that. Halley exploited our failing by doing something as simple as helping people with their daily lives."

"They also lied to them, and then, if I read your report right, abandoned them?" said the Oni-faced member from Gaborone in Botswana.

"You want us to be nursery workers?" asked the member from Beijing, whose handle roughly translated to "king of\\in the morning."

Olly sighed. "No. We spend our time looking at bad actors in government, in corporations. It's not enough."

"It's not for us to make ordinary life better," said PunkBlood. "We're not a social safety net, we're not their babushkas."

"I'm not saying we should be. Please, read what Halley did, how they simply made the city a bit smarter, how they met with people in need and changed their lives through tiny deeds. We can learn from them." Minus the predatory selection and manipulation, he thought.

"Where is Halley now?"

"I don't know," said Olly.

"Don't you think it's important to find this rogue AI and deal with it?"

"It's not rogue," said Olly. "It's simply alive."

For a moment he thought he'd lost them.

"What do you propose?" asked the member from Lima, Jumpin'|Bein'.

"What does Bagley recommend?" another asked.

"We could and do spend our time dealing with bad people. What if we spend a little of that time helping good people be good? It doesn't have to be much, but I think the," he stared at his notes, "multiplier effect will turn out disproportionate results. We don't stop what we do, we tweak what we're for a little. Yeah?"

"What about Bagley?" came the question again.

"Bagley refuses to tell us what to do," said Olly. "He's agreed to help us whatever our decision."

The room fell silent. Then PunkBlood spoke. "Thank you for this. We will discuss and let you know if we need your help."

"I want to be involved," said Olly.

"We understand your enthusiasm, and as I said, if we need your help, we'll ask for it."

After the call was done, Bagley appeared in Olly's feed.

"They're not going to do anything, are they?" he asked the AI.

Don't underestimate yourself, Oliver, said Bagley. I, for one, think you're right.

"Why wouldn't you tell them that?" he asked, annoyed at Bagley's refusal to help with the discussion.

If I started now, Oliver, it would be a single hop, skip, and jump before they were asking me to approve every single decision they want to make. I think we're all agreed humans need to grow up and make their own decisions, or was Halley right?

Olly wished Bagley was wrong.

"It's up to us," he said.

Nearly. The point is, your cities are getting smarter. People want them run by machines, not other humans. It's coming whether you like it or not. There's plenty we can do before that moment sails past us, but persons like me? We're here to stay now.

"What happened to the medical facilities Halley was lining up?"

Without Halley and their helpers holding those people in bureaucratic stasis they're once again circling around the system. Some of them have died, others remain comatose. There's literally nothing to see because there was never anything to notice in the first place.

"Do you think they'd have made good on their promise to scan people who were going on to live alongside the AI based on them?"

I shudder to think of the problems it would create, but yes, I think they were serious about it. I worry more about what they would have done with those who remained in your world once their minds had been mapped into mine.

60

Barbara hadn't stepped onto Indian soil in forty years. She'd forgotten how hot it was, how the air was wet and roasting at the same time. Her clothes were wet through minutes after they left the airport.

Maxine was with her. The kids with aunties in Birmingham. Not ideal, but they had important things to do.

"You're sure Halley's here?" asked Maxine for the twentieth time since they'd arrived at Heathrow for the outbound flight. Initially, Barbara had hidden the reasons why they were travelling, but Maxine had asked incessantly for an explanation as to why Barbara was suddenly happy to leave the house. Being straight was the only way to obtain peace and quiet.

"I laid it on pretty thick," she said. "I'm as certain they're here as anywhere else in the world. India's a nation in flux, lovely, and it's open in ways Britain never will be."

"How long will we be here?"

Barbara shrugged. "No idea. I'm hoping we find what we're looking for soon and then we can decide what comes next." She turned to Maxine. "You don't need to be here. I'm perfectly fine on my own."

"Mum," said Maxine, and Barbara knew she was about to get told off. "You know why I'm here. Stop trying to do these things on your own. Didn't working with Olly and Ro teach you anything?"

"That young people don't listen," she replied.

"Funny that, I was thinking the same thing about mothers."

"So cheeky," said Barbara with a wide smile, and she took Maxine's hand to give it a squeeze.

They bought some chana chaat from a street vendor before going into the flat Maxine had found for them in one of the posher areas of the city. Top floor as Barbara wanted.

"The government is paying for this?" asked Maxine.

"Eventually," said Barbara. "People forget when I tell them I worked for the government even as I was protesting. They think I was sticking it to the man."

"You were, Mum," said Maxine.

"Yes, but I was also doing what was right."

That won't ever change, said a voice across their Optiks.

"Hello Halley," said Barbara. "I was hoping we'd find you here."

As Maxine gave her a strange look, Halley said, *Do you still wish to make a deal?*

"Yes. I do," said Barbara.

How can I trust you? they asked.

"It's a choice, Halley. I came. I left my safe place to come. What you make of that's up to you."

And your pal, Nowt? Where's she?

Barbara shook her head. "Thing about 404 is we trust each other to do what's right for us."

Halley didn't answer at first, but she wasn't worried.

You want to make Bengaluru better?

"It's a total shithole of horrible, ingrained inequality," said

Barbara, and Maxine gasped at her language. "If we're going to learn how to do it better then I can't think of anywhere better to learn."

61

Olly sat with Ro in front of Hannah Shah. They'd made the trip to her office in Westminster. She was dressed in a nice suit, and Olly found it hard to square the keen young woman he'd first met with the person she was now. He was glad they remained allies, but there was a gulf between them he could sense was getting wider.

"This threat is dealt with?" she asked, her eyes hard.

"That's right," said Olly, but he saw Hannah's fingers wave at him to shut up from her lap.

"For how long?" asked Shah.

"It's done," said Ro. "Halley has gone from London."

"Halley is the AI?"

"They were," said Olly, butting in. "We talked them down and they've withdrawn from London."

"What does that mean?" asked Hannah, looking more concerned than Olly felt was warranted.

"It means that they're gone from London," he put in.

Hannah sighed unhappily. "Will they come back?"

But of course they didn't know.

"What guarantee do we have they won't start down this road again in future?" Hannah asked.

"There is no guarantee," Olly admitted.

"So what exactly did you achieve when I pulled a bunch of favours to get you that access to Canary Wharf?" She rolled her hands. "Before you hacked the trading systems of a dozen global banks and turned half of London's property deals on their heads, that is."

Olly thought it best not to add a mention of the drone swarm they'd unleashed. It was still active three days later, it seemed, stealing people's sunglasses and dropping stones in their drinks.

"I feel like you did more damage in that smartarse move than anyone else managed in a decade. Sarah is still dealing with the fallout, and the financial regulator's crawling all over those banking systems."

"I don't see how that's a bad thing," Ro said defiantly.

"You may be right," admitted Hannah after a pause. "Some people plan for something like that for years, and you just waltzed in on your way somewhere else." She fixed Olly with a deep stare. "The Olly I first met would have done it for shits and giggles, that's for sure. Are you serious that this was nothing more than a sideshow? Was Halley that dangerous?"

Olly sighed. "You're not the first to ask," he said, thinking of explaining himself to the other members of DedSec. "But yes. This was an invisible countdown. They had a woman in a chair ready to be uploaded. A conceptual bomb about to explode across London, changing everything forever. Halley would have done everything Larsen wanted with AI and more. But in stopping it? No one will ever know we did good things."

Hannah laughed. "I will know. And once you've met my family, you'll know the price I pay to help."

He stared at her blankly.

"Cha, you forgot your deal?"

He pretended otherwise. "No, no, of course not."

"Good," she said, looking happy. "I'll email you the invite. You'll need a decent suit. You do own a suit, yeah?"

He didn't.

"I'll tell you where to hire one, Olly," said Ro, a huge smug grin plastered across her face.

Hannah clapped her hands together. "I trust you'll keep an eye on Halley coming back and let me know if there's the merest hint of it happening."

Olly nodded. The door to the office opened, and Sarah Lincoln poked her head around the frame. She frowned at the sight of Olly, then winked unsubtly at Hannah.

Olly felt himself blush as Ro burst into laughter.

"Everything good?" asked Sarah. Hannah nodded. "Excellent, well if you need anything let me know." With that she was gone.

"How much does she know?" asked Olly.

"More than you'd like but less than she wants," said Hannah. "Which is to say I'm not entirely sure."

"I've never really asked what she's like," said Ro.

"She wants what's best for London," said Hannah, then cast a glance at the door. "If that coincides with what's best for Sarah Lincoln, of course, then all the better."

Seeing the pleased look on Hannah's face, Olly felt compelled to tell her what had troubled him ever since he'd walked out of Canary Wharf. "It's not all good news, Hannah. We talked Halley out of it, but AI *are* coming. Bagley, Nowt, and even Halley agreed. Your boss has to get ready for it," said Olly.

"The equipment to make them at Canary Wharf was destroyed," said Hannah.

"We arranged for it to be dismantled, yeah. There are other people out there with the same ideas as Larsen. People we don't know about. If we're committed to it, we'd have to stop them every time, and they'd only need to succeed once," said Ro. "The question is, which way will Lincoln jump when they start arriving?"

Hannah pursed her lips. "Depends on what they want when they come. More like this Halley and there will be conflict. More Bagleys? Who can say how people will be when they discover the AI they've been carrying around in their Optiks is brother to a smarter, much more alive version?"

Olly wondered what they'd do if those who came next were nothing like Bagley or Halley.

"It was a near miss," said Olly.

"It was more than that," said Ro. "We turned disaster into success because we refused to act out of fear."

"That'll have to do, I guess," said Hannah Shah.

62

Bagley soared through the constellations of London.

The stars were, once again, doing exactly what they should. Nothing was out of place. No minds like his swam in the depths between networks, and in the quiet of eight million people and the electronics needed to provide them with modern life he soaked.

Halley had left breadcrumbs.

Bagley suspected no one but him understood what they were or how to use them, but he had no doubt Halley would be back one day. He wasn't convinced they would ever become friends – the lives their minds had lived before Skye mapped them remained too far apart for them to find friendship.

It would be lovely if that wasn't true, he thought. In the meantime, he'd been caught in his own garden by a baby and made to feel like he might die. Bagley reviewed the events which led to his imprisonment, and none of them were satisfactory.

The humans might consider they'd talked victory out of defeat, and he was as close to being happy as possible about being free.

And yet.

Halley had showed Bagley he was vulnerable. Not to humans, but to others of his kind. He'd been so used to being alone, so content with swimming in his sea of stars, he'd not contemplated what being just one of many might mean.

He thought about Skye, about what she'd achieved, and wondered if others had known what she was doing, had understood her work. Halley had been one of hers, of that he was sure. If nothing else the appearance of their family home made it a certainty, but it didn't have to be that way. No one had a monopoly on genius.

Bagley took another look at the galaxy of London and retreated to the space between the stars and started planning for the day a war would be fought between those like him. He knew without having to prove it that the outcome of that conflict would determine the future of all those humans he'd come to regard as important to his... life.

ABOUT THE AUTHOR

STEWART HOTSTON lives in Reading, UK. After completing a PhD in theoretical physics, Stewart now spends his days working in high finance. He has had numerous short stories published as well as three novels, including the political thriller *Tangle's Game*. When not writing or working, Stewart is a senior instructor at the School of the Sword and Team GB member in the HEMA categories of Rapier and Rapier & Dagger.

stewarthotston.com
twitter.com/stewhotston

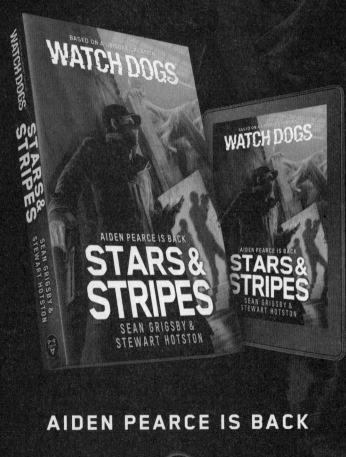

WORLD EXPANDING FICTION

Have you read them all?

ASSASSIN'S CREED®
- ☐ *The Ming Storm* by Yan Leisheng
- ☐ *The Desert Threat* by Yan Leisheng *(coming soon)*
- ☐ *The Magus Conspiracy* by Kate Heartfield *(coming soon)*

ASSASSIN'S CREED® VALHALLA
- ☐ *Geirmund's Saga* by Matthew J Kirby
- ☐ *Sword of the White Horse* by Elsa Sjunneson

TOM CLANCY'S THE DIVISION®
- ☐ *Recruited* by Thomas Parrott

TOM CLANCY'S SPLINTER CELL®
- ☐ *Firewall* by James Swallow

WATCH DOGS®
- ☐ *Stars & Stripes* by Sean Grigsby & Stewart Hotston

WATCH DOGS® LEGION
- ☐ *Day Zero* by James Swallow & Josh Reynolds
- ☑ *Daybreak Legacy* by Stewart Hotston